Praise for *The Outcast*

"This new translation of Pirandello's little-known early work sheds light on the repressive culture of traditional Sicilian village life, prefiguring themes that he would take up in his later fiction and drama. Masoni has done an excellent job in bringing to English-speaking readers this portrayal of a vanished world."

—Susan Bassnett, author of *Translation Studies* and coeditor of *Luigi Pirandello in the Theatre: A Documentary Record*

"A story of forbidden love and humorous misunderstanding, *The Outcast* is innovative, playful, and intellectually challenging writing by one of Italy's greatest modern authors. These traits shine in Masoni's new and much-needed translation. He has captured the ambiguous uncertainties and charming difficulties of Pirandello's first novel, making it available once again to an English-language audience both to study and enjoy."

—Michael Subialka, coeditor of *PSA: The Journal of the Pirandello Society of America*

"Bradford Masoni's masterful translation fills a significant gap in the reception of modern Italian literature in English. A crucial transitional work between realism and modernism, this story of a woman's attempt to take control of her own social image remains powerfully relevant well over a century after its initial publication."

—Luca Somigli, coeditor of *Futurism: A Microhistory*

"Accused of an affair she never committed, Marta Ajala battles against misogyny and malice to create an independent life for herself, her mother, and sister. Masoni's new translation of Pirandello's great work brilliantly captures the novel's unique blend of realism and modernism through to its paradoxical conclusion."

—Ann Hallamore Caesar, coauthor of *Modern Italian Literature*

"Masoni's rendition of *The Outcast* is a much-needed contribution to the dissemination of Pirandello's œuvre in English. Beautifully translated, Masoni's work masterfully captures the linguistic complexity and cultural richness of Pirandello's writing style."

—Lisa Sarti, coeditor of *Pirandello's Visual Philosophy: Imagination and Thought across Media*

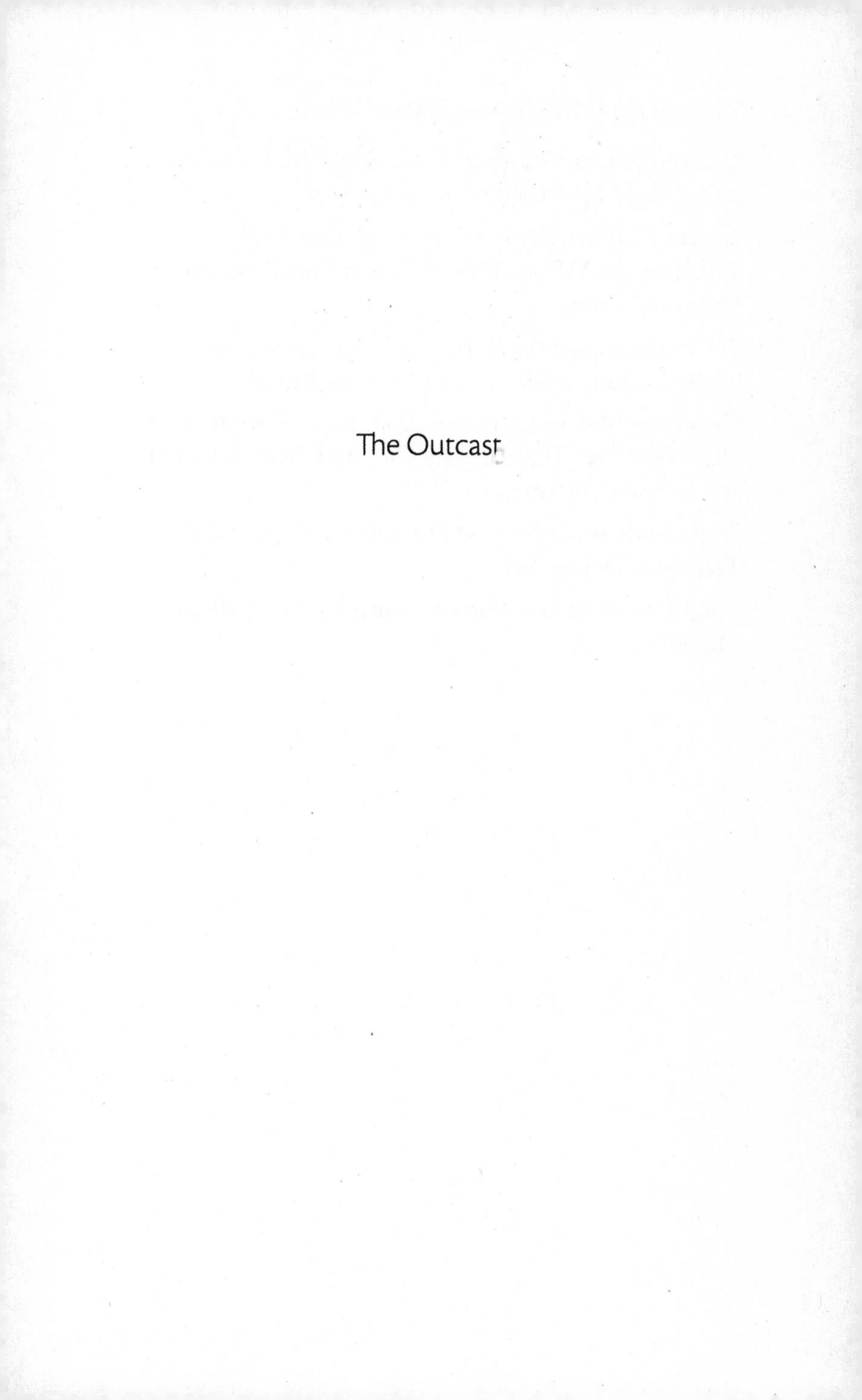

The Outcast

Titles in the **Other Voices of Italy** series:

Giuseppe Berto, *Oh, Serafina! A Fable of Love, Lunacy, and Ecology.* Translated by Gregory Conti

Adrián N. Bravi, *My Language Is a Jealous Lover.* Translated by Victoria Offredi Poletto and Giovanna Bellesia Contuzzi

Shirin Ramzanali Fazel, *Islam and Me.* Translated by Shirin Ramzanali Fazel and Simone Brioni

Geneviève Makaping, *Reversing the Gaze: What If the Other Were You?* Translated by Giovanna Bellesia Contuzzi and Victoria Offredi Poletto

Dacia Maraini, *In Praise of Disobedience: Clare of Assisi.* Translated by Jane Tylus

Luigi Pirandello, *The Outcast.* Translated by Bradford A. Masoni

Other Voices of Italy: Italian and Transnational Texts in Translation

Editors: Alessandro Vettori, Sandra Waters, Eilis Kierans

This series presents texts in a variety of genres originally written in Italian. Much like the symbiotic relationship between the wolf and the raven, its principal aim is to introduce new or past authors—who have until now been marginalized—to an English-speaking readership. This series also highlights contemporary transnational authors, as well as writers who have never been translated or who are in need of a fresh/contemporary translation. The series further aims to increase the appreciation of translation as an art form that enhances the importance of cultural diversity.

The book's title alone highlights important traits that perfectly align with this translation series. The protagonist of Pirandello's novel is, by the author's own definition, *l'esclusa*, the outcast, the woman society rejects for her progressive stance, her attitude, her bold choices. The modernist bent of the novel's style never conceals its realist core. This new combination, typically Pirandellian, further excluded it from mainstream literary taste of the early 1900s, when the book was published. The fact that its first English translation (1925) has been out of print for decades is another factor that marginalizes the text. The translator is a young scholar who has dedicated the last few years to researching this novel and to establishing himself as a translation expert.

The Outcast

LUIGI PIRANDELLO

Translated by Bradford A. Masoni

Rutgers University Press
New Brunswick, Camden, and Newark, New Jersey
London and Oxford

Rutgers University Press is a department of Rutgers, The State University of New Jersey, one of the leading public research universities in the nation. By publishing worldwide, it furthers the University's mission of dedication to excellence in teaching, scholarship, research, and clinical care.

Library of Congress Cataloging-in-Publication Data
Names: Pirandello, Luigi, 1867–1936, author. | Masoni, Bradford A., 1974– translator. | Bini, Daniela, 1945– writer of foreword.
Title: The outcast / Luigi Pirandello; translated by Bradford A. Masoni; foreword by Daniela Bini.
Other titles: Esclusa. English
Description: New Brunswick: Rutgers University Press, [2023] | Series: Other voices of Italy
Identifiers: LCCN 2022045012 | ISBN 9781978836495 (paperback) | ISBN 9781978836501 (hardcover) | ISBN 9781978836518 (pdf) | ISBN 9781978836525 (epub)
Subjects: LCGFT: Novels.
Classification: LCC PQ4835.I7 E713 2023 | DDC 853/.912—dc23/eng/20220920
LC record available at https://lccn.loc.gov/2022045012

A British Cataloging-in-Publication record for this book is available from the British Library.

Copyright © 2023 by Bradford A. Masoni
Foreword copyright © 2023 by Daniela Bini
Translation of L'esclusa. Fratelli Treves, 1908.

All rights reserved

No part of this book may be reproduced or utilized in any form or by any means, electronic or mechanical, or by any information storage and retrieval system, without written permission from the publisher. Please contact Rutgers University Press, 106 Somerset Street, New Brunswick, NJ 08901. The only exception to this prohibition is "fair use" as defined by U.S. copyright law.

References to internet websites (URLs) were accurate at the time of writing. Neither the author nor Rutgers University Press is responsible for URLs that may have expired or changed since the manuscript was prepared.

rutgersuniversitypress.org

Contents

Foreword

Rescuing The Outcast

It seems incredible that so many of Pirandello's small jewels—his short stories—have not been translated into the English language, and that the only English translation of his first novel *The Outcast* has been out of print for decades. Masoni's adept translation, therefore, could not be more welcome. The fact that it was born as a dissertation with an exceptionally erudite introduction makes it all the more praiseworthy. After showing his expertise in translation studies, Masoni explains his approach, writing that "Translation studies is a useful guide, but in the end, it is just that, a guide." Each author is different, each text is distinctive. Translating a text—particularly one as rich as this—cannot be done by forcing it into a unique system and by using a single method. This very diversified translation approach is, in my view, what makes his translation fascinating, and Pirandello would certainly have agreed. Masoni, in fact, succeeds in creating a Pirandellian operating process (I am purposely not using the word "system," which is so anti-Pirandellian). A writer who changes voice, shifts perspectives, engages, and often challenges the readers by putting them off balance can be translated only with a diversified approach ready to change and adapt to the movements of the text.

As a consequence, I am reading *The Outcast* precisely as Masoni does: as a proto- if not fully modernist novel and not as a realist work, as most critics still read it. Of course, nobody would ever deny the presence of realist elements and the strong influence of Luigi Capuana, not only in style but even in content. However, the original aspect of the novel is precisely Pirandello's ability to challenge the very realistic elements he plants in his text, to overturn the reader's expectations, and to give us what Masoni correctly refers to as an "unresolved, and in many ways, deeply unsatisfying ending." He calls the style of Pirandello's first novel "realism with a difference," and he is right on target. In fact, we could say, "with a big difference," since that difference is, as I have indicated above, what challenges and undermines that very realism.

The first and most prominent Pirandellian feature that Masoni has kept in his translation—which was not reproduced in the original Leo Ongley translation of 1925—is the abundant use of free indirect discourse. This is a technique that confuses readers, who, at key points in the novel, cannot tell whether they are reading the character's or the narrator's voice. The use of indirect discourse, therefore, functions as a blow to the conventions of the traditional novel. Masoni's choice to keep it in his translation was also prompted in order to show the presence of this modernist device already in Pirandello's early writing.

Second, I appreciate the choice of maintaining the foreignness of the text rather than domesticating it. I say this not only because Masoni agrees with Lawrence Venuti's arguments about the moral responsibility of the translator not to render the text "transparent," but especially because by maintaining many of the original Italian features, he is truer to Pirandello's "humoristic" vision of the novel, whose purpose was often to be off-putting, to keep readers on their toes. In fact, preserving the humoristic elements in the work is, in my view, a must, once again in order to maintain its modernity and underscore one of the most important features of Pirandello's prose. But more on humor below.

Some examples of Masoni's attempts to maintain the foreignness of the text are first by leaving in Italian the names and nicknames ("Roccuccio," "Mararrò"); terms of endearment ("cara mia"); geographical names, including streets ("Via Papireto," "Monte Cuccio," "Conca d'oro"); titles ("*cavaliere*"); and terms of address ("*Signora*"); by his use of onomatopoeia ("*squee*," "puah!"); and by his making reference to the formal and informal pronoun shifts when that issue arises. He also utilizes the same strategy when encountering more specific cultural references, like the mention in part I, chapter 9 of "lo scialacuore," a frozen dessert specific to southern Italy and for which there is no English equivalent. Even in the translation of proverbs that are specific to Sicilian culture, Masoni, in order to preserve the cultural flavor, always translates them literally when they can be understood by the context.

Pirandello's *umorismo*, as I mentioned above, is another major feature of *The Outcast*, and there are passages that will return almost verbatim in *On Humor* as well as in *The Late Mattia Pascal*. Pirandello himself, in fact, in the dedicatory letter to Luigi Capuana of the 1907 edition of the novel, makes explicit reference to the humoristic quality of his work. However, when it initially appeared episodically in the daily paper *La Tribuna*, he was aware that this quality that he considered "the most original part of the work" and that he had "scrupulously hidden under the completely objective representations of persons and events" could not have been appreciated. Such a statement, therefore, seemed to imply that once it was published as a book, this most original element of the work would be appreciated. There are passages in this letter where Pirandello emphasizes the dichotomy between life and thought; specifically, how the irrationality of reality is completely distant from the orderly system that we impose on it. He is, however, confident that his *Outcast* will show this aspect of our experience to the reader.

One of the instances where the ideas expressed in the essay *On Humor* appears is found as early as part I, chapter 4. Here is Masoni's translation: "Doesn't each of us feel these flashes inside often enough—strange thoughts, glimmers of madness, thoughts that follow from nothing, and that we would never confess to anyone, as if they had sprung from a different mind than the one that we normally recognize as being our own? And then as quickly as they have come, the flashes disappear, and the dreary shadow or the calm light we are used to returns." In part I, chapter 13, we seem to hear Pirandello's later creation Henry IV speaking when Professor Luca Blandino exclaims: "But I don't judge things the way you do! [. . . .] I judge everything according to its circumstance! I don't draw lines in the sand arbitrarily like you do: up to here is good, but past this point, no, that's bad . . . . Let me act like a crazy person!" However, as Gregorio Alvignani continues his pursuit of Marta in part II, chapter 10, we hear echoes of Tito Lenzi in *The Late Mattia Pascal* and his Pirandellian discourse on conscience:

> Oh, *mia cara*, when I say, "My conscience will not permit me," I am really saying, "People will not permit me, the world will not permit me." My conscience! What do I suppose it really is, this conscience of mine? My conscience is

> just other people talking, *mia cara*! My conscience simply repeats to me what the others say, what society says. So then, hear me out! My conscience absolutely gives me permission to love you. And you, you examine your conscience, and you will see that the others have given you permission to love me as well. Yes, just as you yourself said, precisely because of all of those things that they have made you suffer unjustly.

Finally, in part II, chapter 1, we see humorist Marta in action: "Marta had only recently realized that she had a talent for discovering and then mimicking the absurdities hidden just below the surface of everything and everyone, and she could reproduce a person's gestures and voice with an extraordinary imitative faculty." This attention to the façade, to mimicry, to the mask is classic Pirandellian "humorism." The fact that, in this instance, the characters she imitates as entertainment for her mother and sister are the complex, tragicomic couple Don Fifo and Maria Rosa Juè serves to make it an even better example of Pirandello's theory.

It is especially praiseworthy to bring forth Pirandello's original concept of humor in *The Outcast* because, contrary to what happens in his well-recognized humorist works, such as *The Late Mattia Pascal*, *Six Characters in Search of an Author*, and *Henry IV*, where the protagonist/humorist is always a man, in *The Outcast*, the character who is the true protagonist/humorist here is Marta Ajala, a woman. She is, of course, the only character capable of "reading" not only herself but others, and capable of eliciting life's contradictions as well as her own.

Translating Pirandello is certainly a challenge. This is one of the reasons why so much of his work has not yet been translated, or if it has, it has been done poorly. His language is dry, but ambiguous and shifting, as the content is, as reality is. Masoni succeeds in maintaining these characteristics, which are really the essence of Pirandello's prose and philosophy.

A notable little jewel is Masoni's translation of the sonnet that Attilio Nusco writes for Marta. The translator rightly points out that the insertion of this love sonnet is problematic. Its author is a teacher, a colleague of Marta's in the school where she teaches, who is in love with her, but he is completely ignorant of her past. The text of the poem, however, indicates otherwise. It demonstrates that its author not only knows of the vilification she had to endure but admires her for having the courage and strength to bear it with dignity and fight against the slander. The character who is presumed to have authored the poem, therefore, cannot have known enough to have written it. It is difficult to believe that Pirandello would have made such a blunder. Masoni's explanation is absolutely convincing: Pirandello wants the reader to recognize his own authorship in this poetic composition. After all, he was also a poet, and wrote and published hundreds of poems. He must, indeed, have been a frustrated poet, since his poetry never garnered much praise. Perhaps he wanted to show his readers that he had the skill to create a love sonnet in the style of Petrarch, even if it meant juxtaposing it with this original and modern narrative. Given the high opinion he had of his own work, Pirandello was likely disappointed by the lack of recognition of his poetical skills. Thus, he wrote a sonnet whose ownership had to be clearly recognized by any reader. The translation maintains this very quality and succeeds in doing so by keeping the rhyme scheme of the sonnet. It is a remarkable achievement, indeed.

Masoni is unquestionably aware that the perfect translation does not exist, but also, as George Steiner remarked and whom Masoni quotes, that "every act of communication is an effort of translation, and often a failed one." In translating *The Outcast*, Masoni clearly took great joy in addressing this challenge that brings us smack into the heart of Pirandello's philosophy. Not only did Pirandello consider all translators betrayers of the author's intentions (see his 1908 essay "Illustratori, attori e traduttori" ["Illustrators, Actors, and Translators"]), he was also convinced of the impossibility of any kind of completely true communication. It is enough to listen to the words of the Father in his *Six Characters in Search of an Author*, as translated by Masoni:

> All of us have inside ourselves a whole world of things; each of us a world of things all his own. And how can we understand one another, Signore, if in the words I speak I put the meaning and the value of things as I myself see them, the way they are inside of me, while the one who listens inevitably interprets them according to the meaning and the value that he sees in them, as they are in the world he has inside of himself? We think we can understand one another; we never understand one another!

In other words, even if Masoni were able to achieve the impossible—a "perfect" translation of *The Outcast*—it would cease to be so the moment it was interpreted by another person. His acknowledgment of this fact, so in line with Pirandello's understanding of language, adds an uncommon depth to his translation.

Finally, I was pleased to see that at the end of the translation of the novel, Masoni reprinted his own translation of Pirandello's letter to Luigi Capuana, to whom he had dedicated the novel. Masoni therefore realized the importance of letting the reader know what Pirandello thought of his work and what he considered the "most original part" of the novel, disguised as it is under the façade of realism. Moreover, he openly accepted the challenge that this task entailed. In fact, we, readers of this work, can assess the translator's faithfulness to Pirandello's intention and judge the result—and the result, at least for this reader, is undoubtedly successful.

—Daniela Bini

Translator's Preface

Just what is it about the writing of Luigi Pirandello that makes it so compelling? In the many years since my first encounter with the works of Pirandello as a nineteen-year-old undergraduate spending a year abroad at the University of Bologna, I have had ample time to reflect on this question and have discovered that some of the answers my undergraduate self might have provided still ring very true for me today. The Luigi Pirandello that I discovered all those years ago had a very specific mission, it seemed: to make his audience, whether spectators or readers, examine the nature of their reality and the nature of their own relationship to it. The guiding principle that I read, and continue to read, in his works is that the structures of reality that we as individuals are compelled to participate in and abide by, and with which we so often come into conflict, are constructs and too often contradict our natural instincts. This Luigi Pirandello is an iconoclast, a thinker on a mission to expose the true nature of the relationship between the individual and his or her surroundings. These are ideas that many of us find naturally compelling. They are also ideas, I would suggest, that seem to become increasingly relevant and applicable to our own lives as teachers and students, as members of families, as employees, as parishioners, as citizens of states, and as human beings living in societies. Pirandello is not just interested in making a simple statement; he is intent on exploring the often simultaneously comic and tragic implications of the nuances of our complex relationship to reality. In his works, he explores the subjective nature of the individual experience. He puts forward the idea of the individual self not being a perfectly realized, completed whole but a succession of distinct, if overlapping, individuals whose characteristics depend on their circumstance and whose real nature is always hidden beneath a mask, as a work continually in progress. He lays bare our basic inability to tie the loose ends of our experience together into a complete, tidily resolved story. In short, this is heady stuff for undergraduate literature students and mature readers alike, and all the more so given the innovative manner in which these messages are delivered: a style that respects the reader's or spectator's intelligence, that makes him or her work for the message, and that does not condescend or pull punches.

All of the above makes Pirandello an author who is not easy to translate. Of course, no act of translation is simple. But an author so seemingly bent on keeping his readers off-balance presents a particular set of problems for the translator. *The Outcast* is a thought-provoking example of this aspect of Pirandello's writing in that it comes to its readers disguised as a fairly standard nineteenth-century realist novel. I discovered early in this process that in order to do the novel justice in English, I would need to approach it for what it is: an overlooked link to Pirandello's later, more experimental work. As a translator, then, I knew that I wanted the elements of the text that support this reading to come to the fore. *The Outcast* in its original form is characterized by the ubiquitous use of free indirect discourse that in some scenes borders on stream of consciousness; it features the sometimes jarring use of dialect to keep the text off-kilter; it is rife with narrative fragmentation and narrator intervention; it is not structured teleologically and ends in an untraditional, unresolved, and frankly deeply unsatisfying way; and it has a pronounced metatextual component—the novel often feels like it is trying to exclude Marta's voice just as her society is trying to exclude her. These aspects of the work, along with numerous very apparent nods to Pirandello's "humorism"—a philosophy that he would not formally lay out until 1908, almost two decades after he had written *The Outcast*—all feature prominently in the Italian but have been consistently sanitized from previous translations of the text. I have made a point of replicating them here.

A final note bears mentioning for anyone interested in literary history, and specifically in the context in which Pirandello's later works were produced and received. One of the issues that scholars of Pirandello's oeuvre are often asked to address is why this magnificent author's works have fared so poorly outside of his home country. The answers to this question are many and complex. Although in my scholarly opinion they have more to do with factors including the above-mentioned difficulty of translating his writing, it would be remiss of me not to address his association with Mussolini's fascist government roughly thirty years after his having written *The Outcast*. The period of years in which Pirandello wrote and saw his most popular works produced—*Six Characters in Search of an Author* and *Henry IV*—also saw the rise to power of Mussolini's party. Pirandello was, by all accounts, initially uninterested, although as a nationalist, a republican, and, perhaps most importantly, as someone who was anti-clerical and anti-institution, he must have found a great deal of the fascist platform attractive. Pirandello's admiration of Mussolini but well-documented indifference toward his party would change when this suddenly internationally famous author was summoned to the Palazzo Chigi in 1923 to meet with Mussolini himself, who claimed to be an enthusiastic admirer of his works. The result was that Pirandello very publicly aligned himself with the fascist party, and there is no dearth of written evidence that confirms this, including his signing of the 1925 "Manifesto of the Fascist Intellectuals" ["Manifesto degli intellettuali fascisti"] as well as numerous pieces written by Pirandello supporting Mussolini and the party, speeches he delivered, and interviews.

In terms of Pirandello's motivations, biographers like Gaspare Giudice are very clear as to why Pirandello joined the party with such fervor: he was pleased that a man as important as Mussolini had expressed admiration of his work. A number of scholars and critics have also put forward the idea that Pirandello was not especially dedicated to the party, and only joined in order to fund his theater in Rome, an idea that is perhaps at odds with the fact that he would later go on to donate his 1934 Nobel Prize medal to the Italian government to be melted down to aid in funding the Second Italo-Abyssinian War. In any case, it is clear that his association with the party affected his international reception. At the moment when Pirandello's fortunes outside of Italy were on the rise—when he met with Mussolini his works had been performed in New York and all over Europe, and he was about to embark on a tour of the United States—he had chosen to align himself with a political movement that would prove to be extremely unpopular throughout the English-speaking world. Although Pirandello would later judge the fascist party harshly and withdraw his support, interest in his writing and theatrical works would only begin to revive after the Second World War, and Pirandello's fortunes outside of Italy never fully recovered.

It is a struggle to separate great artists from their works, just as it is difficult to liberate great works of literature from their historical contexts. Pirandello is an excellent illustration of this concept. On the one hand, just as a translator must steer away from sanitizing a text, a literary scholar must be careful not to apologize for an author's actions, beliefs, and political affiliations. On the other hand, I have not found it difficult to separate my understanding of Pirandello's affiliation with Italian fascism from his writing. This is, in part, because the works themselves are so boldly critical of the religious, social, familial, and political orders and structures of his day, and so bent on exposing those structures as false, as constructed by those in power to manipulate the oppressed or otherwise powerless.

What, then, makes Pirandello's work so compelling? It is all of these aspects of his writing and more. Reading Pirandello in the ways described above has proven fundamental to my understanding of literature. Translating Pirandello—attempting to preserve the integrity of his vision by conveying his meaning in English—has been instrumental in forming my own view of reality. In the work that follows, I have tried to capture and transmit the virtuosity and modernity of Pirandello's writing, as well as the excitement that his writing instills in me as a reader and translator of his work. In this sense, what follows has been a labor of love.

This project would not have been possible without the encouragement and support of many people. First, I would like to thank the editors of the Other Voices of Italy series at Rutgers University Press—Sandra Waters, Eilis Kierans, and Alessandro Vettori—not only for their editorial insight but for being as passionate as I am about having Marta Ajala's story told in English.

This project started as part of my doctoral thesis and would not have gotten off the ground without the help of many members of the Program in Comparative Literature at the Graduate Center of the City University of New York, especially William Coleman, Giancarlo Lombardi, Carol Pierce, Barbara Pospisil, and my friend and advisor Paolo Fasoli. Here I must also mention the late Robert Dombroski, who nurtured my first forays into Italian modernism and whose important work in Italian studies continues to inspire me and so many scholars in this field.

Over the course of this project, I relied on a number of "expert informants" including Daniela Bini, who, no matter where she was in the world, always made the time to advise me on the nuances of the translation and reflect with me on Pirandello's philosophy, his relationship to women, and his legacy. Michael Debrauw and Dee Schwinn consulted on the Latin portions of the translation, and Michael Podrebarac and Ashley Masoni Huber patiently walked me through the lexicon of nineteenth-century Roman Catholic ritual. Finally, my Italian reader Chiara Beltrami Gottmer was always there with tea and sympathy whenever I encountered difficulties with Pirandello's sometimes thorny prose.

In addition to those mentioned above, there are many people who have had a hand in making this book what it is, including André Aciman, Marga Akerboom, Cory Anotado, Albert Ascoli, Scott and Melinda Berry, Adam Bradford, Daniel Casey, Michael Cuthbert, Shanda Davis, Conrad Del Villar, Michael Donohue, Frank Duba, Wayne Ferrebee, Angus Fletcher, Jonathan Grund, Ana Ilievska, Hannah Joyce, Ian Kilbride, David Kleinbard, Jennifer Kooy, Alison Lipp, Laura Lucci, Joanna Mansbridge, Daniel Masoni, Mark Masoni, Kenneth Muller, Hannah Owens, Burton

Pike, Sherry Roush, Lisa Sarti, Stefan Schear, Paul Stasi, and Jon Whitney. I am humbled by you, and I thank you.

The Outcast is in many ways a book about women, and specifically about the strength of women. There are two such strong women in my life who have had a profound influence on this project. When I was a child, my mother, Elizabeth Masoni, first showed me what literature does and why it is important as we read William Faulkner together over our dining room table. More recently, she has served as my first reader and editor on every draft of this book. Without her keen editorial eye and her ear for dialogue, this project would have fallen at the first hurdle.

Finally, it was my partner and canine co-parent Kelly Marie Webber who first suggested one evening in our sweltering Shanghai apartment that I pursue a project like this one. After a few years of my flirting with translating this novel, she boldly proposed one evening in a restaurant near our new home in Amsterdam that I take time off from teaching to tell Marta's story properly. As has been the case so many times in our life together, her courage and confidence were infectious, and I took the plunge. Kelly, I learn from you and am inspired by you every day, and I am honored to dedicate this translation to you.

—Bradford A. Masoni
Saint Paul, Minnesota, August 2022

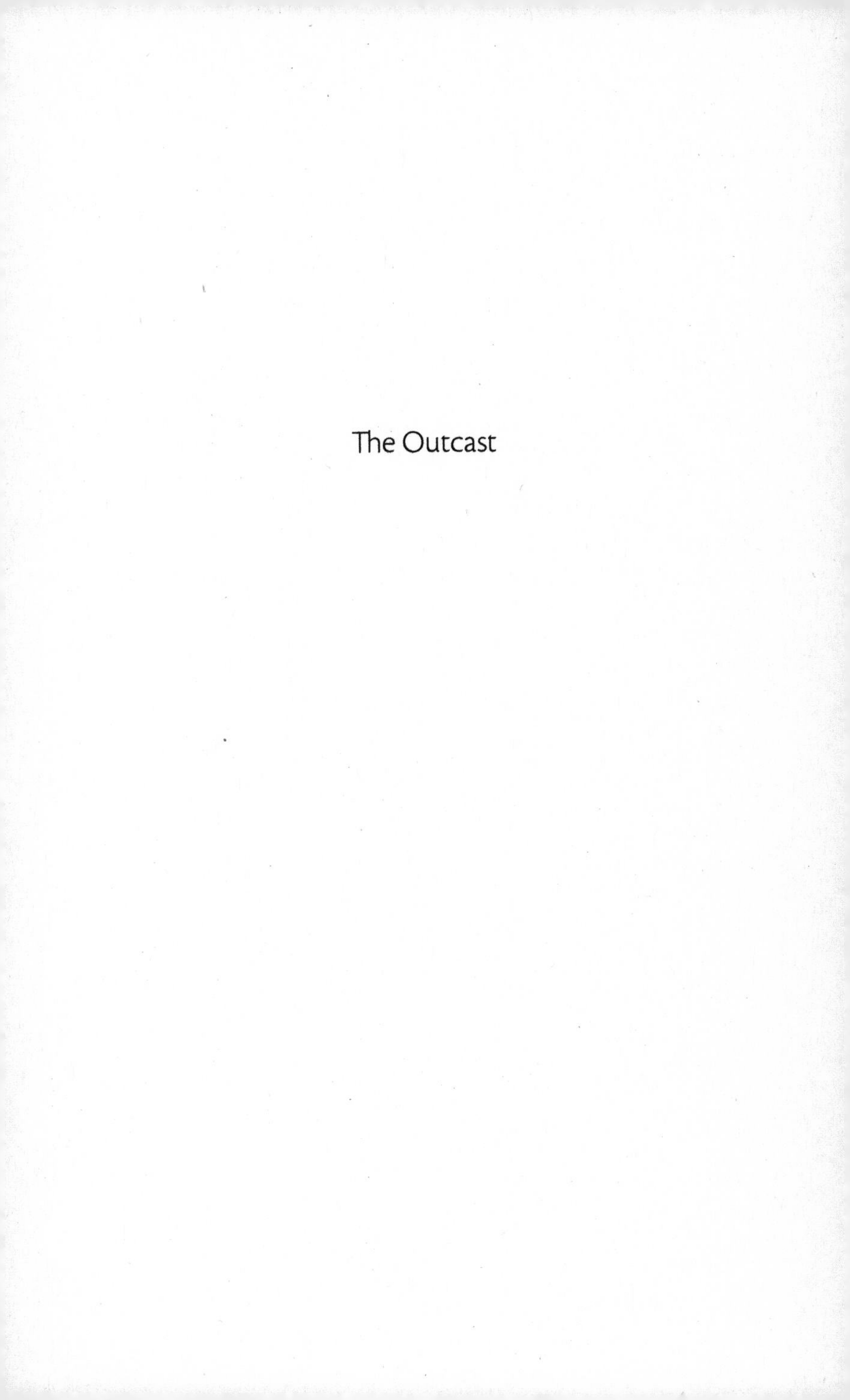

The Outcast

PART I

~ Chapter 1 ~

Antonio Pentàgora was already seated calmly at the dinner table, as if nothing had happened.

His pockmarked face, illuminated by the light that hung from the low ceiling, seemed almost a mask against the rosy whiteness of his skin and the fatty rolls of his neck, which was as hairless as a newly scraped hide. He was jacketless; his limp, faded blue shirt was undone, exposing his hairy chest; and his sleeves were rolled up over his hairy forearms. He was waiting to be served.

On his right sat his sister Sidora, pale and scowling, her sharp eyes angry and elusive under the kerchief of black silk she always wore tied around her head. On his left sat his son Niccolino—the wild one—his pointed bat ears jutting obscenely from his head, which sat atop his elongated neck, his eyes perfectly round, his nose tapered. Opposite him a place was set for his other son, Rocco, who was still on his way home that evening, after the disaster.

They'd been waiting to eat until Rocco got in. Since he was late, they'd all sat down at their places. The three of them sat in silence, in that large, gloomy room with the low, yellowing walls, along the length of which ran two interminable lines of chairs, almost none of which matched. From the sunken redbrick floor arose a vague stench of rot.

Finally, Rocco appeared in the doorway, sullen and exhausted. He was a tall, blond beanpole of a man, with little hair left, and a dark face from which shone brilliant blue eyes—eyes that were almost defeated, almost lost, but that could also turn malicious when he furrowed his brow and tightened his wide mouth with its slack, purplish lips. He slunk in on bowed legs, leading with his chest, followed by his head and arms. Every now and again he had a nervous tic—a trick of the spinal cord—that caused him to stick out his chin while turning down the corners of his mouth.

– Oh, well done Roccuccio! Here he finally is! – his father exclaimed, rubbing his burly hands, laden with heavy rings.

Rocco paused for a moment to stare at the three people seated at the table, then threw himself onto the chair closest to the door, his elbows on his knees, his fists under his chin, his cap over his eyes.

– Oh, get up! – Pentàgora went on. – Can't you see we've been waiting for you? What, don't you believe me? My word of honor, until ten . . . no, longer, longer . . . . What time is it now? Come here; here's your place, all set for you, just like before all this happened.

And he called out, loudly,

– Signora Popònica!

– Epponìna, – corrected Niccolino under his breath.

– Shut up, you—I know her name! I like to call her Popònica, after your aunt. Is that not allowed?

– Who's Popònica? – mumbled Rocco, stirring only slightly from his stupor.

– Ah! She's a woman who's fallen on hard times, – responded his father cheerfully. – A real lady, you know? She hasn't been a servant for long; your aunt has taken her in.

– She's a northerner, from Romagna, – added Niccolino, meekly.

Rocco's head fell again into his hands, and his father, satisfied, slowly brought the full glass of wine to his lips; he took a cautious little sip, and then he threw Niccolino a glance, and, smacking his lips, said,

– It's good! Young wine, Roccuccio. It'll cure what ails you . . . . Try it, try it, you'll get your stomach back. All this is nonsense, my boy, nonsense!

And he drank down the rest in one go.

– Don't you want to eat? – he asked.

– He can't eat at a time like this, – observed Niccolino quietly.

They ate in silence, making sure that their forks did not scrape against their plates, as if worried they would offend the miserable silence that filled the room. In came little Signora Popònica. Her hair was the color of Spanish tobacco and plastered in place with who-knows-what pomade; her eyes were so heavily made up that they looked bruised, and her mouth was painted into sharp creases. She entered, wobbling on her little legs and wiping her tiny, work-gnarled hands on a cast-off jacket, which was tied by the sleeves around her stained smock, serving as a makeshift apron. Her dyed hair and melancholy expression showed at once that this poor, fallen woman ached to be held by more than just those empty sleeves.

Antonio Pentàgora immediately gestured for her to withdraw; she was no longer needed, since Rocco didn't want any dinner. She raised her eyebrows until they nearly reached her hairline, dropped her fleshy eyelids over her melancholy eyes, and left the room sighing, with a dignified air.

Pentàgora finally broke the long silence.

– Remember, Rocco—Hey!—Remember that I *said* this would happen.

His huge voice resounded so jarringly in that silent dining room that his sister Sidora, withdrawn and distracted as she was, leapt to her feet, picked up the salad bowl, grabbed a chunk of bread, and ran off to finish her dinner in another room.

Antonio Pentàgora followed her with his eyes until she was gone, and then glancing at Niccolino, he rubbed his bald head with both hands, his mouth twisting into a frigid, silent grin.

He remembered.

Many years before, he too had returned to his father's house after his wife had betrayed him. His sister Sidora, who had been a nag since she was a child, hadn't wanted anyone to so much as utter a rebuke. She had silently led him to his old, single room, as if she wanted to demonstrate that everyone was waiting to see him emerge again one day, betrayed, regretful that he'd left in the first place.

– I *said* this would happen! – he repeated, managing with a sigh to untangle himself from that distant memory.

Rocco stood up, his emotions high, and shouted,

– Is that all you can think to say to me?

It was then that Niccolino very subtly tugged at his father's jacket, imploring him to be quiet.

– No! – Pentàgora yelled loudly, right in Niccolino's face. – Come here, Roccuccio! Lift up your cap, it's covering your eyes . . . . Ah, here we are; you're hurt! Let me see . . . .

– What do I care about that? – yelled Rocco, almost weeping with rage as he tore his hat off his head and threw it to the floor.

– Your forehead . . . . Water and vinegar, right away: we'll fix you up.

Rocco replied, threateningly,

– You can't be serious! I'm getting out of here.

– So go! What do you want from me? Come on, let it all out! I try to make you feel better, and all I get are kicks and punches . . . . Calm yourself my boy! Now, the letter you could have dealt with a little more tactfully, in my opinion, without, you know, cracking your head open on the cabinet. But enough! It's all nonsense! You have as much money as you like, and you can have as many women as you like. Nonsense!

NONSENSE! was a common refrain for Antonio Pentàgora, and he always accompanied the exclamation with an expressive hand gesture and a tightening of his cheek.

He got up from the table, and leaning against the sideboard on which a huge, gray cat crouched, picked up a candle. He picked off the hardened beads of wax deliberately, wanting to leave no doubt as to his intentions, and then lit it and sighed.

– And now, for God's sake, let's go to sleep!

– You're leaving me like this? – Rocco exploded, exasperated.

– And what would you have us do for you? When I speak it annoys you . . . . Why should I stay? And yet . . . here we are . . . .

He blew out the candle and sat on one of the chairs next to the chiffonier. The cat jumped onto his shoulder.

Rocco paced the room, biting his hands every now and again, or punching at the air in impotent rage. He was crying.

Niccolino, still sitting at his place at the table, was rolling bits of bread into pellets with his index finger.

– You didn't want to listen, – his father began again, after a long silence. – You, – he cleared his throat loudly – yes, you had to go and make just the same mistake that I did . . . . It almost makes me laugh. What do you want to do about it? I feel for you, mind . . . but it was useless, Rocco. We Pentàgoras . . . —be still, Fufu!—we Pentàgoras don't have luck with wives.

He was quiet for another moment, and then he sighed and slowly took up again.

– You already knew this . . . . But when you married, you thought you'd found the phoenix, that rare bird that was different from the rest. And me? I thought the same! And my father, for God's sake? The same!

He made the traditional sign of the cuckold, the "corna," and he waved it in the air.

– My dear boy, do you see these horns? It's our family's coat of arms! More accurate than any coat of arms could be!

At this point Niccolino, who continued calmly rolling pellets, sniggered.

– Idiot, what are you laughing about? – his father said, lifting his ruddy, bald head from his chest. – It's destiny! Everyone has his cross to bear. And this is ours! Our Calvary.

He banged himself lightly on the head with his fist.

– But in the end, nonsense! – he continued. – That cross doesn't weigh anything when we chase away our wives, right, Fufu? They even say it's good luck! A man takes up a wife like he might take up the accordion, and he assumes that anybody can play it. Yes, all you have to do is extend the bellows and then squeeze—anyone can do it! Ah, but hitting the keys in just the right way, that's another story! People say I'm a bad person. But what's so bad about me? I wish everyone were as at peace with the world as I am! But there are those people; whenever they can say something bad about someone, they do. It makes them feel bigger. For my part, it's more useful if I take the blame. You know what I do? I just take the blame. I take it as a lesson and try to learn from it.

He slapped himself on the backside and continued.

– If you want to die, be my guest. I do my best to soldier on. We've got health to spare, and as for the rest, thanks be to God, we lack for nothing. On the other hand, we know that it's the custom of wives to deceive their husbands. When I got married, my boy, your grandfather told me exactly what I am saying to you now, word for word. I didn't want to listen to him, just as you didn't want to listen to me. And I understand! Every man must learn his own lessons in this world. What did I think of my wife, Fana? Exactly what you, my dear Roccuccio, thought of yours: I thought she was a saint! Now I would never say anything bad about her, nor do I bear her any ill will; you all were witness to that. I give your mother plenty of money to live on, and I allow you all to go visit her once a year in Palermo. In the end, she has done me a great service. She's taught me that you should always listen to your parents. That's why I always say to Niccolino, "Save yourself, my boy! At least there's one of us left!"

This part of his father's outburst didn't please Niccolino, who was just beginning to learn about love.

– You just look out for yourselves, and leave me out of it!

– I'm looking out for *him*, eh! *Him*, my boy! – sneered Pentàgora. – By San Silvestro . . . . By San Martino . . . .

– I get it, Papà, – replied Niccolino bitterly. – But what did Mamma ever do to us, poor thing, even if it's true that . . . ?

– Niccoli', now you're starting to make me angry! – his father interrupted, climbing to his feet. – It's destiny, you idiot! And I'm saying this for your own good. Go ahead, go get a wife if the experience of us three isn't enough for you. You'll see—if you're really a Pentàgora, you'll see!

He extricated himself from the cat with a shrug, took the candle from the drawer, and without even lighting it he quickly left the room.

Rocco opened the window and looked out into the darkness for a long while.

The night was damp. Below the house, after a steep decline dotted with a few other houses, a vast, lonely plain stretched out under a veil of fog, all the way to the sea below, faintly illuminated by the pale moon. There was so much air, so much space outside of that high, narrow window. He looked at the façade of the house, so exposed at that height to the wind and the rain, and so gloomy in the lunar damp. He stared down into the dark, deserted alleyway, illuminated by one weeping streetlight; the roofs of the poor houses huddled together in sleep, and he could feel himself becoming more and more distressed. Looking out into the night he was dumbfounded, almost frozen to the core. And just as after a violent hurricane light little clouds float around the sky uncertainly, strange thoughts, vague memories, distant impressions flooded his mind and spirit, although they remained strange, vague, and distant. He remembered that there, in that cramped little street, when he was a little boy, just down there by that feeble, flickering light, one night a man was killed in cold blood; that later a servant girl had told him that the dead man's spirit still walked the alley, that many people had seen it; and he thought of how afraid he had been, and how for a long time he couldn't bring himself even to look out the window, down that street . . . . And now, after two years, here he was moving back into his father's house, full of memories, of ancient oppressions. He was suddenly free, almost like being a bachelor again. And he would have to sleep alone that night, in that unfurnished room, in the same little bed as before. Alone! And his own house, the one he had shared with his wife, with its heavy new furniture, would remain empty, dark . . . ; the windows would be left open . . . , and that moon, waning as it shone through the haze on the distant sea; surely it could be seen from his bedroom . . . his room for two . . . peeking between the curtains of rose-colored silk . . . Ah! The muscles around his eyes tensed and he clenched his fists. And tomorrow? What would happen tomorrow when the whole town would know that he had run off his unfaithful wife?

There, immersed in the vast, melancholy silence of the night, broken here and there with moonlight, alive with the squealing of invisible bats, his fists still clenched, Rocco cried out, exasperated,

– What will I do? What will I do?

– Go down and see the Englishman, – he heard the soft, quiet voice of Niccolino, who hadn't left his place at the table, his eyes fixed on the tablecloth.

Rocco started at the sound of his voice, and he turned, surprised by the advice as much as by the fact that his brother was still there, sitting impassive under the light.

– Bill? – he asked, frowning. – Why?

– If I were in your shoes I would challenge this man to a duel, – Niccolino said simply, and with conviction, as he collected in his cupped palm all of the little rounded pellets of bread and got up to throw them out the window.

– A duel? – repeated Rocco, who stood stunned for a moment as he let his brother's suggestion sink in. Then he erupted: – But of course, yes, yes, yes! That's it! How did I not think of it? Of course, a duel!

From the church nearby they heard the slow chime of midnight.

– It's midnight.

– The Englishman will be awake.

Rocco picked up his crushed cap from the floor.

– I'm going!

~ Chapter 2 ~

On the stairs, in the dark, Rocco Pentàgora was suddenly unsure whether to knock on the door of the Englishman or on that of Professor Blandino, another lodger, who lived on the floor below.

Antonio Pentàgora had built his house in the shape of a massive tower, floor by floor. He'd stopped, for the time being, at the fourth. But the fact was that Pentàgora had never once managed to find anyone to live in any of the small apartments. Whether because the house was too far out, or because no one wanted anything to do with the landlord, the first floor had sat empty for years. On the second floor, Professor Blandino rented the only room that was occupied, which he left in the care of Signora Popònica. The third floor, like the second, had only one inhabitant, the Englishman Mr. H. W. Madden, known to all as "Bill." All of the other rooms in the house were left to the mice. The doorman had the dignified solemnity of an accountant, but he only made five lire a month, and so never greeted anyone.

Luca Blandino, an instructor of philosophy at the local high school, was around fifty years old, tall, thin, and completely bald, a deficiency he made up for with an enormous and fantastic beard. A peculiar man, known across the region for his incredible absent-mindedness, Blandino taught out of necessity and with sad resignation, for he was continually rapt in his meditations and no longer cared about anyone or anything else. Nonetheless, those who had been able to make a strong impression on the professor—and who thus allowed him, at least for a little while, to descend from the lofty peaks of his own abstraction—were able to pull him out of his shell and, in return, received useful and selfless advice. Rocco had managed to make such an impression.

Madden was a no less peculiar man. He was also a teacher, but of a very different kind, a private tutor of foreign languages. He gave lessons for practically no money in English, German, and French, and even in his terrible Italian. In this way, his vast mind was something of an international meeting place. His fine, golden hair seemed to be keeping its distance from his forehead and temples, perhaps for fear of his large, hooked nose, and two bulging veins snaked up from his eyebrows in search of his hairline, as if running for cover. Below his eyebrows shone two little gray-blue eyes, sometimes clever, sometimes achingly sad, as if burdened by his broad forehead.[1] Under his nose he wore a straw-colored mustache, which he trimmed religiously to keep it from invading his upper lip. His monumental forehead notwithstanding, Nature had gifted Mr. Madden with a physical agility that was positively monkey-like. And Mr. Madden soon discovered that he could even profit from this gift: in his idle moments, he gave fencing lessons—but without any pretenses to being a master, mind you!

Probably no one, not even poor Bill, would have thought to laugh about how in God's name he had ended up leaving his native Ireland and had been reduced to living in a little village in Sicily. He never received even a single letter from his homeland. He was entirely alone with the misery of his past behind him and the misery of his future undoubtedly ahead of him. But even as he twisted in the fickle wind of destiny, he was not discouraged. In truth, for all his bad luck, Mr. Madden had in his head more words than thoughts, and these he continually ran over in his mind.

As Niccolino had predicted, Rocco found him awake.

Bill was sitting on an old, rickety sofa in front of an end table, his magnificent forehead illuminated by a lamp with a broken shade. He was shoeless with one leg crossed over the other, taking tiny, angry bites of an overstuffed sandwich and staring religiously at an uncorked bottle of cheap beer that sat on the table before him.

Every inch of that floor was begging for a broom, and maybe a spittoon for Mr. Madden; the walls and the few pieces of decrepit furniture were screaming for a serious dusting; the meager little bed with its exposed frame required the arms of a strong serving girl, and one who would come back at least once a week; Mr. Madden's suit demanded less a lint brush than a horse brush.

The room's one window was open; the blinds were up. Mr. Madden's shoes—one here, one there—looked as if they'd been thrown to the middle of the room.

– Oh, Rocco! – he exclaimed in his barbaric accent, as if he were gargling, chewing, and violently spitting out his consonants and vowels, his emphasis on all the wrong syllables. He sounded as if he were speaking with a hot potato in his mouth.

– Excuse the hour, Bill; I know it's late, – said Rocco, his face colorless. – I need to speak with you.

Bill almost always repeated the last words of the person with whom he was speaking, as if to better latch on to a response:

– Speak with me? One second. First I have to put my shoes back on.

At this point he saw the gash on his friend's forehead.

– I've had a "*lite*."

– . . . I don't understand.

– A "*lite*!" – shouted Rocco, fingering his forehead.

– Ah, a "*lite*," of course! A fight, *der Streite*, *une mêlée*, yes, I understand perfectly. You say "*lite*" in Italian? LEE-TAY, excellent. What can I do for you?

– I need your help.

– (LEE-TAY). Help? I don't understand.

– I want to have a duel.

– Ah yes, a duel. You? I understand perfectly.

– But I don't know . . . well, I don't know anything, really, about . . . about fencing. How do you do it? I don't want to get myself killed in the street like a dog, if you know what I mean.

– Like a dog, yes, I understand perfectly. And so, some . . . *coup*? You wish to strike some blow, as you might say? Yes, *coup infallible*, I will teach you. Very simple, yes. Do you wish to start now?

And Bill, with a movement like that of a well-trained monkey, took down from the wall two old, rusty foils.

– Hold on, hold on . . . – Rocco said to him, agitated by the sight of those foils. – First, explain it to me . . . . I'm the challenger here, right? Or I challenge, and I am challenged in return. Our seconds discuss it; they agree. We decide on sabers. We meet at the agreed-upon place at the agreed-upon time. But then what? Tell me everything I need to know, and in order.

– Yes, of course, – responded Madden, who liked order, in a manner of speaking, as he liked not to get turned around; and so he put himself to explaining to Rocco, in his own meandering way, the preliminaries of a duel.

– Naked? – asked Rocco at one point, alarmed. – What do you mean, "naked"? Why?

– Naked . . . in the sense of "shirtless," – responded Madden. – Naked, your . . . how do you say? *Le tronc du corps* . . . ! *Die Brust* . . . ! Ah, yes, yes, torso, the torso! Or on the other hand, not naked. Yes . . . it's as you wish.

– And then?

– Then? Um . . . well then you duel . . . *La sciabla*; *en garde*; *à vous*!

– That's exactly my question, – said Rocco, – so, for example, I pick up the sword . . . ; come on, teach me . . . . How do you do it?

First, Bill showed him the correct form, placing his fingers between grip and bell guard. He then left Rocco to lunge, straighten, and lunge again, which he did, awkwardly. Rocco was, however, soon disheartened by these new and uncomfortable positions, which felt so unnatural to him. – I'm falling! I'm falling! – and his constantly flexed arm wore him out and made him sore; it must have been the foil, no? It weighed too much. – Eh! Eh! There! Again! – incited Madden, however. – Wait, Bill! – In making that kind of lunge, how was it possible to keep the left foot from moving? And the right, good God! He was no longer able to even draw back and defend himself! Every time he moved, Rocco felt the blood flow to the cut on his forehead, throbbing. In the meantime, the shoddy furniture, which had been pushed to the sides of the room, seemed to jump with fright, astonished at the ridiculous dances the two monstrously enlarged shadows of these two nocturnal duelists were performing.

BUM! BUM! BUM! – the angry pounding of the neighbor below could be heard through the floorboards.

Madden stood up straight, his thighs practically dislocated, his broad forehead glistening with sweat. He strained his ears.

– We've awakened Professor Luca!

Rocco had given up; he was finished. He collapsed into a chair, his legs dangling, his head drooping, tilted against the wall behind him, almost swooning. It seemed, from that position, that he had already completed the duel with his adversary and had received a fatal blow.

– We've awakened Professor Luca, – repeated Bill, staring at Rocco, to whom such news didn't seem such an unpleasant surprise.

– I'm going to see Blandino, – he said in the end, lifting himself to his feet. – This all needs to be done with by tomorrow. Blandino will be my second. Good night, and thanks, Bill. I'm also counting on you, you know.

With a candle in his hand, Madden accompanied his friend to the door; he waited on the landing for Professor Blandino to open his door, and only when the door had been opened and shut again did he return to his room, making a strange gesture with his hand, as if catching an obstinate fly from the tip of his nose.

Rocco found Luca Blandino in a terrible mood that evening. He was muttering and stumbling about as he led Rocco through a series of deserted rooms, and finally into his own room. Then, with his grizzled gray whiskers and the swollen, red eyes of someone whose sleep has been interrupted, he sat down on his bed, his bare, hairy legs dangling.

– Professor, forgive me, and have pity on me, – said Rocco. – I need your advice.

– What's happened to you? You're hurt! – cried Blandino in a hoarse voice, staring at Rocco with a candle in his hand.

– Yes . . . ah, but if you only knew! It all started ten hours ago, when . . . . You know, my wife . . . ?

– Bad news on the home front?

– It's worse than that. My wife, she . . . . I've sent her back to her family . . . .

– You have? But why?

– She betrayed me . . . . She betrayed me . . . . She betrayed me.

– Are you mad?

– Crazy? No! What are you talking about?

And Rocco began to sob, hiding his face in his hands. He hesitated,

– What do you mean crazy? What do you mean by that?

The professor looked at him from the bed, almost not believing his own eyes or ears, overcome as he was with weariness.

– She betrayed you?

– I surprised her . . . . She was reading a letter . . . . And do you know from whom? From Alvignani!

– Ah that scoundrel! Gregorio? Gregorio Alvignani?

– Yes, sir – (Rocco held back his rage). – Now you've got to understand, Professor . . . ; in this way . . . he can't finish it this way! He's run off.

– Gregorio Alvignani?

– Yes sir, he's escaped. This very evening. I don't know to where, but I'll find out. He was afraid . . . . Professor, I put myself into your hands.

– Me? What have I got to do with it?

– I must take my satisfaction in front of the whole town, Professor, and you have to help me to do that. Don't you think so? How can I live like this?

– Easy now, easy . . . . Calm down, my boy! What does the rest of the town have to do with it?

– My honor, Professor! How can that not matter? I have to defend my honor . . . in front of the whole town . . . .

Luca Blandino shrugged his shoulders and seemed annoyed.

– Leave the town out of it! You need to reflect on this, to be reasonable. First thing, are you absolutely sure?

– I have the letter I tell you, the letter that he passed to her through the window!

– Him? Gregorio? Why, he passed it to her through the window . . . like a schoolboy! Are you absolutely sure what you're telling me is true? Hmm . . . hmm . . . hmm . . . . He passed her the letter through the window, you say?

– Yes sir, I have it right here!

– But look, look, look . . . . This is your wife we're talking about, for the love of God! Your wife, the daughter of Francesco Ajala! That man's a beast. Look here . . . . You're about to start a bloodbath . . . . What are you telling me here? Just what are you telling me? Get out of here . . . through the window? He passed the letters through the window, like a schoolboy?

– Can I count on you, Professor?

– On me? For what? Ah, I see what you're thinking . . . Wait, my boy, you must think this through . . . . You've gotten me out of bed . . . . Now is not the time. It's not possible right now . . . .

He climbed out of his bed; he approached Rocco and clapped him on the shoulder and added,

– Go back upstairs, my boy . . . . You're in too much pain right now; I can see that . . . Tomorrow, eh? By the light of the sun. We'll talk about this again tomorrow; it's late now . . . . Get some sleep, if you can manage . . . ; get some sleep my boy . . . .

– But you must promise me . . . . – Rocco insisted.

– Tomorrow, tomorrow, – Blandino interrupted him again, pushing him toward the door. – I promise . . . . But what a scoundrel, oh! Passing her letters through the window? You never know what this terrible old world will throw at you, eh my dear boy? Poor Roccuccio—she was betraying you . . . . Out, out, get going now . . . .

– Professor, don't abandon me, please! I'm counting on you!

– Tomorrow, tomorrow, – repeated Blandino. – Poor Roccuccio . . . funny thing, life, eh? What a misery . . . . Good night, my boy, good night, good night . . . .

And Rocco felt the door shut softly behind him. And there he was, in the dark, on the landing, in the middle of the silent staircase. Lost. Did no one want to know about it—about him—any longer?

He sat on the lowest steps like an abandoned child and leaned against the railing with his elbows on his knees and his head in his hands. The dark, the silence, his predicament tightened itself around his heart like a fist and left him desperate to the very depths of his soul. His face contracted, and he began to weep, all the while lamenting under his breath,

– Oh *mamma mia*! *Mamma mia*!

He wept and wept. Eventually, he reached into his pocket and pulled out the crumpled letter. He struck a match and tried to read it again, but he felt on his hand something wet, and very soft, and slightly viscous. He raised the match to see what it was. The long strand of a spider web hung from above the staircase. As he sat and stared at it in the matchlight, he didn't feel when the match had burned itself down to the nub between his fingers. He burned himself and shouted in the dark,

– Damn! Damn! Damn!

He lit another match and went back to reading the letter, which was almost indecipherable, scrawled as it was in tiny handwriting on gray paper. He read the first words mechanically: "*I have been writing to you for three months (yes, it's already been three months) and still* . . . ." He skipped over a few lines and let his eyes fall on the underlined "*When?*" He then threw the match away and sat there with the letter in his hand, his eyes no longer able to make anything out in the darkness.

The scene flashed again before his eyes.

He had forced the door open with a violent thrust, screaming, "The letter! Give me the letter!" In the commotion, Marta had taken cover by the open cabinet of the large chest of drawers, next to which she had been reading. He had forcibly removed her from behind the cabinet and was dragging her forward by the wrists. "What letter? What letter?" she stammered, staring back at him with terror in her eyes. But the letter, which she had crumpled up in the sudden fright of his discovery and shoved between her dress and a shelf of the chest, had fallen like a dead leaf to the floor. In launching himself at it and getting to it before she could, he had cut his forehead on the open drawer as he'd smashed his head into it. He was blinded by his anger, by his pain, and so he had railed against her without regard for her incipient maternity, pursuing her through the house, beating her.

Then there was that other scene, with his father-in-law. Rocco had gone to show him that letter and the others he had discovered in the drawer. Was she guilty? "And what exactly would constitute guilt for her?" he had asked. "Forgive my saying so, but maybe that's because she's your daughter?"

Francesco Ajala pounced like a tiger. "My daughter? What are you saying? That my daughter is a tramp?" But then he suddenly seemed very calm. "Careful, Rocco, careful what you do . . . . Do you see what this is about? Letters . . . ? And you're ruining two lives here: yours and mine. Maybe you could still forgive her . . . ." "Oh yes? And would you forgive her if you were in my place, if instead of her father you were her husband?" And Francesco Ajala did not know how to respond.

"Her father couldn't, but I am supposed to? Unbelievable!" thought Rocco in the silence of the stairwell.

"It's all over! Now it's all over!"

He pulled himself to his feet and, striking another match, began to climb back up the stairs, his eyes still fixed on the letter in his hand.

"What does that mean? . . ." he asked himself, trying to decipher the Alvignani family motto embossed in red at the top of the page:

NIHIL – MIHI – CONSCIO[2]

~ Chapter 3 ~

Shadows and then, little by little, darkness had invaded the room where Marta's mother had welcomed her with open arms after her husband had kicked her out. In the darkness, the glassware on the table, which had been laid for supper before Marta arrived, reflected the last flicker of daylight from the street.

Signora Agata Ajala was a very tall, very heavy woman, but had a sweetness in her face and voice that seemed to exist for the sole purpose of attenuating the negative impression aroused by her body in everyone who spoke to her or looked at her. Reentering from the adjoining room, where she had been briefly occupied, she suddenly caught a glimpse of her two daughters, who were sitting on the couch, illuminated in the light threading in through the open door: Marta with a handkerchief to her face, her head thrown back against the back of the sofa, and Maria, who was bent over her, holding her hand.

– She wants to leave this place . . . . – Maria announced, almost unable to speak as a result of this unforeseen tragedy.

– Mamma, he found out . . . . He found out, – said Marta, her head lolling as she wrung her hands. – He found out and now he does not want to come home. He is not going to forgive me. I know it. Please go and find him: tell him he can come back, Mamma, that I'll be gone. I know he no longer believes me fit to live under the same roof as him. Tell him that I came to you . . . like this, because I didn't know where else to go. I'm leaving. I didn't know where else to go.

Two loving arms, stretched out in a rush of excitement, latched around her.

Her mother said,

– Where else would you have gone? Where *could* you have gone? Stay, stay here, with Maria. I'm going to go speak to him . . . .

And she threw a black wool shawl over her head, fastened it around her neck, and left.

The wide suburban street, so animated during the day, was silent and deserted at that hour of the evening, like a street in a dream. The moon shone a green light that reflected on the windows of the tall row of houses, and a heavy but broken line of smoky clouds now and then veiled that pale, cool lunar serenity casting gloomy shadows on the damp street.

– Oh, San Francesco! – said the mother as she raised a hand in the direction of the church at the end of the street.

There, only a few paces from her home, on the same suburban street, the huge tannery owned by her husband, Francesco Ajala, rose before her. As she came closer she caught sight of her husband on a first-floor balcony. She trembled at the thought of confronting him, of his inevitable anger and disappointment, knowing all too well the terrible emotional excesses they might inspire in him. He was even taller than she was, and the light of the balcony door outlined his huge frame.

There were two tragedies here, not just one. And the misfortune of the father was, in this case, far more serious than that of Marta. Perhaps Marta's misfortune could be resolved by using a little bit of levelheaded reasoning and waiting a few days. But there was no reasoning with her father.

Signora Ajala had learned long ago to measure every disappointment, every little cause for grief, not with respect to herself, to whom it would have meant little or nothing, but instead in light of the anger it would rouse in her husband. On occasion, good God, the breaking of some household object, say—even if it were of little value, but difficult to replace—would plunge the whole household into terror and confusion . . . . The neighbors, people outside of the house, laughed about it when they found out, and they were right to. Really? All that rage over a bottle? Over a little picture frame? Some little knickknack? But they didn't understand what it meant to him, to him as a husband. It meant a lack of respect not for the object, which was worth little or nothing, but for him, for him because he had bought it. Was he just stingy? Certainly not! For the sake of one little trinket that had cost only a few cents, he could tear the house to pieces.

Over their many years of marriage, she had managed with her sweet disposition to tame him to some extent, and also to forgive him again and again for the serious wrongs he committed, and all the while without losing her own dignity and without allowing him to feel weighed down by her many reprieves. But still, from time to time, some trivial little thing was enough to set him on a wild rampage. It's possible that after such fits he felt sorry; he would never want—or even know how—to apologize. That would have been a humiliation, an admission that he had indeed been wrong. Instead, he wanted the others to have to guess his apology, to understand that he was sorry without his ever saying those words. At that point, however, everyone was still reeling in the wake of one of his outbursts, and no one dared so much as to breathe, much less to say anything. And so he would close himself into a silent, black rage for weeks on end. To be certain, he noticed, and with a secret spite, the efforts of his family members to never do anything that might give him the slightest pretext to complain, and he suspected that many things were hidden from him. If one of these secrets did come to light, even after a very long time, he let loose his accumulated scorn in a rage, without reflecting on the fact that his rage was out of place by then, and that, in the end, the only reason anything had been concealed was so as not to displease him.

He felt like a stranger in his own house. Or at least it seemed to him that his family treated him like a stranger, and he distrusted them. He especially distrusted *her*, his wife.

And Signora Agata, in fact, was the victim above all of two false impressions, burned into her husband's soul: one was that she was guilty of malice; the other, that she was hypocritical. And she suffered all the more inasmuch as she herself was often forced to recognize that these impressions were not wholly without reason: she had to admit that, in truth, owing to the discord between them, she was sometimes forced to hide from him things of which he would most certainly not have approved. In such situations, she would have to deceive him simply in order to survive.

– Francesco! – she called to him humbly, in the silence of the street.

– Who's there? – shouted back Ajala, starting violently and bending himself over the railing of the balcony. – You? Who told you to come here? Get out of here! Get out of here right now! Don't make me yell from here!

– Open up, I beg you . . . .

– Get out of here I said! I don't want to see anyone! Go home! Go home immediately! No? Don't make me come down there!

And Francesco Ajala, with one final, mighty shake of the iron railing, withdrew from the balcony.

She waited for him with bowed head, leaning against the outer door like a beggar woman, drying her eyes every now and again with the same handkerchief she'd been wringing in her hands for the last four hours.

The sound of footsteps reverbated along the long corridor, echoing darkly. The little window just to the right of the door opened, and Ajala, bending over and sticking his head out, seized his wife by the arm.

– What did you come here for? What do you want? Who are you? I don't know anyone anymore; I don't have anyone anymore! No family, no home! Get out, everyone! Out! You disgust me! Get out! Out!

And he gave her a violent push.

– She stood in front of the window, still wincing from the blow, and then she entered like a ghost, resigned to wait until he had emptied his heart of all its anger, pouring it out onto her. She resolved to stand her ground, even if it meant taking a beating.

In the dark of the entryway, Ajala, with his fingers clasped behind the nape of his neck and his arms pressed tightly around his head, was staring at the great glass door at the end, turned opaque in the pale moonlight. He turned, hearing his wife sobbing softly in the dark; he came toward her with his fists clenched, roaring at her mockingly,

– Did you take her back into the house? Did you kiss her and stroke her and pet her, that fine daughter of yours? So what do you want from me now? What are you expecting to happen? Will you tell me that?

– You want to leave us . . . . – she sobbed softly.

– Yes, right away! My luggage . . . .

– Where will you go?

– Why should I tell *you*?

– Because, well . . . I have to know what to pack . . . . How long you'll stay away . . . ?

– How long? – he screamed. – Do you really think I can ever come back here? That I can ever set foot again in your . . . house of shame? I'm getting out for good! For me, it's prison or the grave—I'll catch up to him! I'll find him, no matter the cost . . . .

– And does that seem right to you? – she ventured, bleakly.

– No! Come on . . . of course not! – he exploded with a terrible sneer. – It is *right* that a daughter soils her father's name! It's *right* she gets herself chased out of her husband's house like a whore, and then runs home to teach her wicked ways to her little sister! *That* is *right*! At least that's what the word means to you, apparently!

– As you wish, – she said. – But I was only asking whether, before getting so carried away, it doesn't seem to you that it would be better to . . . .

– To what?

– To see if it might be possible to avoid scandal.

– Scandal? – he shouted. – But Rocco has already come here!

– Here?

– To show me the letters!

– So you've seen them? – she asked, anxiously. – And the last one? It's proof that Marta . . . .

– Is innocent, right? – he snapped, seizing her roughly by the arm, jostling her, pushing her, and pulling her again. – Innocent? Innocent? You dare say the word in my presence? Do you have no shame? Where is your blush? – And in saying this he furiously slapped her cheeks, again and again. – Is it here? Or here? Or here? Here? Here? Here? – he slapped her face until her cheeks were red. Then he picked up again,

– Innocent . . . with those letters? Would you have done the same, then? Quiet! Don't you dare try to excuse her!

– I do not excuse her, – she moaned softly, with agony. – But if I have proof . . . me . . . proof that my daughter does not deserve the punishment that you want to inflict upon her . . . .

– Ah, that, – intoned Ajala darkly, – that's what I said to that imbecile . . . .

– You see? – cried his wife, almost happy at this glimmer of hope.

– But then he asked me if I, in his place, would have forgiven her . . . . And, no! Because I, – he added, seizing her again by the arms and shaking her violently, – I would not have forgiven you! I would have killed you!

– Even if I weren't guilty . . . .

– For that letter? Isn't that enough?

– Marta is guilty, it's true, – admitted her mother, – but of acting foolishly, and of nothing more. But now what do you want to do? Do you want to go away? To confront this other man? But if you do that, this misunderstanding will . . . . Let me speak, please! I have faith, myself. Faith that one day, soon, the truth will come out . . . .

– Stop making excuses for her! There is no excuse!

– I am not excusing Marta, no. I am accusing myself, alright? I blame myself because I should never have let that marriage take place . . . .

– So you're blaming me too, then?

– But you said so yourself! Didn't you regret it too? We were too quick to marry her off! Admit that we made a bad choice! And all that she had to suffer under the tyranny of that witch of an aunt, and that dreadful father, before Rocco finally decided to get them a place of their own! This doesn't excuse her, it's true, I know; but it seems to me that it might render our judgment of her less . . . severe. That poor, poor girl . . . yes, a . . . .

She could not go on. She hid her face in her handkerchief, shaking with uncontrollable sobbing.

Leaning on his elbow against the wall, his forehead in his hand, he tapped his foot rhythmically on a pile of scrap iron in the hallway, his thick brow furrowed. He seemed solely intent on this exercise. Then he said in a somber voice,

– Since the fault is ours, let this be our punishment, and let's pay it all. Listen! I will go back to the house: it will be, from now on, our prison. I will not leave it until I die!

– He went upstairs to close the balcony window he had left open. His wife waited for him a bit in the dark of the hallway. Then, because he was taking so long, she went upstairs herself. She found him alone, his face against the wall, weeping.

– Francesco . . . .

– Out! Out! Out!

– He pushed her ahead of him in a rage. He closed up the tannery, and they made the short trip back to the house in silence. At the front door, he ordered his wife to go ahead of him, adding, threateningly,

– Don't let me see her!

A little later, he too went upstairs and locked himself into a room, in the darkness. He threw himself on the bed, fully clothed, his face buried in the pillows, with one hand clinging to the head of the bed.

He lay that way all night long. Every so often, he pulled himself into a sitting position and strained to hear. The house was silent, but certainly not because anyone was sleeping.

The heavy silence of the house only irritated him, deepening the dull but violent turmoil that plagued his soul. As he sat there, he dug his fingernails into his legs and arms, choking with a raging, impotent desire to weep, to cry out. Then he would fall back again onto the bed, and bury his face again in the pillows, which were bathed in tears.

What? Had he been crying?

Little by little, under the nightmarish weight of thoughts that presented themselves again and again, in the same form and in the same order, his head began to spin and he remained motionless for a long while, almost unconscious, wearily breathing ragged breaths in fits and starts. Then he would wake up confused, aware only of how dry his eyes felt, opened wide and unblinking in the darkness of the room.

Then the cracks in the shutters began to lighten. Little by little, tiny threads of humid dawn crept farther and farther into the room, shining golden in the darkness: the sun!

He lay in bed, his hands clasped behind his neck, staring at the shutters. The carts had already begun passing continuously in the street below, and it was as if they were passing through his head. He saw them as he lay there, idle and barely conscious, still wrapped in the warmth of the bed and of the room. Outside that window, the day . . . work to be done . . . the workmen, sitting one next to the other on the curb waiting for the doors of the tannery to open . . . . There, the bell is ringing, and they enter, two by two, in groups of three, cheerful or withdrawn, bundles of sticks under their arms. And there's old Scoma, the one who never speaks . . . his daughter . . . .

And my daughter too! Mine too! Worse than his! At least his didn't betray anyone but was herself betrayed! And now . . . misery . . . .

He sprang from the bed, as if to run to Marta and take her by the hair, drag her about the house, and beat her until she bled.

Two timid little knocks at the door.

– Who is it? – he shouted with a start.

– It's me . . . . – sighed the voice behind the door.

– Go away! I don't want to see anyone!

– If you need . . . .

– Go away! Go away!

And he heard the footsteps of his wife as they moved away from the door, slowly and softly. He followed her in his mind as she wandered the house. But where was *she*? What was she doing? Did she dare say a word, or look her mother and sister in the eye? And what could she possibly say? For shame! For shame!

The thought of her, his curiosity to see her, the *need*, one might say, to hear her weeping and see her trembling on bended knee before his eyes, begging for forgiveness, which he would not grant, kept him agitated all day long. He kept the room dark, and even felt horror at the few rays of light coming from the slits in the shutters, which hurt his weary eyes every time he passed them as he turned and paced the room.

Late in the day he opened the door for his younger daughter. He opened the door and lay down on the bed again.

– Close the door immediately!

Maria closed the door and set down a mug of broth on the bedside table.

– Do you not feel well?

– I do not feel anything, – he responded harshly.

Maria sat at the foot of the bed, sighing softly, with a napkin in her hands.

He raised himself onto an elbow, trying to make out his daughter in the darkness.

Maria had never been the favorite. She had grown up very much in the shadow of Marta, one might say, and it almost seemed that she had assigned herself the task of being the opposite of her adored older sister in every respect: talents, spirit, looks. No one had ever paid any attention to her, nor did she ever complain about it, won over as even she was by Marta's charms. She locked her thoughts and feelings deep inside herself, for no one, it seemed, ever asked her to reveal them. And it seemed that neither her father nor her mother had realized that she was grown up now, that she had become a woman. Not beautiful, not graceful, but from her eyes and voice there emanated such goodness, and there was such a timid grace in everything she did, that it was impossible for anyone not to be won over.

– Maria, – her father called out in a hoarse voice, still in the same position.

Maria ran to the bed and suddenly felt herself embraced and held tightly in his arms, feeling his head pressed against her chest. In this position, they wept together, wordlessly, holding each other more and more tightly, for a long time.

– Go, go . . . . – he said, finally, in anguish. – I don't want anything . . . . I want to be alone . . . .

And his daughter obeyed, still trembling from this unexpected rush of tenderness.

~ Chapter 4 ~

Maria had given up her little bedroom to Marta, the same room that had been Marta's when she was a girl. Nothing in the room had changed; Maria hadn't added a thing.

There stood the quaint old wardrobe, the rustic pastoral paintings on the panels seeming to have improved with age. And there sat Grandmother's little worktable, its veneer all burnt and cracked since the evening long ago when she had dropped the oil lamp on it, almost setting fire to her skirts in the process. And there beside the little brass bed was the glass basin for holy water and underneath it, the palm frond with its pink ribbon, now hopelessly faded.

Was there holy water in that basin? Oh, of course there was. Maria was nothing if not devout!

And over the bed was the ivory crucifix, hanging on a concave slab in a black oval frame, the same *Ecce Homo* that she had seen nod his thorn-crowned head in assent, as she and Maria had rushed to him, one after the other, to pray for their mother when she had suddenly fallen ill.

Marta had never been superstitious, but all the same, that image had a permanent place in her memory, and it was always accompanied by the strange wonder of knowing that her sister too, although some time later, had seen the very same *Ecce Homo* bow his head in assent, a sign that their prayers would be answered.

Hallucinations, surely! But all the same, why couldn't she bring herself to raise her eyes now to look upon that sacred image above the bed?

Wasn't she truly innocent? Had she perhaps really loved Alvignani? Ridiculous! To her mind no one could take such a notion seriously. Her only fault was centered on not having known how to stop his letters, which she should have. Rather, she had tried to stop them, but in just the wrong way—by responding to them . . . . In any case, she did not feel the slightest bit of guilt regarding her husband.

The only parts of that furtive correspondence that she had read with any interest were those referring to a very serious issue concerning the nature of conscience, her own in particular. It was a problem that she had innocently revealed to Alvignani in her responses to his early letters, which were indeed overly philosophical despite all of their composed sentimentality.

All of those fine phrases of love she simply ignored, or else laughed off as superfluous and innocuous gallantries. In a word, what had passed between them was a purely sentimental, almost literary discussion, which had lasted around three months. And perhaps, yes, she had enjoyed it to some extent; she was idle, after all, more often than not abandoned in solitude by her new husband. Sculpting the form, choosing her phrases as if for a school essay, she was actually quite proud of her performance in that secret intellectual duel with a man of Alvignani's caliber; he was, after all, a famous and admired lawyer, and beloved by the townspeople, who were on the point of electing him deputy.

The bursting of her husband into the room while she was reading that last letter, in which, for the first time, Alvignani had ventured to refer to her by the informal "*tu*," and the violent scene that followed had astonished and frightened her all the more since she felt so calm and indifferent about it; "innocent," in her words.

And couldn't this have easily happened to any honest woman, so long as she wasn't hideously ugly? Being stared at by someone with a strange persistence was only troubling if you weren't prepared for it, and a woman aware of her beauty could, in fact, get pleasure from it. In that moment of annoyance or pleasure, though, no honest woman would think deep in her heart that she was committing a sin, even if she temporarily embraced that kindled desire, imagining, in that fleeting instant, another life, another love . . . . And then the sight of the familiar things around her called her back to reality, reminded her of her situation and her station, of her duties. And everything ended there . . . . Mere moments! Doesn't each of us feel these flashes inside often enough—strange thoughts, glimmers of madness, thoughts that follow from nothing, and that we would never confess to anyone, as if they had sprung from a different mind than the one that we normally recognize as being our own? And then as quickly as they have come, the flashes disappear, and the dreary shadow or the calm light we are used to returns.

Without wanting it, without knowing exactly how, Marta found that she had been completely enveloped, caught in a web.

From the terrifying surprise of seeing Alvignani throw down the first letter from his window, and from the torturous uncertainty as to which road she should take to ward off the advances that would inevitably follow, she no longer understood how she—honest, the honest daughter of honest parents—even she had managed little by little to let it develop as it had, without even knowing it! Ah, how many unwise decisions had that man made even before he threw down that first letter! And how many more after! Only now was she noting them; only now did they offend her. The shutters of his window, opposite hers, would not stay still; up they went, from bottom to top, and then suddenly down, where they remained for a while before being jerked back up again. And then the sudden disappearances from the window and certain signals from the head and hands . . . . She had been able to laugh, then, laugh at that man who, even though already middle-aged and respectable, rendered himself so ridiculous in her presence, who seemed so infantile . . . . But by what desperate means should she have tried to make him stop bothering her? Compromise her father? Her husband? She was exasperated, discouraged; and yet her eyes were nonetheless always drawn there, to that window opposite hers, involuntarily, as if something beyond her control drew her gaze there, always there . . . . As a result, she went out often, to eliminate that childish temptation; she went, for days at a time, to her father's house, and there she made Maria play for her, always the same thing, a sad, old barcarole.

– Well, Marta?

And she, sunk deep into the divan, responded in a feeble voice and distant eyes,

– I am far away . . . far away . . . .

Maria had laughed, and her innocent laughter now rang in Marta's ears. And the memories continued to appear, flash before her in her mind's eye. She saw her mother enter the room, asking after her husband.

– He's as usual . . . . – she responded.

– Are you happy?

– Yes.

And she was lying. Not that she had anything to complain about in terms of his conduct. But there was something there, at the bottom of her heart, a hostility that was not clearly defined, but also not new. It had been there from the first day of their engagement, when she, only just sixteen, had been taken out of school, taken away from the studies she had followed with such fervor, and Rocco had been presented to her as her fiancé. Even then, there was the vague feeling of oppression that she always pushed deep inside herself, allowing that feeling to be suffocated by the sage advice of her parents, who had seen in the Pentàgora boy an excellent match. "What a nice young man! And so rich!" Oh yes; and she had repeated her parents' sage reflections to her school friends as if they were her own. The truth was that she'd wanted to take her leave of them, just as if overnight she had grown from a little girl into an old woman, experienced in and weary of the ways of the world.

Here and there the walls of her little room still held some of the dates she had scribbled, memories, of course, of old school triumphs, or of naïve festivities among friends or family. And on those walls and on all of those simple, humble objects that were so dear to her, it seemed as though time had somehow fallen asleep and forgotten to move forward, that everything there still held the fragrance of the breath she had breathed on it as a child. And in this way, Marta began to sift through her past, taking stock of the life she had lived as a child.

How many times had she stood here like this with her eyes intent and her spirit wandering, listening to those first drops of rain pattering on the windowpane? How many times had she seen that pale, sad light in that same narrow room and savored the sweet sensation of the coming cold weather, the end of the cloudy autumn, the shivers that one gets on winter nights, just before dawn?

Maria stared at her sister, amazed at her calm, and almost couldn't believe her eyes. She was hurt by Marta's seeming acceptance of this disgrace, as though the storm was not passing over her head right at that very moment. "And yet she cannot ignore the state that Father has been reduced to on her account!" thought Maria. She almost wept at the pain of not seeing Marta behave as she had wanted her to behave: humbled, remorseful, overcome by her grief, inconsolable, just as she had been in those first days after her return home.

In fact, Marta had stopped crying altogether. After having confessed everything to her mother—everything, down to the tiniest of details, down to the most intimate and secret of sentiments—she had hoped that her father would at least treat her justly, if her husband would not, and that he would abandon his resolution never to leave the house again. For her, her father's open condemnation was a message to the whole village and constituted a far more serious reproof than the one her husband had wished to inflict with so little reason when he had thrown her out of their conjugal home.

In this way he, her own father, confirmed her husband's accusations and slandered her irrevocably. Could he not see that this was what he was doing?

Marta had asked her mother anxiously if she had relayed her confession to her father, and her mother confirmed that yes, she had.

And? Still so obstinate?

From that moment forward, she had not shed another tear. She had felt the shift inside her, as that restrained rage had hardened into a cold disdain, into that indifferent mask, sneering at the suffering of her mother and sister, who, rather than condemn Marta's father for his blind, bullheaded sense of justice, showed him nothing but pity, mainly for the ill that this would certainly do to his health, as if it had been her fault.

And then Marta would deliberately ask Maria for news of some friend or other of their mother's who used to come visit; and, when Maria would answer with obvious embarrassment, would exclaim with a strange little smile,

– Of course, everyone knows that no one will want to visit our house anymore . . . .

And so everything was just going to end this way? Was she to remain imprisoned in that stifling little room, in that darkness, in mourning, as if the world had ended?

The rest of the family had removed themselves to the rooms farthest away from those in which Francesco Ajala had imprisoned himself. No voices, no noises at all reached his ears as he sat in the armchair at the foot of the bed staring at the stripe of light that shone under the darkened door. He sat there listening for the apprehensive shuffling of feet, barely audible on the other side of the partition of the next room, and every time someone slipped past on tiptoe, he guessed at who it might be. Surely not *her*! It was Agata . . . . It was Maria . . . . It was the maid . . . .

– And the tannery? – his wife reminded him one day. – Do you really want us to lose everything this way?

– Everything! Everything! – he responded. – We will die of hunger.

– And Maria? Isn't she your daughter too? Why should poor Maria be punished?

– And what about me? – screamed Ajala, raising himself up darkly before his wife. You talk of punishment? Why should *I* be punished? You're the one who wanted this!

He regained his composure, sat back down; then he went on in a hollow voice,

– Bring your nephew Paolo Sistri to me. I will entrust him with the direction of the tannery. There's no sense in being proud, not now. He wanted to marry her once? He can have her! Now everyone can have her.

– Oh, Francesco!

– Enough! Send for Paolo. Leave me alone!

It was from this same Paolo Sistri—the son of one of Signora Agata's sisters, now deceased—that the three women had received word of Rocco Pentàgora's recent escapades. It seemed that he had gone out with Professor Blandino and Madden the day after the scandal broke, looking for Alvignani. When they found him in Palermo, Gregorio Alvignani had not initially wanted to accept the challenge; he had in fact managed to persuade Blandino to lobby Pentàgora to take it back. But then the young man attacked him publicly in an attempt to force him into a fight. The duel had taken place, and had gone poorly for Rocco, who had received a long gash down his left cheek. Three days later, he had returned home in the company of a prostitute, whom he had brought into his house and forced to wear Marta's clothes, and much to the outrage of the whole town, proceeded to make a spectacle of himself, taking her on walks and for drives in his carriage dressed that way.

After that news, how could her father not recognize how unworthy and vile his daughter's husband was? Was he not, even then, ashamed to be subjected to that man's disreputable condemnation of his daughter, of his family?

Marta shook with contempt and rage but got into the habit of taking great pains to contain herself in front of her mother and her sister, who began to look more dejected and beaten down every day.

– But why are you crying, Maria? – she asked disdainfully one morning as her sister entered her room with eyes red from weeping.

– Daddy . . . you know why! – responded Maria with difficulty.

– Eh, – sighed Marta. –What can we do about it? Maybe he's resting. He's not hurting anybody . . . .

She was standing there without her bodice in front of the mirror. As she drew the tortoiseshell combs from her dark, fragrant hair, it cascaded down her shoulders and over her bare arms. She threw her head back and shook out that beautiful, heavy mane; then she sat down, and her perfectly formed shoulder, white as polished ivory, appeared from among those tresses as they parted between her breast and her back. And on that shoulder, there was a small, violet mole that had colored slowly over the years; it shone like a single star on her back, where Maria had first discovered it when they were only children and still shared a bed.

– Come and brush my hair, Maria.

~ Chapter 5 ~

Paolo Sistri was very tall and haggard with disproportionately long legs, a face perpetually drained of color and dotted with freckles, and tufts of red fur on his throat and chin. And now he came every evening to submit his report of the daily goings-on at the tannery for his Uncle Ajala's approval.

After about a half an hour, he would exit the room of the shut-in, dejected and confused, and, with a tilt of his head, would respond in the same way every evening to his aunt Agata and to Maria, who anxiously awaited him:

– He says that everything's fine.

But it seemed that he was neither convinced nor satisfied by his uncle's endorsement, as if he secretly suspected that his uncle was praising him in jest. Flopping onto the nearest chair he would take the deepest breath he could manage and then release it slowly through his nostrils, shaking his head in resignation.

Now that he was a businessman, or at least dressed as one, he had renounced his romantic ambitions toward Marta. In those first days, he was very awkward in her presence; then, slowly but surely, he began to regain his composure. When speaking, however, he addressed himself either to Maria or to his aunt. In a confused tangle of words, he would tell of all of the little ups and downs of the day, falling back into his chair at the end of each line and rolling his eyes back and forth as he sweated and swallowed. Every dense, circuitous sentence that came out of his mouth was either left hanging pregnant in the air, or it vanished, fading into an exclamation. If, however, one of them was unlucky enough to be brought to its natural end, he repeated it three or four times before putting himself to the task of spinning another.

His aunt demonstrated that she was listening attentively by nodding in agreement at nearly every word, and often when he was finished, knowing that, in any case, he had no one to go home to, invited him to stay for dinner.

Paolo almost always accepted. But they were cheerless, these silent suppers, interrupted only when they sent food to the room of the shut-in, and they were chilled by Maria's expression as she returned all the more troubled, weighed down with sadness.

Marta took note of everything with a strange expression in her eyes, at times almost derisive, at other times merely disdainful. Wasn't their obvious misery a reproach to her and an assumption of her guilt? She often stood up and left the table without a word.

– Marta!

She would not respond, locking herself in her little room. Then Maria would stand at the door and beg her to open it, to return to the dinner table. Marta listened with a mix of pain and pleasure to the entreaties of her sister, and she didn't open the door, nor did she respond; then as soon as Maria went away, tired of her appeals falling on deaf ears, Marta would grow angry with herself for not having given in and would burst into tears. But quickly her remorse would be transformed into hatred for her husband. Ah, at that moment, with that rage in her heart, if only she had been able to get her hands on him! And she would wring her hands, weeping, raving. And to think that in the meantime his child was growing in her womb . . . . She would be a mother, and so soon! Her situation horrified her; she argued with herself until she fell into convulsions, and these violent attacks left her exhausted.

Sometimes Paolo Sistri would stay for a little while after dinner, to keep them company. After the table had been cleared, a little bit of family life flickered timidly there under the lamp. But then that voice would issue sadly from those lips, as if frightened of the silence imposed upon that unfortunate house. Every so often, Maria would slip away on tiptoe to listen at her father's door.

– He's sleeping, – she responded to her mother's anxious looks as she returned and sat down again.

And her mother closed her eyes on her grief, sighing and putting herself back to the chore of making clothes for the grandchild that was on the way.

And they would have to work quickly; no one up to that point had thought about preparing at all for that poor, innocent child, who would be born into such difficult circumstances. Someone had been thinking about the child, however—a friend from many years past with whom Signora Agata had broken off relations at her husband's orders . . . .

Her name was Anna Veronica, this friend. When Signora Agata had met her for the first time, Anna lived with her mother, who proudly provided for her by teaching primary school. At that time, there were many young men courting her, hoping to take advantage of her passionate nature. But although Anna was truly consuming herself from the inside out, waiting for a man upon whom she could bestow her ardent and devoted love, she had always known how to defend herself from such men. A bunch of flowers, the exchange of a few little letters, speeches, and dreams, maybe even a few furtive kisses—and that was all.

And then a little while after the death of her mother, she fell into the trap. She was vilely taken advantage of by the brother of one of her wealthier female friends, in the very house she customarily visited as a respite after her long hours of school. She had always been welcomed there because of her willingness to help with the needlework, and because she always managed to lighten her hosts' spirits with her quick and ready wit, and indeed she often stayed for dinner, and sometimes even stayed the night.

That first fall from grace had been kept carefully hidden with prudent self-interest by the parents of the young man, such that no definite information of any kind had been leaked out into the community. Anna had secretly wept for the lost flower of her youth, for her shattered future, and had for some time hoped that the young man would repent. Many of her girlfriends, either because they were unaware of her situation or simply kind, had remained friends with her, and Agata Ajala, who was at that time newly married, was among these.

After a few years, however, Anna Veronica had the misfortune of falling in with another young man; sickly and sad, he had come to live just around the corner from her in three modest, drafty rooms, with a terrace full of flowers. He had asked for her hand, but Anna, in her honesty, had wanted to confess everything to him. Once she had done so, however, she had not known how, or perhaps had not been able, to deny him that same proof of love she had already conceded to the other. This time, after she had been forsaken and abandoned, a scandal had sprung up immediately, for, this time, Anna was pregnant by her sentimental seducer, who had quickly fled town. The baby, luckily, died not long after being born. Anna, relieved of her teaching position, had managed to obtain a meager charity pension, by virtue of which she had been able to survive in that state of solitude and shame to which her sad suitor had relegated her. And then she had turned to God and sought His forgiveness.

Signora Agata often saw Anna Veronica in church, but she pretended not to notice her. Anna understood and did not wish her ill. She kept her eyes raised high, and, in those eyes and on those lips, her prayers were still more fervent, prayers nourished by that time with a love that encompassed everyone, her friends as well as her enemies, as if it fell to her to show them all by example what forgiveness means.

When news of Marta's fall from grace became public, Anna Veronica began to see Signora Agata in another light, those Sundays, at Mass. She knew that Marta was pregnant, and one day, as she exited the church, she humbly drew close to her friend, who was still praying, and hastily deposited a package in her lap, saying to her only,

– For Marta.

Signora Agata had wanted to call her back, but Anna had barely managed a wave of her hand and had run off. In the package, she found some crocheted lace, three embroidered bibs, and two bonnets. She was moved to tears.

Of Agata's many friends, not even one had stood by her after the scandal had broken. But before her very eyes, in their place, this old friendship was almost furtively renewing itself. Indeed, the very next Sunday, she saw Anna Veronica again in church, and sat right next to her. After Mass, they had spoken at length and wept together as they recounted stories and shared memories of their old friendship, and of the happy and sad times they had endured.

And now that Francesco Ajala was always locked away, couldn't Anna Veronica come without his knowing to keep her friend company, to help her with her sewing, just as she had done so long ago?

Of course she could! And soon there she was, on tiptoe, crossing the room adjoining that of the shut-in. She freed herself of her long black prayer shawl, and smiling at Marta and Maria with two different smiles, whispered,

– Here I am, children. Now what needs to be done?

In the evening, Marta helped her mother and her mother's friend in that labor of love, and often, looking at the strips of cloth, the little shirts and infant camisoles and baby caps there in the basket, her eyes would darken and fill with silent tears.

Meanwhile Paolo, speaking in a low voice, was trying to make Maria understand the machines in the tannery: the millstone that crushed the myrtle and sumac bark, the trestles for hanging up the hides, the mortar . . . . Or he would relay the latest goings-on of the village. Everything was a mess because of the upcoming political elections. Gregorio Alvignani had put his name up as a candidate. The Pentàgoras were spending excessive amounts of money fighting him. Manifestoes, canvassers, meetings, pamphlets . . . . For his part, Paolo did not know which side to support, how to position himself. Not being on the Pentàgoras' side, he didn't want to demonstrate support for the opponents of Alvignani, whom he would never have voted for. Given the authority vested in him at the tannery, which employed more than sixty workers, it didn't seem like good form to ignore the election altogether . . . .

Poor Maria pretended to listen in order not to hurt his feelings, and her torture often lasted hours.

– Do you want to bet? – Marta said smiling one evening before going to bed. – I'd be willing to bet that Paolo is in love with you.

Marta! – exclaimed Maria, blushing to the whites of her eyes. – How can you say such things?

Marta burst into a shrill laugh:

– What did you expect? Or haven't you heard? I'm a fallen woman!

– Oh Marta, my dear, dear Marta, please . . . ! – moaned Maria, burying her face in her hands.

Marta seized her sister by the arm, and shaking her violently, she shouted, lit up with a sudden rage,

– Are you all trying to drive me crazy with this tragedy that you are constantly acting out around me? Is everyone in on it? Do you want me to leave? Out with it! I'll go! I can leave tonight, right now . . . . Let me go, let me . . . .

She threw herself toward the door, Maria trying to hold her back. Their mother rushed in.

– Be quiet, Marta, for goodness' sake! Hush . . . . Are you crazy? Where do you think you're going?

– Down there! To the streets, to shout for justice! Crazy . . . yes, maybe it is!

– Don't shout like that . . . . Your father will hear you!

– All the better! He should hear me! Why is he staying locked up in there? It's not for nothing that he's locked himself up in the dark; like that, like a blind man, he condemns me . . . . I don't want this. I don't want to stay here with you anymore . . . . Without me here you'll be content and happy . . . .

And with that, she was suddenly overcome with weeping; she writhed violently until deep into the night in a tremendous convulsion of nerves, as her mother and sister kept watch at her bedside.

~ Chapter 6 ~

Her head thrown back onto the headrest, and her beautiful, delicate hands resting on its arms, Marta would sit now for hours on end in the oversized armchair. Her body was overcome with a lethargy that she could not seem to shake. She would contemplate some piece of furniture or other in the room. It seemed to her that only now were the meanings of individual objects becoming strangely clear, and as she examined them, she was almost able to understand their existence independent of the relationship between her and them. Then her eyes would come to rest once again on her mother, on Maria, on Anna Veronica, who were working in silence there in front of her. Her eyelids would drop, and she would let out a long, weary sigh.

And so passed these days of sad, slow waiting.

Finally, one morning, a little bit before noon, her labor pains were suddenly upon her.

She was freezing cold, her forehead damp with sweat, as she paced the room, agitated, finding that she could no longer stave off the sharp pangs of childbirth. Meanwhile, she looked on in terror as the old midwife and another woman, who had come to help, prepared the bed. She shuddered with irritation at each and every calm, sensible piece of advice they gave her.

A young doctor—tall, pale, fair-haired—had been called in by the midwife, who was very worried about the state of her patient. He was now in the next room, quietly unpacking bandages, compresses, rubber tubing, receptacles for liquids, and a number of curious-looking instruments, laying them out with tremendous care on a side table. And every time he selected a new object, he placed it in a precise, deliberate manner on the table before him with an air of pretentious satisfaction, as if he were saying to himself as he laid down each one, "Ah, that's done." Every now and again his ears would perk up as the woman in labor in the adjoining room would wail terribly, and he would smile to himself.

– Mamma, I'm dying! – moaned Marta, rolling her head from side to side. – Mamma, I'm dying! Oh, Mamma! Oh, Mamma! – as she clung tightly to her mother's arm.

Signora Agata, for her part, encouraged her daughter as she looked on with infinite pity through the tears coursing down her own face; she was torn apart by her daughter's groans, sometimes low and dull, sometimes piercing, and by her continual wailing. The two women stayed together in a tiny corner of the room, as if doing so might help Marta suffer just a little less.

Maria had withdrawn with Anna Veronica to a room on the other side of the house, close to their father's, and in a low voice Anna tried to soothe the girl's anxiety and impatience.

– When the little one comes down this hall to knock with his little hand on that door, calling *Grandpa! Grandpa!* with the smell of milk in his little voice, ah, then tell me he won't open up! He'll open that door . . . . And then, my child, I will no longer be able to come visit you anymore; that's true, but by then it won't matter! I pray every night to my Jesus that he grant you this favor.

All of a sudden Marta burst into the room with arms raised, stumbling and shouting, frantic with pain and fear. She was half-dressed and disheveled, and followed by her mother and the other two women. Maria and Anna Veronica stood up, and they too began to follow her, frightened. Marta pounded on her father's door and, beating it with both her head and her hands, she called to him, imploring,

– Papà! Open up! Don't let me die like this! Open the door! I'm dying! Forgive me!

The women, crying, shouting, were trying to tear her away. The doctor took her by the arm.

– This is madness, *Signora*! Come, come: your father will join us later. You must do as we say now . . . .

The women surrounded her and half dragged, half carried her back into the room where she was to give birth.

Here they were finally able to lay her down, and she collapsed onto the pillows, exhausted.

Not long after, Maria, who had snuck back to eavesdrop at her father's door, entered her sister's room with a frightened look, her whole body trembling, and called her mother. She brought her to the door of the shut-in, and after listening carefully, said to her,

– Do you hear? Do you hear? Mamma, do you hear?

From his room, through the door there came a low, dull, continuous sound, like the growling of an angry dog.

– Francesco! – cried Signora Ajala loudly.

– Daddy! – cried Maria, on the verge of tears.

There was no response. The mother grasped the doorknob with a tremulous hand and pushed and shook it. All in vain.

She waited. The wheezing continued, growing in pitch and volume into what sounded like a snarl.

– Francesco! – she called out again.

– Mamma! Oh Mamma! – cried Maria with foreboding, wringing her hands.

Signora Ajala threw herself against the locked door with her shoulder—a second time, and on the third attempt the door gave way.

In the dark of the room lay Francesco Ajala, facedown on the floor with one arm extended, the other twisted under his chest.

The sharp screams of Maria and her mother were answered by a long, wild howl from the room of the birthing woman. Anna Veronica came running, the doctor trailing behind her; they threw open the shutters, and laid the inert, stricken body of Francesco Ajala on his bed with useless caution, almost into a sitting position, propped up on pillows.

– Stop screaming, for heaven's sake, stop screaming! – pleaded the doctor. – Or we may lose both of them!

– Lose? He's lost? – screamed Signora Ajala.

The doctor made a frantic gesture, and before running back to the room of the birthing mother, he ordered the servant girl to go immediately for another doctor at the nearest pharmacy.

Maria, weeping, was wiping away the blood that trickled from a small cut on her father's forehead with a handkerchief. Oh, if only this had been his only injury! Still, she put all of her attention, all of her love and effort into stopping those few little droplets of blood, as if her father's life depended upon this and this alone. Her mother seemed to have lost her mind. She insisted that her husband speak to her, and she embraced him and squeezed his icy, lifeless hands. Francesco

Ajala, his face ashen, continued to make a dull rattling sound, his mouth wide open and his eyes closed.

Another doctor, a bald little man with a lazy eye, rushed in.

– Let me through! What's the matter? Let me see . . . . Ah! – he said with a high, nasal voice that betrayed severe nasal congestion, striking his hips with his fists.[1] – Poor Signor Francesco! We need ice . . . . Someone go to the pharmacy across the street, quickly, and also ask for a mustard plaster, and a hot water bottle . . . . Who will go? Who can run? Move away from the bed . . . . Air! Air! Oh, poor Signor Francesco . . . .

Through the closed doors, there came a prolonged cry that seemed to express a sort of maniacal rage. The doctor turned suddenly, and for a moment everyone was tense and distracted.

– My poor daughter! – Signora Agata finally managed to moan, breaking into sobs.

The other women began to weep and wail in unison. The doctor looked around, lost, confused, stunned, and scratched his temple with his finger; then he sat and clasped his hands in front of him, and began twiddling his thumbs.

A single tear trailed slowly down the face of the dying man, stopping only when it reached his thick gray mustache.

Every remedy was in vain.

His agony lasted until that evening. That perpetual, monotone rattle was the only evidence that any life at all persisted in that gigantic body, folded in half such that it sat almost upright on the bed.

It was only much later that Signora Agata thought of Marta, and she returned to her room. As she opened the door, she was struck with the twin odors of ammonia and vinegar. Had the birth, then, already taken place?

Marta was lying pale and immobile on the pillows and seemed lifeless. The assistant was bent over the recovering woman applying a compress, and the doctor, who was very pale in his shirtsleeves, was throwing bloodstained cotton swabs into a basin on the floor.

– In there, – he said to the mother, nodding toward the door of the adjacent room.

Signora Agata silently beheld her daughter for a moment.

– Dead . . . . – whispered Marta as if only to herself, with a voice so empty of expression that it almost seemed to come directly from her lips, without thought.

Signora Agata entered the next room emotionlessly, like an automaton. There the midwife showed her a barely formed, monstrous little creature, wrapped in gauze. It was black and blue, and smelled of musk.

– Dead . . . .

From the street below rose the shrill sound of a bell ringing, and a nasal, almost childish chorus of women in a hurried procession:

Today and forever be praised
Our blessed God . . . .

– The Viaticum! – cried the old midwife, dropping to her knees in the middle of the room, the dead child in her arms.

Signora Agata left the room in a hurry and ran into the entryway. The priest in his robes was already entering, the pyx containing the Eucharist in hand, and a man trailing behind him, his eyes wild with fear, was closing the *baldacchino*, the symbolic protection of the white umbrella no longer necessary. The sexton, carrying the small tabernacle that had housed the sacrament, followed the priest into the dying man's room. The women and children who accompanied the

Viaticum knelt in the little antechamber, whispering among themselves.

Francesco Ajala did not hear, did not understand any of this. He received extreme unction, and in the presence of the priest, he breathed his last.

As soon as they reached the street, the strident ringing of the bell and the rosary of the women was drowned out by the resounding cries and applause of a crowd of rowdy men, who, a flag waving ahead of them, were celebrating the announcement that Gregorio Alvignani had been elected to the House of Deputies, in Rome.

~ Chapter 7 ~

After the birth, Marta spent three months suspended between life and death.

"Divine providence, that illness," Anna Veronica would say. Yes, because otherwise those two poor, superstitious ladies—the widow and the orphan—would undoubtedly have gone mad. Eventually, however, as they struggled desperately against Marta's seemingly indomitable illness, their lips, which had seemed as if they would never curl into smiles again, did so a mere two months after that disturbing, almost violent death of the master of the house, at the first signs of Marta's recovery.

Undaunted even after so many nights sitting up with the patient, Anna Veronica began bringing her little perfumed pictures of saints each morning, bordered with quilted cardboard dotted with gold, and with golden halos.

– Here, – she would say, – now put these in an envelope under your pillow. They will heal you. They are blessed.

And she proceeded to show her images of the two patron saints of the village, San Cosimo and San Damiano, with their robes down to their feet, crowns on their heads, and martyr's palms in their hands. These were two true miracle workers, and their saint's day would be celebrated soon; indeed, Anna Veronica had promised them an offering if they would heal Marta.

– These two, – she added, – can do more for you than that bald old doctor, with his one eye on Christ and the other on Saint John . . . .

She then did an impression of the doctor, with his perennially high, nasal voice: – *"I suffer from lithiasis, Signora!"* – "And what might that be?" – *"Gall stones, Signora, gall stones!"*

Marta would smile palely from her sickbed, following Anna Veronica's performance with her eyes, and even Maria and her mother would smile.

In the evening, before she went home, Anna would recite the rosary in Marta's room, along with Agata and Maria.

The sick woman would listen to the murmur of their prayers in that dimly lit room, a single lamp with a green shade its only source of light. She would watch the three kneeling women, bent over their chairs, and when they came to the litany, she would often join them in responding to Anna Veronica's invocation:

– *Ora pro nobis.*

As evening fell, however, that sweet feeling of serenity, of the renewal and lightness that usually accompanies convalescence, would slip away from her. To her eyes, the light given off by that lamp with the green shade was too little, far too little to combat the shadows that invaded the house. And she felt a gloomy anguish, a dark anxiety, a profound emptiness and confusion creeping in from the other rooms in the house, through which her thoughts would wander uneasily if she let them stray for even a moment. Then she would suddenly draw them back to her by fixing her gaze on the lamp, feeling its familiar comfort. Out there in the shadows, in the darkness of those other rooms, her father had disappeared. Out there, now, he no longer existed. There was no one out there, not anymore . . . . The shadows. The darkness. It is true, of course, that he had been a nightmare for her. But at what cost had she now been freed from that nightmare? The gloomy anguish, the dark anxiety, the profound emptiness and confusion . . . didn't these all, in fact, come from thinking of him?

– *Ora pro nobis.*

She often fell asleep with a prayer on her lips. Her mother often lay beside her in the same bed, but she too struggled to fall asleep every night, not only because of the agonizing and very present memory of her husband, but also because of her assiduous worry about her nephew, Paolo Sistri, upon whom the entire existence of the family now depended.

After this most recent disaster, Paolo no longer stopped by the house at his usual time every evening. His aunt even had to send for him two or three times in order to get news of the tannery. And when he finally broke down and came, he seemed more dejected and bewildered than before.

Once he even turned up with his head bandaged.

– Oh *Dio*, Paolo, what's happened to you?

Nothing. In one of the rooms of the tannery, in the dark, someone (perhaps deliberately!) had forgotten to close the . . . . What do you call it? Yes . . . the . . . the . . . trapdoor, that's right, and as he was passing by, wham! down he went. He had tumbled down the . . . the what-do-you-call-it-made-of-wood . . . the floodgate ladder, right! It was a miracle he had even survived. But all was well—better than well!—at the tannery. Maybe, though . . . let's see . . . maybe it would be better if we tried a certain French tanning method . . . that way of tanning where you . . . right, yes! You pulverize the . . . what do you call it? . . . the cork, beech, and oak bark . . . . With our method, on the other hand, when the oak is poured into the myrtle water . . . .

– For goodness' sake, Paolo! – his aunt interrupted him, her hands together as if in prayer. – Let's not try anything new! Everything was going so well at the tannery doing things our way when my poor husband was looking after it, may he rest in peace . . . .

– Good God, what does that have to do with anything? – Paolo retorted arrogantly, now that his uncle was no longer around. – This is another process entirely! Because . . . do you see how it is? You take . . . no, do you take that before? Boiling water. Oh yes, and now you take distilled water . . . wait! With the pulverized oak bark, instead . . . .

And he went on like this for a little while, digging himself deeper into a hole, starting over again from the beginning, all in an attempt to make sure his aunt understood that important and complicated French tanning method.

– Have I made myself clear?

– No, my dear. But maybe it's just me. Please, please just be careful!

– Just leave it to me.

And really you couldn't blame him. Night and day, he was always in the thick of it. By day, he was either in the lime pits overseeing the mixing of the different tanning liquids, or at the tanks, or the baths, then at the racks for the skinning and scraping of the hides, and so it went, on and on. By night, there he was going over the books, making sure the numbers added up. At four in the morning, he would hear the roosters crow . . . . What did she know, his aunt? The roosters, word of honor, at four . . . . And there he was, still on his feet! The ink in the inkwell didn't spare any of his ten fingers, and had even left smudges as high as his nose and forehead.

– If only she were here to see it! – he would huff as he sat in his shirtsleeves, his head thrown back on the headrest of the oversized chair, staring up as though the figures of his ledger were traced in the spiderwebs on the ceiling. And then to distract himself he would blow smoke at them, which he took in great mouthfuls from his pipe – *fffff.*

Meanwhile, out on the street and in the huge building, everything was silent as a tomb. On the bare, yellowed walls the candle flickered its tremulous light each time Paolo puffed. His enormous shadow stretched out distorted and monstrous on the office floor.

– Puah! – Right in a creditor's face! And he would shout the man's name as he spat on the wall. A spider passed before his eyes, silently, cautiously, as if frightened of the light, tottering lightly on its eight spindly legs. Paolo was as horrified by these little creatures as women often are of mice. He would quickly jump to his feet, raise a slipper, and paff!— he would crush the spider beneath his sole. Then, his face twisted in disgust, he would hesitate awhile, gaping at his victim plastered against the wall.

After the death of his uncle, he had pitched his tent definitively at the tannery, throwing everything he had into the work. He ate there, and he slept there; and he never permitted anyone so much as to enter his moldy little room. He took care of his own meals, made his own bed—all him. But things never went right! Was he looking for his knife and fork? The meat would burn on the fire. Did he want something to drink? He found drops of grease floating in his wine. Who had poured oil into his glass?

– Puah! Damn it . . . .

And he'd sit there, tongue hanging out, his face twisted in disgust.

But all this was nothing. What really got to him was his battle with the cloud of crows that had descended upon the tannery since his uncle had died! He defended the interests of his poor widowed aunt with ferocious zeal; the courtyard of the tannery resounded with his violent arguments. But in the end, he was always forced to give in, and to pay, and to pay. They sold less and less each day, and each day, the debts and claims increased. The leather merchants canceled their contracts, or they took back their hides and sent them elsewhere. His aunt, ignorant of all this, asked him for the same amount of money as she had been used to receiving before, as if business were going as well as ever. And he—who didn't have the courage to admit the miserable state of things—tried everything he could so that every month he could at least come up with the money for her.

Marta eventually was able to get out of bed, and, supported by her mother and Maria, was already taking her first steps, from the armchair to the foot of the bed, and even all the way to the mirror on the wardrobe.

– Look at me! Good Lord, I'm a mess!

She removed her arm from Maria's shoulder and with a pale, trembling hand she delicately swept aside the hair that had fallen across her forehead, and as she looked into her own eyes, she smiled with a sort of bewildered compassion for her poor lips, burned as they were by the intense heat of her fever. Then she went to sit in the leather armchair by the window. Anna Veronica came and, in her unassuming, sweet way, told Marta about the May vespers in honor of the Virgin: the cool church, smelling of roses; then the blessing; and at the end of the service, the sacred songs, sung with organ accompaniment;

the last rays of golden sunlight as they entered the church through the high, wide windows, open at the top; and even a little swallow that had entered and fluttered about, lost, while outside the others chirped and chased after each other like women who had drunk too much wine.

Marta listened, her mind wandering, disconnected from her senses.

– We'll take you there . . . . We'll go all four of us, together, before the end of the month. Oh, you'll be well enough, don't worry!

But she said that no, that wouldn't be possible.

– Yes, the church is just around the corner, but if I can barely stand . . . .

The third Sunday in May, after Mass was over, Anna rushed in, exultant, from the church.

– For you, for you, Marta! They've brought her out just for you!

– What? – asked Marta, looking up from the armchair, almost dismayed.

– The Madonna! The Madonna! For you! Do you hear? The Daughters of Mary are bringing her to you! Do you hear the drum? The Madonna is coming to visit you in your home!

Every Sunday in May, after the sermon and the benediction, the devout of the church would carry a little wax Madonna out into the neighborhood, housed in a bell-shaped case of crystal.

– What? How can that be? – said Marta, entirely bewildered as she heard the chorus and the roll of the drum grow ever louder.

– Every Sunday, I took a number for you. Today, my heart told me, today Marta's number will come up! And that's just what happened. I let out a shout of joy right there in the church, so loud that everyone turned around. And here is the Madonna, coming to see you . . . . Here she is, here she is, *Vergine santa*!

A delegation of girls entered the room, each with a little medal hanging from a blue ribbon around her neck. Then the sacristan of the church entered carrying the wax Madonna in its glass case, which in his large, rough, blackened hands seemed all the more fragile. On the stairs, the drum rolled noisily.

Those girls were all used to smiling in precisely the same way, accustomed to seeing and hearing the expressions of joy with which the devout received the little Madonna. Seeing now that Marta remained seated, pale, stunned by all the commotion, which was too much for her weakened constitution, at first they remained a little disconcerted; then they gathered around her and began to chatter, each one repeating the words of the others: – Now surely you will be healed . . . . The Madonna . . . . The visit of the Madonna . . . . No more doctors . . . . You can throw your medicine away . . . .

The roll of the drum had meanwhile ceased. Signora Ajala had given the drummer and the sexton some small change, and shortly thereafter, everyone had left.

Marta could not get enough of the little Madonna as it sat there on her knees, and she steadied the glass bell jar with her waxen fingers.

– How beautiful! How beautiful she is! Oh Maria!

And before the month was through, Marta was indeed able to carry herself to church to give thanks to the Madonna, accompanied by Anna Veronica, her mother, and her sister.

~ Chapter 8 ~

"Merciful Jesus, I wish to reconcile myself with You, confessing to Your minister all of the sins with which I have offended You. Great must my misery be if I have been able to forget You so easily. I am ungrateful, and I do not know how to live without offending You, my Father and my most beloved Savior. And now that I have borne witness to my own guilt, I hold myself accountable. I repent, and I beg for Your mercy. Weep, my heart, for you have offended God, Who has suffered so much for your sins. Oh Lord, receive this, my confession; accept and acknowledge with Your grace my act of contrition and the resolution of my heart, as I say these words with Santa Caterina da Genova, – '*My love, let there be no more world, no more sinning; only love, only faithfulness and obedience to His holy commandments.*' – In the name of the Father, the Son, and the Holy Spirit. Amen."

Having made the sign of the cross and closed her prayer book, Marta directed an anguished glance at the confessional, before which, on the other side of the confessional, there knelt an old, penitent woman who had been there when Marta arrived. On Marta's side of the confessional the wood was all pockmarked and yellowed and worn smooth. It held the vague imprint of legions of sinful foreheads. Marta noted this with disgust, and she pulled the hood of her long black shawl even tighter around her, until it almost hid her face. She was very pale and trembling as she waited for her confession to be heard.

The church, all but deserted now, held a mysterious, absorbing silence that hung in the harsh stillness of the incense-permeated chill. Penitents could feel the weight of the solemn emptiness of that holy space, as it hung almost palpably from the enormous pilasters and wide arches, pressing down on their souls in the semidarkness. The whole central nave was occupied by two wings of caned chairs, organized into long rows on a dusty floor that periodically sprouted into worn-down, ancient tombstones.

It was on one of these stones that Marta remained, kneeling as she waited for the elderly woman to cede her place at the confessional.

Oh, but how many sins that old woman seemed to have! Were they her own, or were they the sins of her poverty? And what might they be, anyway? The old confessor listened to her through the latticed wooden portal, his face impassive.

But then she lowered her eyes and, trying to pass the time as best she could, Marta attempted to decipher the inscription on the tombstone, only barely visible on the stone, which also bore a worn-down effigy. Underneath must lie a skeleton . . . . What did the name matter now? How much more secure and protected—cozy even—did that restful sleep of death appear!

The two wings of chairs stretched all the way to the columns that supported the choir stalls. Behind these columns were two long benches, and when she had entered Marta had seen an old farmer sitting there with his arms crossed over his chest, rapt in prayer, his eyes deep set and dried out by the years. Oh, those gnarled, muddy hands, that neck, limp from years under the yoke and scarred with a black furrow that ran from his chin to just under his throat, and those flattened temples, the wrinkled forehead underneath that shock of bristling white hair! Every so often the old man would cough, and it would echo raucously throughout the empty church.

Through the large, high windows the pale blaze of the dying day streamed in, illuminating the huge frescoes in broad swaths amid the deafening chatter of the swallows.

Marta had come to the church at the suggestion of Anna Veronica. But as her wait had grown longer she had begun to get a terrible impression of herself, kneeling there like some pathetic beggar woman. She could understand that humility in Anna, which served the latter as a source of such serene sweetness. But Anna had truly sinned. She had thus sought—and found—comfort in her faith, had found in the church a refuge. But as for herself? She was absolutely sure, Marta was, that she would never have failed in her duties as a wife, not because she felt her husband worthy of such respect, but rather because she considered betraying him unworthy of her, and no pandering on his part would wring even the tiniest concession from her. But seeing her now in the church, humble and prostrate, wouldn't people suppose that she had accepted her punishment as just, and that she was kneeling before God in order to beg for comfort and refuge, that she recognized that she no longer had the right to hold her head high before all? But it was not for this that she had come, it is true—not for her undeserved punishment, not for her father's tragedy, for which she refused to accept any responsibility. No, none of these were the reason she had allowed herself to be persuaded by Anna to come to the church and confess. She had come for herself, to feel the peace and comfort of God. What was she going to say, however, in just a little while to that old confessor? What was she supposed to repent? What had she done? What sin had she committed to merit all of this reproach, all of the suffering, the tragedy of her father and child, the perpetual mourning in her family home, and maybe, come tomorrow, complete poverty? Should she accuse herself? Should she repent? If any sin had been committed, hadn't it been unintentional, for lack of experience? And hadn't she paid an exceedingly high price already? The priest would most certainly advise that she accept with love and resignation the punishment mandated by God. But was it really from God? If God were just, if God could see into people's hearts . . . . Or was it rather from men . . . . Were they instruments of God? Had God told them the extent to which she should be punished? No, men went too far, whether as a result of their baseness of spirit or a perversion of their honesty . . . . To accept the punishment with humility, without argument or reflection, and to forgive? Would she be able to forgive? No! No!

And so Marta raised her head and looked around the church, as if all of a sudden she were lost. That silence, that solemn peace, the height of the vaulted ceilings, and just ahead of her that little confession booth, that ancient, prostrated lady, that motionless, stone-faced priest—all of these suddenly faded away from her rebellious spirit, like a frivolous dream into which she had wandered while her consciousness slept, and which, as the viciousness and sadness of her reality came rushing back to her, she now watched melt away.

She got up from her knees, still confused. Her legs faltered, and she dizzily shielded her eyes with one hand, as she steadied herself on the back of a chair with the other. Then she made her way across the church, almost teetering as she went. On the bench under the choir stalls, she saw the little old farmer again, in the same position, with his arms crossed over his chest, absorbed in his prayers, ecstatic.

All the way home she turned the image of that penitent man over and over in her mind.

That was the degree of faith she was missing! But she could never have it. She could not forgive. Inside her skull, her brain felt shrunken, like a dry sponge from which she couldn't manage to wring a thought that would comfort her or that would give her even a moment's peace.

It was an illusion, of course, this sensation. But it did cause her real anguish, which she tried in vain to wash away with tears. And how many, *Dio*, how very many had she shed! So many now that crying no longer helped. There was always a knot in her throat, always irritating her, oppressing her. Before her very eyes a sort of ungodly entity seemed to be taking shape, coming into being around her. It had initially been just a shadow, an empty shadow, a fog so negligible that, with a breath, one could have dispersed it, but then it became hard and heavy as a stone, crushing her, crushing her home and family, everything . . . and she could no longer do anything to stop it. That was the fact of the matter. The thing, which had taken on a life of its own. Something that she could no longer fix, enormous for everyone and especially enormous for her, even if in her own conscience she felt it to be insubstantial, a shadow, a fog that had now turned to stone. And her father, who might have been able to vanquish it with his proud disdain, instead became its first victim. Had she been changed by this *thing*? She was the same. She felt the same—so much so that it often did not seem the catastrophe had even occurred. But now she too was turning to stone. She could feel herself losing the ability to feel anything any longer—not grief at the death of her father, not pity for either her mother or her sister, not friendship for Anna Veronica—nothing, nothing!

Should she return to the church? Why? She had prayed, and her prayer was just a meaningless movement of her lips; the meaning underneath the words escaped her. Often, during Mass, she caught herself staring at the feet of the priest as he stood on the altar step, the flecks of gold on the chasuble, the lace of the missal. Then, at the elevation of the host and chalice, she was awakened by the scraping of the chairs on the cathedral floor and by the ringing of the silver bell, and she rose with the others and knelt, watching with astonishment as certain of her neighbors beat their breasts and wept real tears. Why did they do that?

In order to distance herself from the jagged rocks of senility onto which each of her thoughts, each of her feelings was in danger of shipwreck, she tentatively attempted to apply herself to her studies again, or at the very least, to read. As she reopened those old abandoned books, an indescribable tenderness swept over her. She revisited some of the sweetest images of her past, and it was as if they pulsed with life before her eyes. There was her school, the different classes, the benches, the teacher's desk. And there they were, all of her professors following each other one by one over the course of the school day, and then the din of the park where they would spend their breaks, the laughter as she walked arm in arm along the paths with her closest friends. Then the sound of the bell, and back to class; the director and his wife . . . the rivalries . . . the punishments . . . . On the little table before her sat an open book, a geography text. She flipped through a few of the pages. In one of the margins, there was a little drawing, and these words written in her hand:

"Mita, tomorrow we leave for Peking!" Mita Lumia . . . . What an abyss now stood between her and her old school friend!

How was it that, in certain people, there was no drive, no aspiration to be better than anyone in anything, to excel in even the smallest way?

And yet this is what she found, more or less, in all of her old schoolmates, and even in her own sister, the good Maria. Her husband was squarely one of this tribe as well, and happy and proud to count himself among its members. Oh, if only she had stayed in school! At this point . . . .

She remembered all of the praise and encouragement that her professors had given her, and also . . . yes, also the praise that *someone else* had given her, in response to her letters: Alvignani. What was it that he had said? She had discussed with him a woman's place in society . . . . "She is able to reconcile her incredibly acute feelings," Alvignani had written her in one of his letters, "her incredibly acute feelings with a keen observation of the real world." This compliment had made her laugh so much. And that "*reconcile* her senses"! Perhaps it was well written . . . . Alvignani was, after all, very cultured . . . , but in her opinion, his writing was too painterly. On the other hand, when he spoke . . . . Oh, in Rome, with him, if only she had not been tied down . . . . In Rome, the wife of Gregorio Alvignani; in a different place, a vast city full of intellectual light . . . far, far away from all of this mud.

She bowed her head over her books, moved suddenly to action by an old zeal, almost as if by an irresistible need to breathe life into a longing that seemed unable to withstand the slightest blow from reality, like the creak of the door when she had to enter the next room, where her mother and sister sat dressed all in black.

She knew nothing about what was happening in her family. She had noted only the way Maria and her mother stared at her, as if they were hiding something. But this was just an impression, a feeling . . . . Perhaps they didn't like her spending all day by herself? Were they excusing her? Pitying her? Her mother's eyes were often red with weeping, and Maria, who was sprouting up in height, was wasting away to nothing; she had a disoriented air, a grief that seemed to follow her around. To make her happy, Marta would ask her,

– Shall we go to church, Maria?

For Maria the question meant, "Shall we go and pray for father?" And she always answered yes, and they went.

One afternoon as they were exiting the church, they were set upon by a little boy who was almost naked, wearing only a rag of a dirty shirt, which fell in tatters over his filthy, spindly legs. His face was jaundiced and unwashed. With his little hand he grabbed hold of Marta's shawl and refused to let go, begging them to help his father, a bricklayer who had fallen from a wall at the factory.

– His story is true, – confirmed Maria. – Yesterday he fell from a scaffold. He broke an arm and a leg.

– Come, come with me you poor child! – Marta said then, starting out.

– No, Marta . . . – said Maria, looking at her sister with pity; but she soon lowered her eyes as if she were embarrassed, and had changed her mind.

– Why? – asked Marta.

– Nothing, nothing . . . let's go . . . . – Maria responded, hurriedly.

Having reached their house, Marta asked her mother for some money to give the child.

– Oh my dear child, we don't even have any for ourselves . . . .

– What?

– Yes, yes . . . . – her mother went on, through tears. – Paolo disappeared two days ago, no one knows where . . . . The tannery is closed; they've sealed up the doors . . . . We are ruined! Stay here, both of you. You tell her, Maria . . . . I have to go speak to the lawyer right away.

~ Chapter 9 ~

Before dawn the following day they were awakened with a start by a wild clamor on the street below: shouts and haphazard cries to the heavens, and the deafening blowing of the boat horns in the harbor.

– *The fishermen* . . . . – Maria said under her breath with a sigh in the darkened room.

Ah yes, it was the feast day of the patron saints of the region. Who would have thought it had come so soon?

Every year on this day at daybreak, the so-called "fishermen,"—that is, just about everyone who lived on the shore, and not just the ones who made their living by the sea—descended upon the town in droves. Ancient custom dictated that every year these people who lived at the edge of the sea should triumphantly parade the bier of their two patron saints through the streets of the city. It just so happened that it was in the sea that they had suffered their first martyrdom, and thus it was especially to the seafarers that they accorded their protection.

And so every year the city was awakened by that deafening invasion, like the sea itself during a tempest. Along the streets, the windows were hastily flung open, and bare arms stuck out, only to be replaced by faces pale with sleep, sometimes in old shawls, in caps, in kerchiefs.

Not one of the three dejected women even considered getting out of bed. They lay still with their eyes open in the dark, and images of the wild figures passing below them in the streets played in their minds. Amidst the smoke and the bloodred flames of the torches flickering in the wind, the *pescatori* were dressed all in white, in shirts and underclothes, feet bare, red sashes around their waists, yellow handkerchiefs tied around their heads. They had watched them from their windows many times before, in happier days.

Once the infernal rampage had passed by, the street fell again into nocturnal silence. But not long after, the festivities began again. Maria buried her face into her pillow and began to weep silently, tormented by memories.

Then came the first shouts of the shoeless mass of villagers the saints had helped in their time of need:

– *Behold the Saint of Miracles! Arise, faithful ones!*

They were boys and teenagers and men, who, by some miracle of San Cosimo and Damiano (the people had long ago made the two into a single saint in two persons) had escaped some peril or had been healed of some infirmity. Every year, as a show of faith, they went around the region in their stockinged feet, dressed in white like the *pescatori*, each with a tray hanging from his neck by a strip of white silk. On the trays were images of the two martyrs, each available for a penny, or two, or three.

– *Behold the Saint of Miracles! Arise, faithful ones!*

These *miracolati* went into people's houses to sell their pictures, and as a fulfillment of their vows to the saints, the families offered one or more gilded candles and one or more chickens adorned with festive ribbons. These offerings and the pennies they received for the pictures were then turned in every hour on the hour to the Commission for Local Celebrations, which was headquartered at the little church dedicated to the two saints, in the center of town.

In addition to the candles and the chickens, larger offerings were ostentatiously paraded to the little church, to the sound of drums: lambs, ewes, and rams with their fleece brushed and snowy white, lavishly decorated mules loaded down with grain, all adorned with multicolored ribbons.

In the early hours of the morning, Anna Veronica arrived, dressed all in black as usual, and wearing the long shawl of the penitent. She needed to fulfill the vow she had made during Marta's illness to bring the two candles and the embroidered tablecloth to the church as she had promised.

And Marta was to go with her. In the madness of those last few days, after Paolo's running away, she had forgotten to let Marta know the night before.

– Come, come child, have courage. You can't break a vow.

Marta was completely consumed by her own thoughts, wrapped up in a gloomy silence. She responded immediately, annoyed.

– I'm not going . . . . Leave me alone! I'm not going.

– What! – exclaimed Anna. – What are you saying?

And wounded, she stared at her friend and at Maria.

– Yes, you're right, – she responded, shaking her head. – But who can help us?

Marta leapt to her feet.

– So in addition to everything, I have to show my gratitude, is that right? For the grace that I have received, for getting well . . . .

– But it's easy to die, my child, – sighed Anna Veronica, half closing her eyes. – If you have remained alive, doesn't it seem like a sign that God wanted you to live? That He has some purpose in mind for you?

Marta did not respond. Perhaps the words her friend was saying, pronounced with her usual sweetness, had responded to one of her own secret feelings, to a secret purpose. She furrowed her brow and moved off in the direction of her room.

– You also need to take your mind off things, – added Anna.

In the streets below, the people were in a frenzy. From the seashore and the mountains, from all the villages surrounding the town, people had streamed in in a number of groups, which now proceeded awkwardly through the streets. Villagers were in groups of five or six, holding each other by the hand so as not to get lost. The women were gaily dressed in long embroidered shawls or with short cloaks of white, blue, or black cloth, enormous cotton and silk handkerchiefs in a variety of floral patterns around their heads or across their chests, and thick gold hoops hanging from their ears, and necklaces and brooches and bracelets and beads. The men were farmers or sailors, or they worked in the sulfur mines, and they were clumsy in their stiff new clothes and awkward in their hobnailed shoes.

Marta and Anna Veronica, hiding the candles and the tablecloth under their shawls, moved as quickly as they could through the heaving, directionless crowd.

They eventually reached the piazza in front of the church, which was brimming with people. The noise was deafening and incessant, the confusion indescribable. All around the square people had improvised stalls made of giant, billowing bedsheets. From these, vendors were shouting until their voices gave out, selling toys and dried fruit and sweets. Figurine makers were making their rounds, selling painted plaster images and repeating the stories of those shoeless witnesses who had been miraculously saved. The toy sellers pulled relentlessly on the strings of their spinning toys, and the gelato vendors—their pushcarts decorated in colored lanterns and piled high with clattering glasses—shouted – *Lo scialacuore! Lo scialacuore!* – hawking their most popular flavor.

This cheerful announcement was followed by a generous distribution of slaps to the most mischievous of the young rascals who surrounded the carts like a cloud of obstinate flies.

In contrast to the genial barking of the vendors was the melancholy refrain of a group of beggars on the steps directly in front of the main door of the church, where the people were packed, trying to elbow their way in. Marta and Anna Veronica found themselves carried, almost crushed, by that press of people, and in the end, without having moved a foot, they found themselves inside the dark church, crammed in among the curiosity seekers and the devout.

From where they had been deposited in the middle of the central nave, the enormous bier loomed over them, its massive frame ringed with iron so that it could better withstand the inevitable wear and tear of that disorganized, frantic procession. On the bier stood the statues of the two iron-headed saints, their expressions almost identical, in robes flowing down to their feet and a palm frond in each of their hands. At the back, under an arch of the nave, between two of the columns on the left side of the church, the Festival Committee sat around an enormous table, busily receiving the offerings of the devout: votive tablets containing crude representations of miracles obtained in the most disparate and strange circumstances; candles; dressings for the altar; and legs, arms, breasts, feet, and hands made of wax.

Among the members of the board this year was Antonio Pentàgora.

Luckily, Anna Veronica realized this before encountering him at the table; she froze for a moment, startled and unsure what to do.

– Stay here a moment, Marta. I'll take them up myself.

– Why? – asked Marta, who had suddenly grown very pale. And she added, her eyes lowered, – Nicola is here in the church, isn't he.

– His father is there at the table, – said Anna under her breath. – It's better that you stay here. I'll hurry.

Niccolino was not expecting that encounter with Marta. He hadn't seen her since the evening before her break with his brother. He stood and gawked at her, wide-eyed, and then he stole away dejectedly, disappearing into the crowd, ashamed. He had always been shy in her presence. He had wanted so much for her to love him like she would a little brother, raised as he was without a mother, without sisters. From the midst of that bustle of heads, he tried to catch a glimpse of her again from a distance, without being seen. He caught sight of her and stood still for a moment observing her, considering her, turning that image of her over in his mind. Then, slipping silently through the crowd, he followed her with his eyes until he reached the door of the church. For a moment, he neither saw nor heard the festival that surrounded him. He suddenly came back to himself in the middle of the packed piazza, not quite sure how he had gotten there, pressed on all sides by the crowd, which had grown enormous as they now awaited the processional of the bier from the church. Apoplectic, perspiring faces sat atop craning necks, trying desperately to see over that crowd of bruised bodies, desperate for breath in the cramped heat of the square. Some had a tortured, despairing look in their eyes, others wore cruel, ferocious expressions. The bells high above sounded over that ferment, and the bells of other churches responded in the distance.

All at once the whole crowd began to move, pushed and pulled by a thousand opposing forces, paying no attention to the collisions, the bruises, or the suffocations, intent only on seeing.

– There it is! There it is! It's coming!

The women sobbed, and the men swore angrily as they pushed against the crowd that blocked their view. All shouted, exhausted, and the bells pealed as if they too had been angered by the roaring mob below.

Suddenly the bier burst violently from the great main door, and stopped with a thud there in front of the church. Then the frenetic shouting escaped thousands of throats:

– *Viva San Cosimo e Damiano!*

And thousands upon thousands of arms waved in the air, as if the entire population of the town had joined together to fight some desperate battle.

– Make way! Make way! – was heard from every corner not long after. – Make way for the saint! Make way for the saint!

And before the bier, all along the piazza the people began to stand aside here and there, always with difficulty, pushed back violently by the guards, who tried to clear a path. Everyone knew that the two saints proceeded through the town quickly, like a storm. They were the saints of good health, the saviors of the region during the cholera epidemic, and so they had to run about, here and there, continuously. Their breakneck speed was a tradition, and without it, the festival would have lost all of its vivacity and its character, even if everyone was afraid of being crushed to death.

A bell rang stridently in front of the church. Then, between the strong iron poles supporting the bier, there started a scuffle among the *pescatori* charged with carrying it on their shoulders. At every stop along the way, they repeated this scuffle, quieted with some difficulty each time by the members of the Festival Committee, who were doing their best to guide the procession.

One hundred bloodred, unkempt, brutish faces were slotted between the poles in front of and behind the great machine. It was a tangle of bare, sinewy arms, faces purple with strain and streaming with sweat, torn shirts, anguished muttering and heavy breathing, shoulders crushed beneath the iron poles, calloused hands that clutched fiercely at the wood. And each of the frantic men under that impossibly heavy load, infected with the madness of his suffering even more than with love of the saints, pulled his bar toward himself, and so they were constantly working at cross-purposes. The saints staggered drunkenly through the crowd, which pushed and shouted back at them wildly.

At each short stop, after a run of relatively unhindered "progress," the women, crowded onto balconies or into windows, would show their devotion by throwing slices of dark, spongy bread from chests and baskets down onto the crowd and onto the bier. And below, the crowd went wild as everyone wrangled for the bread. In the meantime, the pallbearers were guzzling bottle after bottle of wine, and were getting progressively drunker, even if most of that wine was pouring out again as sweat.

Every now and then, the bier became ominously light; at such times, it moved forward as if on its own, leaping through the lively squall of the crowd. At other times, it became impossibly heavy. The saints did not wish to go any farther, and suddenly became obstinate. Such moments were when accidents would happen; someone in the crowd was always trounced. A moment of panic, and then to bolster their courage, everyone would shout, – *Viva San Cosimo e Damiano!* – and they would forget the danger and press on. But many times, the bier would return to a spot where it had previously rested, and once again, it would suddenly refuse to move. And all of the eyes would then turn to the windows, and the crowd, threatening and cursing, would force whatever faces they saw there to move away. For this was a sign that among these must be someone who had either not fulfilled promises to the saints, or who had caused people to speak badly of him or her and so was not worthy of viewing the saints.

In this way, the people took it upon themselves to act as ethical magistrate, even if only for one day.

Marta and Anna Veronica stood facing each other on the balcony, flanked by Agata and Maria. Antonio Pentàgora had already signaled the pallbearers some time before. At first, the four poor ladies did not understand the movements of the saints; they saw that they wouldn't budge, but did not suspect that it had anything to do with them. When the bier moved once again to just below their balcony and once again came to a jarring halt, the whole crowd raised their eyes and their arms against the women, shouting and cursing, exasperated at the fate of an unfortunate boy who had been thrown to the ground and who now lay there crushed and bleeding. Marta and Anna Veronica left the balcony immediately, followed by the weeping Maria. Signora Agata, very pale and trembling with disdain, closed the shutters with such violence that one of the glass panes broke into pieces. To the frenzied crowd below this seemed like a direct affront, and they hurled abuse and insults up at them. And as that tempest raged below their house, the four poor women trembled, huddled together, holding each other close in a corner of the room. In that anguished pause, they heard the powerful head of one of the saints ram once, twice, three times against the iron railing of their balcony. At each blow, the whole house shook.

Then the fury gradually subsided. A deep silence fell over the street.

– Cowards! Cowards! – Marta said through clenched teeth, pale and trembling.

Anna Veronica wept with her face hidden in her hands. Maria approached the balcony timorously, and through the window saw that the blows from the saint's iron head had twisted the bars of the railing.

~ Chapter 10 ~

– Too much, eh? – Antonio Pentàgora said, his customary cold sneer congealed on his lips, and his eyes full of pity for Niccolino.

– Cowardice! – exploded Niccolino, savagely. – You ought to be ashamed of yourself! The whole town is talking about yesterday's scandal. Well done!

– And the same to you, Niccolino! – said his father calmly. – I really must congratulate myself on having a son I can be so proud of! These are noble, generous sentiments . . . . Bravo! Tend the roots of these thoughts well, boy, and you'll see how they mature in time . . . .

Trembling with rage, Niccolino rushed out of the room in hopes that he wouldn't lose control of himself. It was just the way Rocco had left the night before after a violent fight between father and son had almost come to blows.

Left alone in the room, Antonio Pentàgora slowly shook his head a few more times and sighed,

– They're poor in spirit, my two boys.

And he sat there thinking for a long time, his broad face flushed, his chin on his chest, his eyes closed, and his brows furrowed.

He knew, he *knew* everyone hated him, first and foremost his own sons. Mah! . . . So what? There was nothing he could do to avoid that; it was meant to be that way. There was no escape for the Pentàgora family! Fate had played a joke on them, branding them with the horns of the stag, and there was no escaping fate.

"Ha! We're doomed to be either hated or mocked. Better to be hated then. It was meant to be!"

All men, according to Antonio Pentàgora, came into this world with their roles assigned, and it was ridiculous to think that anyone or anything could change his. When he was a young man, even he had thought it possible for a moment, just as his sons did now! He had hoped, he had lied to himself . . . . It had seemed to him, just as it seemed now to poor, foolish Niccolino, that his heart was full of noble, generous sentiments. He had put his trust in them, and where had that gotten him? Round and round, but always back to being deceived by their wives. This was the role of the Pentàgora men. This was their destiny.

Old Pentàgora was so set in this way of thinking that if, by chance, someone came to him for help as the result of some emergency, he, upon feeling himself almost give in, indeed already moved by the man's plight, would check himself, grumbling, and, opening his mouth with that sneer of his, would counsel the poor soul to go elsewhere for help, to so-and-so, for instance, who was known to be one of the great philanthropists of the region.

– Go to him, my dear man: he was born to help people. Not me, though; that's not my department, you see. I'd be offending that worthy gentleman whose job it has been for years, and who can't really do anything else. My trade is in cuckoldry.

He had become that cynical when he spoke, quite unintentionally; he said these things in a completely unassuming and open way. And he was always the first to poke fun at his own conjugal misfortune, both in order to prevent others from doing so and to disarm them. When he was out in the world, he felt like he had crossed into enemy territory. And his signature sneer was like the snarl of a cornered dog that has turned on its pursuers. Thank goodness he was rich, and thereby, powerful. He didn't need to fear anyone. In fact, everyone gave him a wide berth: make way for the calf, as they say, especially the golden calf!

– Nonsense!

After his daughter-in-law's betrayal, a betrayal that to his mind was, of course, inevitable, Antonio Pentàgora had been enormously entertained by Rocco's shameless carrying-on with one of the local bawds.

– Bravo, Roccuccio . . . I love it! Now you're getting the hang of it! You'll see that little by little . . . . Let me feel your forehead . . . .

But no. That idiot son of his had refused to sit back and enjoy the part fate had assigned him. He was always pouting, always irritable and rude. Then they heard about Francesco Ajala's death, out of the blue! And that crazy Rocco had suddenly felt crushed by the pity that the death of that angry old fool had provoked on the part of everyone in the village. Very quietly, so as to avoid any more scandal, Rocco had gotten rid of his mistress, and had returned to his father's house as if it were a funeral.

– And why? You think maybe it was you who killed Francesco Ajala?

For a long time, there had been no way of convincing him even to leave the house, to get his mind off of things for a little while. Horses . . . saddle horses and cart horses . . . he had bought that boy six of them! After a couple of weeks, he wanted nothing to do with them. – And so, what then? A little trip maybe, on the mainland in Italy, or abroad? – No, not even that! – Gambling, at the club? – Nine thousand lire lost in a single evening. And he had paid his son's debt without uttering a word.

And so, what remained to be done? The opportunity of the saints' day presented itself: "Extreme ills call for extreme remedies!" And so he had arranged for that scandalous scene under the balcony of the Ajala house.

Pentàgora wasn't sorry. Rocco had run away like an ill-tempered bull, kicking and stamping at the touch of the branding iron. Yes, maybe he had given him a little bit too strong a dose, the poor kid. But that's what he needed! In time, he would calm down. In time, he would thank him.

"Listen, just listen to that crazy woman!" Antonio Pentàgora muttered to himself, hearing the nonsensical grumblings of his sister Sidora, who was indeed wandering around the house like a crazy woman.

Perhaps even she had heard news of the scandal. What did she think of it? No one knew but the fire in the fireplace, which she kept lit year-round. Pentàgora used to joke that she kept it going because she wanted to burn up all of the horns of the family, but that she never succeeded.

For several days, Rocco made sure not to see his father, even from a distance. Niccolino kept him company and gave him a chance to vent, like a good brother.

– Wasn't throwing her out enough? Wasn't it? I was vindicated, and . . . enough! But no, her father had to go and die. I'm not saying that it's my fault, but I definitely contributed to it in some way. And then the baby dies, and she almost dies herself . . . and when she is finally up and getting well again, he, the coward, goes and makes that ugly scene in front of her and everyone! Why keep insulting her? And who asked him to do anything anyway? The coward! The damn coward!

He wrung his hands in rage.

Meanwhile, the news grew worse from day to day: the tannery closed; Paolo Sistri run off (and people were accusing him of having stolen from the register money that, in fact, had never been there). And so misery was knocking on the door of those three poor, forsaken women. How were they going to make do? Alone, without help, looked down upon by the whole village?

And at night, Rocco seemed to find himself in the presence of an enormous Francesco Ajala, whose pale, puffed-up figure was shaking his fists at him, "*You are ruining two households, yours and mine!*" On other nights, he would see his mother-in-law (from the first day of their engagement she had been so good to him!) in rags, desperate, and Marta weeping, her face hidden, and Maria dazed, moaning, "Who will help us? Who will help us?"

So on the day he learned that the tannery was being put up for auction, Rocco rushed to his father almost against his will, and proposed—somber and without looking him in the eye—that his father buy it himself.

– You're crazy! – responded Pentàgora immediately. – Not even if they marked it down for me to three cents. What's more, look here: up 'til now I've let you do as you please with my money. Now, I've thrown away enough. It's not sand, you know! And now charity? It's not my job. We Pentàgoras, our trade is in cuckoldry.

And he left Rocco flat.

~ Chapter 11 ~

Marta, Maria, and their mother hadn't been out of bed long when they heard the distinct *ring-ringing* of the doorbell. Maria went to the door and, looking first through the peephole, saw a poorly dressed old man, accompanied by two young men, waiting on the doorstep.

– What is it that you want? – she asked, uncertain, from behind the peephole.

– Ziro, the bailiff, Don Protògene, – responded the little old man, pulling on the white curls of the beard around his neck. – Will you please be so kind as to let us in?

– The bailiff? But who are you looking for?

– Is this not the house of Francesco Ajala? – asked Ziro, the bailiff, of the two young men that accompanied him.

Maria timidly opened the door.

– A thousand pardons, Miss, – said one of the two young men. – Don Protògene, if you would be so kind as to hand her the document. There you are, Miss, please show this paper to your mother. We'll wait here.

As it happened, Signora Agata was making her way to the door at that very moment.

– Mamma, – called Maria, – come see . . . . I'm not sure what . . . .

– Ziro, the bailiff, Don Protògene, – the little old man presented himself once again when Signora Agata arrived, this time lifting from his shriveled head the worn bowler hat, sunk all the way down to the nape of his neck. – My orders are not . . . let's say, *pleasant*, but . . . the Law demands it, and, however unfortunate, it's fallen to us to carry the gavel.

Signora Agata stared at him for a moment, stunned. Then she unfolded the paper and read it out loud. Maria watched her mother with frightened eyes. The old bailiff nodded his head at every word and, when the lady had raised her eyes from the paper, not having understood its contents very well, he said in a humble voice,

– This is the order of the magistrate. And these two gentlemen are the witnesses.

The two young men raised their hats, bowing slightly.

– But how can that be? – Signora Agata exclaimed. – They told me that . . . .

By now, Marta, too, had come to the door to listen, and at the sight of her, the young men winked and nodded from the landing, elbowing each other furtively.

– But how . . . . – Signora Agata repeated, turning to Marta, confused. – The lawyers told me that . . . .

– Lawyers say lots of things . . . . – one of the boys, the stocky blond one, interrupted with a little smile, blushing. – Just leave it to us, *Signora*, and you'll see that . . . .

– But if you take away our things . . . .

– Mamma, – Marta interrupted her, not hiding the contempt in her voice. – It's useless to stand here talking. Let them come in. They're just following orders; they must do as they're told.

– With much sadness, yes, indeed . . . . – added Don Protògene. – Eh, unfortunately . . . .

He closed his eyes and shrugged his shoulders with his palms upward, running the pointed tip of his tongue across his upper lip.

– Let's be patient, – he continued just after. – Now, where shall we begin? If the *signora* might find it in her heart to . . . .

– Follow me, – Marta ordered. – This is the parlor.

She opened the door and went in before the others in order to let some light into that room, which for so many months had lain dormant behind closed shutters, abandoned. She then turned to her mother and sister, adding,

– You may leave now. I'll attend to these gentlemen.

The two young men looked at each other, mortified. The blond one was studying to become a lawyer and had already risen through the ranks to become Gregorio Alvignani's errand boy. In fact, he had begged the older bailiff to bring him along as a witness, for no better reason than to see Marta up close. He now made a show of examining his long, well-groomed fingernails, and said,

– Please believe that we are sorry, *Signora* . . . .

But Marta interrupted him, with that same contemptuous gaze.

– Just be quick about it. All this talk is useless.

Don Protògene, having drawn from his breast pocket a piece of paper, an inkpot made of bone with a stopper, and a goose quill, began taking an inventory of the parlor. Looking around and seeing only upholstered chairs and sofas, on which he did not suspect it would be polite to sit, he asked Marta with a humble smile,

– Would the *signora* be so kind as to have me brought in a chair that . . . ?

– Sit there, – said Marta, indicating one of the armchairs.

And the old man sat down obediently, but only on the very edge of the chair. With quivering hand, he perched his spectacles on the very tip of his nose and, spreading out the sheet of paper on the little round table that stood before the settee, he solemnly wrote at the top of the page "Parler," with an *e*. That accomplished, he tucked his pen behind his ear and, rubbing his hands together, said to Marta,

– Naturally this furniture will remain, most esteemed lady. Now I will just be making a little inventory of the things here, with the values.

– But you can take it all away with you if you wish, – said Marta. – In a few days, we'll be leaving this house, and all this furniture will never fit in the new one.

– Which means you're furnishing it yourself, – concluded Don Protògene. And he began to write, – One piano . . . .

Marta looked over at the piano Maria had so often played, as she herself had too, from when she was a little girl until her passion for her studies left her no time for music. And as the old man and the two young men went through the room piece by piece, identifying and writing down the names and numbers of various objects, Marta's eyes would rest on one of them for a moment, evoking a memory.

In the meantime, Anna Veronica had arrived, and Signora Agata, demoralized and in tears, told her about this most recent disaster.

– Now this! And thrown right out onto the street! . . . Oh Lord, have you no pity? Not even for this poor, innocent girl, Lord?

And with that she gestured toward Maria, who stood with her forehead pressed against the glass of the window, trying to hide her silent tears from her mother.

– And Marta? – Anna Veronica asked.

– In there. With *them* . . . . – Signora Agata responded, drying her eyes. – If only you could see her; as cold as ice, as if this had nothing to do with our home or us . . . .

– Courage, my dear Agata! – Anna said. – God is only testing you . . . .

– No! This isn't God, Anna! – Signora Agata interrupted her, taking her by the arm. – Don't say it's God. God cannot want this!

And she gestured again toward Maria, adding under her voice,

– This is torture! Torture!

Then Anna Veronica, attempting to distract her, spoke to her about the new house.

– Oh, I am just coming from there. You ought to see it! Three little rooms, full of light and air . . . . No, not small—that's not what I meant . . . . Oh, you'll love it . . . . And the most adorable little terrace! Perfect for hanging out the laundry! Yes, and there are even metal clotheslines already hung. And four posts at the corners of the terrace, and if you turn just a little bit, you see, we can shake hands for how close we are . . . . The window of my little room opens right out onto it . . . . Just think of the moonlit nights . . . .

Anna caught herself. All of a sudden she revisited a night long past; a sentimental suitor of hers had lived in that little house, where, in a few days, her friends would go to live. Shaken, she hurried on to another subject.

– But where is my mind! So . . . I had completely forgotten why I came over in the first place! I have good news for you. Yes . . . . – and she called out, – Maria! Come here, my child . . . . Come now, dry those tears . . . . Take my handkerchief . . . . Just like that . . . there's a good girl! So, I have an announcement: Baron Troisi's daughter is getting married . . . . I'll wager that doesn't mean much to you, but to me it does, my dears. The lady *baronessa*, you see—it seems impossible!—has actually deigned to have her daughter's trousseau made here in the village! Do you see? And I've taken a good part of that responsibility on myself. So you see, we will all work on it together, and God will help us. To the new house!

– Hello? – Ziro, the bailiff, interrupted at this point. He was bowing awkwardly in the doorway, with his goose quill behind his ear, his inkpot and the paper in one hand and his hat in the other.

The two young men trailed behind him. Marta suddenly appeared behind them, corralling them forward.

– That's right, go right in. Mamma, you can leave now. Oh, you're here, Anna? You can take Maria and my mother into the other room.

– You see? – said the mother to her friend. – You see how cold she's become?

– Oh, Agata, – observed Anna Veronica. – Do you really believe that she is not suffering as much as we are? She is not letting herself show it in this moment in order to keep your spirits up . . . .

– Maybe, – sighed the mother. – But you know as well as I how she reacted when this inferno was let loose upon our poor home, this storm that continues to rage. You were here; you saw! She stayed locked up in there, as if she hadn't wanted to know or see anything. It's a miracle to me that she's even out of her room today, that she's showing the slightest interest in us . . . . What is she writing in there? What is she reading? I am ashamed, my dear Anna, to be reduced to noticing these little things myself. Maria and I go to bed early to save on lamp oil, and she keeps hers lit until midnight, until two in the morning, even . . . studying . . . studying . . . . And I ask myself if maybe the sickness hasn't reached her brain . . . . "How can you do this?" – I say. – "You know the state we have been reduced to . . . . Your father, dead. The ruin. The poverty . . . and you just lock yourself away, reading by yourself, calm, as if nothing has happened."

Anna Veronica listened, full of sadness. She couldn't understand Marta's behavior either. Why so little concern, or even worse, so little feeling? It couldn't be called egotism exactly, for she herself was too involved in the affair.

– If I may . . . ? Ziro, the bailiff, repeated his entreaty not long after his first attempt, now in the doorway of this room, again followed by the witnesses.

And so from that room, too, the three women were compelled to leave. And in this way, they were pushed, room to room, from the house which three days later they were to abandon forever.

In the new house, after the sad clearing out and tidying up, Anna Veronica brought them the fragrant linen, the soft napery, and the laces and the ribbons for the wedding of the young Troisi *baronessina*.

Signora Agata, watching Maria concentrating on her work, had difficulty holding back her tears; ah, the girl would never get the chance to do the needlework on her own trousseau. She would remain this way, a poor child, orphaned and alone, forever . . . .

In the new house, Marta continued to lead the same sort of life as before. Anna Veronica, though, was no longer so astonished by this, for Marta had revealed her plan to her, on the condition that she not divulge it to Signora Agata or Maria.

She eventually revealed it herself one evening, rushing out of her room with a troubled look on her face. She had been preparing for the examinations for her teaching license, which were to begin the next morning at the *Scuola Normale*. Anna Veronica had submitted the application for Marta, and had paid—from her own savings, no less—the fees.

Her mother and sister were struck dumb.

– Let me do this, – said Marta, disappointed by their shock. – Do not stand in my way, for pity's sake . . . .

And she went back to her room and locked the door.

It had not been so long since she was in school that she could avoid taking the exams with some of her old classmates. She would have to see them then! She had no illusions about how they would receive her. She would meet them head-to-head, with the attitude of one ready to launch an attack—yes, and not just against them, should it come to that, but against the whole town. In her mind, she went over the roads she would travel the next morning to the exam. She would look those cowards, who had publicly insulted her on the day of that savage festival, directly in the eye.

As she thought of that enormous sea of people undulating under the balcony of her former home, arms upraised, turned into beasts by the wine and by the sun, Marta felt even more strongly the desire to fight. On that long night of vigil, she truly felt that she would rise above these cowardly, unjust wrongs. And then, armed with disdain, she would have the pride of being able to say, "I have raised my mother and my sister out of poverty and misery; they are alive now by my actions, because of me."

Little by little, comforted by these thoughts, her dreams of a brighter future overtook her apprehension about the looming exam, and she managed to overcome her anxiety. But she could not overcome her resentment, which awakened and grew until, by the time she got up the next morning, it had become paralyzing.

She no longer knew what she should do. She looked around her bedroom in search of herself, seeking the familiar, half expecting the spare furnishings to offer some suggestion: there was the basin, in which she would wash, and there was the chair, on which she had laid out the clothes she would wear. Before long, she was washing and dressing hurriedly.

While she was doing her best to arrange her hair with no mirror, her mother entered, already dressed to accompany her.

– Oh thank goodness, Mother! Help me finish my hair, please . . . . It's getting late!

And her mother started brushing her daughter's hair, as she had done every morning before bringing her to school. Finished, she looked at her daughter. Good Lord! She had never looked so beautiful . . . . She attempted to show a deep restraint, thinking that she would now have to go out with her daughter into the city, navigating among people's vicious glances, and all for the sake of a mission that, in the timid humility of her own character, she could neither appreciate nor fully comprehend. She was worried that Marta's great beauty, that air of defiance and provocation in her eyes, might cause people to reproach her openly for her shamelessness, to cry out, "Look at how brazen she is!"

– You're flushed . . . . – she said, looking away from her daughter, and she had wanted to add, "Keep your eyes lowered as we go through the streets."

They finally went downstairs, and they walked straight ahead, side by side, while Maria, behind the glass of the front window, nervously followed them with her eyes.

Signora Agata wished that she were half as tall as she was, so as not to attract so many glances, and to pass by unobserved, or that she could run, in a flash, down that interminably long street. Marta, on the other hand, was thinking of the imminent encounter with her old schoolmates and was in no hurry to get there.

They were among the first to arrive at the college.

– Oh, *signorina bella*! What's this? You've come back? My, how you've grown! And that pretty face of yours . . . . – exclaimed the old caretaker woman, gesturing extravagantly with her head and hands to express her expansive admiration.

– No one's arrived yet? – asked Marta, a little embarrassed, smiling kindly at the old woman.

– No one! – she responded. – You were always first . . . . Remember when you were only this high, and every blessed morning, bump! bump! bump! There you were kicking the door because you couldn't reach the knocker . . . . Lord, it was still dark out! Do you remember?

Ah, yes! Marta smiled . . . . Ah, the good memories!

– Will you come in? – the old lady continued. – The *signora* must be tired . . . .

And looking Signora Agata in the eyes, she sighed, shaking her head tentatively:

– Poor Signor Francesco! What a loss . . . . They don't make gentlemen like him anymore, my lady! But enough. May the blessed Lord receive him in glory! I think the door to the waiting area is locked. Just be patient and wait a second, and I'll run to get the key.

– A good soul! – said Signora Agata to Marta, grateful for the gracious welcome.

After a minute, the old caretaker returned from her errand, and said,

– My daughter Eufemia is also taking the exams with you today, Marta!

– Eufemia? Really? How is she?

– Poor thing. She hasn't slept in days . . . . Ah, if she doesn't do well, it won't be for lack of hard work . . . . You with all your talent, *Signorina*, if you can, help the poor girl a little in there today! They say that it will be the most difficult exam of them all! Let me run up and tell her to come right down, so she can keep you company . . . . Here now, sit down and make yourselves comfortable.

And with that, she dusted off the leather sofa with a corner of her apron.

– If Eufemia is studying, please don't call her down, – said Marta to the old woman, who was already on her way out the door.

– Oh, she wouldn't miss a visit with you for all the world! – the old caretaker responded without turning around.

From the very start, Eufemia Sabetti and Marta had been classmates, although she was older than Marta by at least six years. She had grown up in the school, among a group of students of a much higher social status than she was, and had learned from them a certain air of civility that made her mother immeasurably proud. Indeed, her mother had paid for that satisfaction with numerous sacrifices. Eufemia, it is true, spoke to her classmates with the familiar "*tu*," wore hats, and had the manners and affectations of a real "lady." But still, in their eyes she remained a janitor's daughter. They did not rub her nose in it, of course . . . no, the poor thing! But they did make it clear, whether in the way they looked at her clothes and her hat, or in the way they would occasionally drop her in the middle of a conversation and crowd around another *of their own kind*. And Eufemia pretended not to notice any of this. She wanted to stay friends with them.

– Oh Marta! What luck! – she exclaimed as she ran into the room, greeting Marta with a kiss, unembarrassed. Smiling, she greeted Signora Agata and sat down on the sofa, so that Marta was in between them. – What luck! – she repeated. – How are you? What's new? And you're really taking the exams?

She was dark and very thin, a tiny little thing in her caffè-latte-colored, black-trimmed dress. When she spoke, her whole body trembled, and she continually fluttered her eyelids over her beady eyes, which shone like a ferret's. When she laughed, she showed her gums and her incredibly white teeth.

The embarrassing questions began right away, and Marta felt she had to respond, at least to the more discreet ones. The other questions, though, the ones she saw in Eufemia's eyes, made Marta more evasive.

Signora Agata stood up.

– I'm going home, Marta. I will leave you with your friend. *Coraggio*, little ones!

As she left the waiting room, she saw in the atrium a cluster of young girls in bright summer dresses, among whom she recognized some of Marta's old schoolmates. They suddenly went quiet and lowered their eyes as she passed. No one acknowledged or greeted her. One girl only—Mita Lumìa—gave her a slight nod of the head.

The old caretaker woman had announced to the girls that Marta had come.

– What nerve! – said one.

– Well, I refuse to go in, if she's there, – said another.

– What has she come here for? – asked a third.

– Oh, to take the examinations, of course. What, do you want to stop her from taking them? – responded Mita Lumìa, who was also shocked, but not as worked up as the other girls.

– Fine, but I'm not sitting next to her, – protested a fourth, – not even if the director himself orders me to!

And a fifth said to Mita Lumìa: – We don't even know what to call her! Pentàgora? Ajala?

– Oh Lord, call her Marta, like we used to call her! – responded Mita, annoyed.

At that very moment, Marta, with a bitter smile, was saying to Eufemia,

– Who knows what they're saying about me out there . . . .

– Let them talk all they want! – responded Eufemia.

Suddenly four of the little group burst in and crossed the room almost running, without so much as a glance at the sofa.

As grateful as Marta was deep down to Eufemia for the company, she couldn't entirely overcome a sense of humiliation at being seen sitting next to her; not for herself, but for those gossips that saw the two of them together, saw her accepted, that is, only by the janitor's daughter.

They got up. Just then Mita Lumìa came in, unhurried.

– Oh, Marta . . . . How are you?

And she attempted a smile and held out a soft, damp hand.

– Dear Mita . . . . – responded Marta.

And they just stood there for a moment without knowing what more to say.

~ Chapter 12 ~

Envy on the one hand, and on the other, thwarted intrigues and dashed hopes happily combined in slander to explain how they had been vanquished.

It was so clear!

There was one reason and one reason alone that Marta Ajala had been given the post of substitute teacher in the first preparatory classes of the *collegio*; she was the "protégé" of Deputy Alvignani.

And for the first few days after her appointment, there was a procession of fathers of families to the school, demanding to speak with the director. Oh, but it was scandalous! Their daughters would simply refuse to go to school! And no father could in good conscience force his daughter to attend, given the circumstances. Something had to be done immediately, whatever the cost!

The old director referred the fathers to the school inspector, but only after having defended the future substitute on the grounds that she had submitted examinations of the highest quality. If some other young woman had done better, she would have been appointed. No injustice had been committed, nothing unusual . . . .

– But yes!

The school inspector, the *cavaliere* Claudio Torchiara, was from the area, and was a close friend of Gregorio Alvignani. Naturally by the time the complaints reached him, they had been twisted into another form and tone altogether. Did Alvignani really want to risk becoming unpopular with voters by using his influence so scandalously?

It was useless for Torchiara to protest that Alvignani had nothing whatsoever to do with it, and that, indeed, Ms. Ajala's position was not even a government appointment. Oh, come now! If the director of the school was going to talk that way, so be it. But he, Torchiara, who was a Sicilian and from the town? Come now! Had he forgotten the recent scandals? Had he lost his memory?

Had Ajala's appointment come out of thin air then? And if Torchiara had a daughter, would he in good conscience send her to be taught by a woman about whom people had said such terrible things? What a shining example for our daughters!

If Marta, ever more oppressed by their growing poverty, closed in her little room preparing those exams, had for even one moment entertained the thought that she would soon meet almost exactly the same cowardice and abuse, this time in another guise, perhaps her spirits would have been dashed. But her youthful boldness was spurred on by, on the one hand, her eagerness to rise above her present condition through her own efforts, and on the other, by the poverty into which she and her family had been plunged, by the understanding of her own worth and the sanctity of the sacrifice she was making for her mother and sister. At that moment, she was thinking only about passing the test; she would only be able to carry out her plan once she had done so.

Now, though, she understood the disappointed astonishment of her mother and sister when she had announced her ambitious plan to them. And she had not yet even heard the slanders with which the respectable people of the town were arming themselves to attack her, to shove her back down into the mud from which she was so determined to escape!

In the meantime, the old caretaker, Sabetti senior, came to her sadly with the announcement that the position she had been promised was to be awarded to one Ms. Breganze, a niece of one of the members of the city council.

In the interim, at the unexpected news that Marta intended to become a teacher, Rocco Pentàgora's pity, which was on the verge of becoming remorse, was turned into contempt at his having been so suddenly pushed aside.

He did not see in Marta's decision how dire her straits in fact were, financially, nor her urgency to provide even the most basic needs for her family (which he himself would have been happy to provide, in secret, naturally). Instead he saw only her insolent and contemptuous determination to defy the whole village. It was as if she were saying, "I don't need anything or anyone but myself and my family. I don't care about your condemnation." And he felt as though he had been left out of her plans; not only did he feel not looked after, but he also felt openly disregarded and despised by his wife! And a restless anger began to overcome him, which manifested itself particularly in an incomprehensible disdain for the profession she had chosen.

– A teacher! A teacher! – he grumbled. – The woman who was once my wife now wants to be a teacher!

And he had no peace after that, as if her being a teacher somehow dishonored the name she had once carried.

But how could he stop her? How could he bring himself back to life, and make her feel like she could not ignore him? How could he make her feel that she could not break this chain, not escape from the dead weight of a bond to which she had not, in any case, been faithful?

And his rage grew . . . . A new scandal? Some new punishment? Could he bring himself to fan the flames of the slander that had resulted from the presumed relationship between Marta and Alvignani by publishing the letters the latter had written to her? No! No! The ridicule such an act would engender would fall more openly on him than on her. In any case, everyone in town believed that the scandalous relationship had happened, and to participate in the spreading of the slander would only have made him feel more keenly his powerlessness against a woman who openly did not care for him or for anyone else. Instead, it would be better for everyone if the vilification died down. Yes . . . but how? And here a surge and immediate rejection of contradictory proposals filled his head, some dictated by his hatred of Alvignani, and, equally savage, some were dictated by his anger. Some were the result of the pain of his lost love, and some were even the result of his generosity.

Some evenings he would leave the house, directionless. Suddenly, he would find himself on the road leading to the outskirts of town, close to Francesco Ajala's tannery. What had he come here for? Oh, if only he could see her! . . . Look, there was the old house . . . . Now she was living farther down . . . just past the church . . . . And carefully he would continue walking, peering into the few lit balconies under cover of darkness. At the first sound of footsteps on the lonely road, however far in the distance, he would turn back, careful not to be seen in that neighborhood, and would return to his house.

But the next day, he would do the same thing all over again.

Why this obsession with seeing Marta again? Or better still, with being seen by her again? He himself didn't know. He imagined her dressed all in black, as Niccolino had seen her that day in the church.

– More beautiful than ever before, you know?

But she would certainly not have looked at him; she would have lowered her eyes as soon as she saw him from across the room. Would he dare stop her on the street? Madness! And what would people have thought? And what would he have said?

It was in this frame of mind that one morning he found himself at the house of Anna Veronica.

Seeing him there, pale and clearly upset, Anna stood.

– What do you want with me?

– Please excuse the inconvenience . . . . Sit, sit please. I'll get a chair myself.

But all the chairs were covered with piles and piles of linens, and Anna had to get up herself in order to free a place for him.

– What beautiful things . . . . – said Rocco, embarrassed.

– They belong to the Baronessa Troisi.

– For her daughter?

Anna nodded, and Rocco let out a sigh; his eyes narrowed and his face darkened. He remembered the preparations for his own wedding, and Marta's trousseau.

– Here's your chair, – said Anna, with an awkward haste.

Rocco sat down sullenly. He didn't know where to begin. He sat for a moment with his eyebrows furrowed, his eyes lowered, his shoulders sagging, as if he were waiting for some great weight to fall on his back. Anna Veronica, still startled, scanned his face.

– You . . . know already . . . I imagine, – he finally began, emphasizing each word without raising his eyes. – I know that you're the friend of . . . and so . . . .

He broke off. He couldn't continue in that tone, with that attitude. He shook himself, raised his head, and looked Anna directly in the face.

– Listen, *Signora maestra*, I believe that . . . that is, I don't believe the things that people are saying against . . . Marta now . . . about this new crazy passion of hers.

– Ah, – said Anna, shaking her head with a wistful smile. – You call it crazy, do you?

– Oh, it's worse than crazy! – Rocco shot back angrily. – I'm sorry, but . . . .

– I don't know what people are saying, – responded Anna. – I can only imagine . . . . And you do well not to believe it, Signor Pentàgora. All the more so since no one can know better than you . . . .

– We must not speak of that! We must not speak of it, please! – Rocco begged her, holding his hands out in front of him. – I didn't come here to talk about the past.

– And so? I beg your pardon, but if you yourself say that you don't believe . . . . – Anna attempted to continue.

– Believe what? Do you know what people are saying? – Rocco asked with a voice that had suddenly changed. – That her association with Alvignani has continued! There, I've said it!

– Continued?

– Yes, *Signora*. And why? It's this obsession of hers with calling attention to herself! "But you know what is weighing on you now," they say to her, "what you have done! How do you find the courage even to go out in the square and face the terrible gossip of the village?" People are talking . . . and I believe it! How did she get that appointment?

– But everyone knows! – retorted Anna, sneering scornfully. – It's the only way anyone can get a post these days! And it's those people, those many upholders of honesty all over our village, who show us how things are done, how to get positions like these! "Might as well," they say, "because look . . . whether you do it or not, it's all the same. For us, it will be the same whether you've done it or not." Silly Marta, then, who didn't do it, right? What good did being honest do her? Who believes she didn't do it?

– I don't believe what they are saying, I've already told you, – responded Rocco, his face darkening even more. – And yet I maintain that if people are talking, it isn't entirely their fault . . . . What can you expect them to understand about whether an exam result was good or bad, really? The scandal, that's all they can think about! The intrigue! And you, *Signora*, you don't want to see it from this other angle . . . . That's why you can make excuses for her . . . .

– Oh, it's not only that, – shouted Anna, rising, – but also that I admire her, Signor Pentàgora! I admire Marta, and I sing her praises! Because I know that poor girl's conscience. I know her remorse for the others who suffer unjustly because of her. But there is neither stain nor sin there, hand to God! There I find only the pain of the offenses made against her, of the outrages she has suffered! And I hear a shout in the darkness, "Enough!" But do you know what they have been reduced to? Do you know that they don't even have food to eat? Who did you expect would provide for her mother and her sister? Who would lift them up a little bit out of their poverty and misery? I know; I know the sacrifice she had to make, my poor Marta! Or would you have had her let them all die of starvation just to please you and the rest of the village?

Rocco Pentàgora was on his feet now too, his mind a mess, his pale face splotched with red. He paced the room nervously, skimming the backs of the chairs with his hands, his fingers a blur of motion. Then he drew near to Anna with a menacing look in his eyes and grabbed both of her hands in his.

– Listen to me, *Signora maestra* . . . . For pity's sake, tell her . . . . Tell her to give up this idea of . . . of being a teacher. So that . . . so that these people talking won't have anything to talk about, and . . . and that I'll provide, say it just like that, for the needs of the family, without . . . without letting anyone know . . . . Not even my father, you understand! I promise on the saintly soul of Francesco Ajala! I am not doing this for love, believe me! I am doing this for her reputation and for mine . . . . Tell her so . . . .

Anna Veronica promised to deliver the message, and not long after, repeating his instructions and promises, he went away, seeming more upset and obsessed than when he had arrived.

– For reputation, not for love. Tell her so. For decency's sake, understand!

~ Chapter 13 ~

Just as soon as Rocco Pentàgora had gone, Anna Veronica ran as fast as her feet would carry her to the Ajalas.

– Where is Marta? – she whispered to Maria, putting a finger to her lips.

– In her room . . . . Why?

– Shhhh! Quiet!

She motioned for Agata to come nearer, and she looked around nervously.

– Let me sit down . . . . I'm trembling all over . . . . Oh, my dears, if you only knew! You'll never guess who came to see me, just a moment ago. Marta's husband!

– Rocco? Rocco himself? – exclaimed everyone at once, still whispering. Maria and her mother were shocked.

Anna put her finger to her lips again.

– Like a crazy person, – she added, waving her hands in the air. – Oh, I was so afraid! He still loves her, let me tell you! If it weren't for . . . . But listen . . . so . . . he came to see me. He said, "I don't believe the slanderous things people are saying . . . ."

– And? And? – was all her hopeful mother could manage.

– Exactly. "And?" I asked him, just as you would have. But he says, "Marta,"—wait a minute!—"Marta," he says, "must not expose herself to the malice of those people . . . . In short, that she shouldn't be a teacher . . . . It offends him and saddens him. But enough of this. Do you know, my dears, what he has proposed to me? That I persuade Marta to drop the idea . . . . He will provide, he says, for all of your needs himself, just so there won't be any more of this evil gossip.

– Is that all? – sighed Signora Agata. – Ah, so with just a little bit of money, handed out in secret as if we were charity cases, he thinks he can close people's mouths? And the day after won't people just say that the money is coming from someone else's pocket? Stupid, cowardly boy!

– No! No! – replied Anna. – Don't say that . . . . He loves her, take my word for it . . . . But there is that Jewish dog of a father of his, you understand? And as long as he's around . . . . If Marta would at least write him a note . . . .

– Who?

– Him! Her husband! To . . . soften him a little. A letter like only she can write . . . . This would be just the moment! "You know very well," it needs to say, "what is and isn't true . . . . And now see how they're treating me? What they're saying about me?" Oh, if she would write him just a few words . . . . And all the more because he asked for a response . . . . What do you think?

– Marta will never do it, – said Maria, shaking her head.

– Well let's at least try! – Anna replied. – Should I be the one to speak to her? Where is she?

– She's in there, – nodded Signora Agata. – But I'm worried that now is not the right time . . . .

– I'll go in alone, – added Anna, standing up.

Marta was stretched out on her little bed with her arms folded over a pillow and her face hidden. As soon as she heard the door open she pulled her arms in closer and buried her face deeper.

– Marta, it's me, – said Anna, closing the door softly.

– Leave me alone, Anna, please! – Marta responded without raising her head, fidgeting on the bed. – And please don't try to make me feel better!

– No, no, – Anna Veronica was quick to reply as she approached the little bed and placed her hand gently on Marta's shoulder. – I only wanted to see you . . . .

– I don't want to see anyone! I can't bear to listen to anyone, not now! – replied Marta feverishly. – Leave me alone, for goodness' sake!

Anna quickly withdrew her hand, and said,

– You're right . . . .

She waited a moment, and then went on, sighing,

– It's too good . . . . It would have been too easy! You imagined that people wouldn't block your way on the path that you created yourself, through your own hard work, your own intelligence and courage . . . . But what have these things gotten you, my dear? It's protection you need! And do you have that? No . . . . But there's no other way of moving forward. And remember, everyone will always judge you as they see fit . . . .

Marta suddenly raised her head from her cheek and said angrily,

– But they promised that position to me!

– Yes, – Anna replied quickly, – and in fact just that one simple unkept promise was enough, because then the people began to shout that you were being protected by someone . . . .

– Me? – said Marta, not comprehending at first and looking deep into Anna Veronica's eyes. Then she screamed, – Ah! . . . I . . . I . . . – and she couldn't say anything more, but pressed her face into her hands. Then she exploded, – Of course! Yes . . . yes . . . of course people believe that! Someone is spreading this new lie about me!

– *He* isn't, though, you see? Your husband isn't, – said Anna quickly. – He came to see me just to tell me so.

– Rocco? – Marta exclaimed, stunned, trying in vain to furrow her eyebrows. – Rocco came to see you?

– Yes, yes, just a little while ago . . . to tell me that he doesn't believe them.

– To see you? Rocco did?

Her astonishment was still getting in the way of her understanding the reason for his visit.

– And what does he want?

– He wants . . . – Anna responded, – he wants you to . . . .

Marta was silent for a moment.

– Do you want to know what he wants? – Marta lashed back, her eyes flashing. – He's lost his courage. On the one hand, he feels remorse, and on the other . . . . I've tried to keep my head held high, haven't I? But he wants me to bow! He wants to throw me back down to the ground, down! Down! Back into the mud where he threw me in the first place! *This* is what he wants! I'm not so much as to breathe, not permitted to remove from my forehead, here, this brand, the brand he thinks he's stamped me with! *This* is what he wants! Oh, and if I give him this satisfaction of lying flat in the mud, like a frog that he can crush under his boot if he so chooses, if I would only give him that satisfaction . . . then he would be able to take care of me, to buy me clothes to wear and food to eat, for me and my mother and my sister . . . .

Anna stared at her, surprised and saddened.

– Isn't that what he wants? – Marta pressed her. – Have I guessed it? Do you really want to tell me? I can read his mind like a book. It's clear as day what's going through his head!

– But if only you would write this to him . . . . – risked a suddenly timid Anna.

– Me? Write to him?

– Because he wants a response . . . .

– He wants a response from me? – asked Marta scornfully. – Me, write to him? But I . . . instead of that . . . since nothing has gotten through to these people, and just like me, Mamma and Maria have had to lower themselves to servitude . . . . I, well, there's one more person I can write. I can write to Rome, to him.

– No, Marta! – Anna exclaimed, distressed.

– No . . . no . . . – Marta quickly took back her threat and turned back over on the bed, burying her face once again in the pillows. – No . . . I know. It's better to die of starvation . . . .

Anna Veronica didn't know how to respond. Her compassionate eyes drifted over the bed and rested on that lovely young body, wracked with sobbing. With one hand, she pulled out a corner of Marta's skirt that had been tucked up under her leg and covered her leg with it.

She sighed and left the room.

When she came back in, neither Signora Agata nor Maria asked her anything. The three of them sat in silence for a long while, staring into space.

– And what if you went to see Torchiara? – suggested Anna, finally breaking the silence.

Signora Agata stared at her, as if to say, "What for?"

– It's an injustice, – Anna went on. – Torchiara will have to tell you something . . . . Also, for you to feel that you . . . . Do you think you can go on like this?

For two days, in fact, Marta had barely eaten, would do nothing more than throw herself on the bed, where she lay motionless.

– What do you want me to say? – sighed Signora Agata. – The position has been given to someone else at this point . . . .

– But it was promised to Marta first! – said Anna. – He will explain it to you . . . . I don't want to give you false hope, God knows, but at least he will tell you something . . . something that can lift this poor girl's spirits. Up, my dear! Let's at least try! Yes, right now! I know, it's a sacrifice . . . .

– For me? – said Signora Agata disconsolately, getting up and holding out her arms.

Nothing meant anything to her at this point. She no longer had the will to do anything. She placed her widow's bonnet over her hair, which had turned gray just over these last few months.

– I'll go right away.

She scuttled through the streets avoiding people's glances as if she truly had something to be ashamed of. There were so many . . . the whole village supported this injustice, this condemnation. Even her husband, the man who had never asked anyone for anything, who never bowed to anyone, even he had hidden himself away from it. What was she in the face of this? Only a poor woman, saddened by this injustice, saddened by the tragedy of it. And she was ashamed, yes, ashamed of her poverty, ashamed of the very clothes on her back. Marta . . . Marta should have resigned herself to this. She should have stayed humble and waited for the slow justice of time. The three of them could have worked together, in the shadows, and made the best of things without going and breathing new life into this war.

Here was Torchiara's house. She climbed the stairs with effort, out of breath, and stood before the front door. Before she rang the bell she hid her face in her hands.

– Is he alone? – was the first thing she asked the servant who opened the door.

– No, he is with Professor Blandino, – she responded.

– Then . . . shall I wait here?

– As you wish . . . . In any case, I will let him know you are here.

Not long after, *Cavaliere* Claudio Torchiara entered, drawing back the curtain that hung by the door with one hand and with the other pushing back up his nose eyeglasses with lenses so thick that in correcting his extreme myopia they made his eyes appear incredibly small. He called out,

– Please do come in, *Signora*! Welcome!

He took her by the hand and led her forward to the settee in the study.

Signora Agata, bowing her head with a melancholy smile, sat in a corner of the sofa.

– Professor Luca Blandino, – added Torchiara, by way of introduction.

– We know each other . . . . – interrupted the bald, bearded Blandino, who offered his hand distractedly to the embarrassed woman sitting opposite him. – Francesco Ajala's widow? He was a great man, your husband.

Torchiara let out a sigh and pushed his thick, gold-rimmed glasses up his nose for a second time. There was a moment of silence, during which Signora Agata tried with difficulty to keep her tears in check.

– How true it is, – Blandino went on, his eyes closed, his arms folded, – how true it is that our conduct is judged by others as either just or unjust, and not by virtue of its intrinsic nature, but according to its external circumstance . . . . How have we judged Francesco Ajala? We have judged him using a vocabulary that serves us communally, speaking of duties, and of obligations, that is to say, without cracking the particular code prescribed to him by his own nature, and modified, edited, so to say, by his education and experience. This, however unfortunately, is how we judge people!

And with that, he stood up.

– Are you leaving? – asked Torchiara.

Blandino did not respond, but began to pace the room with his eyebrows drawn together and his eyes half-closed. He was so absorbed in thought that he was not aware in the slightest of how inappropriate his presence there was, and what pain and embarrassment it caused the *signora*.

– So then, I imagine that you do me the honor of this visit on behalf of your dear daughter. Is that not so, *Signora*? – Torchiara asked softly, eyeing her with an air of both resignation and of apology for the presence of Blandino, as if to say, "Patience! We must excuse the man; he can't help it . . . ."

Torchiara, however, didn't regret Blandino's presence in the slightest. In fact, he had purposely asked Blandino to stay once this new guest was announced in order to ensure that the visit didn't go on for too long and that it wasn't too overwhelmingly painful for his, Torchiara's that is, delicate sensibilities. And now it fell to him to take away that poor mother's last hope . . . . But it was too early, yes, that's right, too early for an appointment even if it were temporary, for a simple substitute . . . . It's a difficult career, teaching, so difficult . . . . She would just have to wait a little longer, that's all . . . . Oh, the future would be full of great opportunities for that young schoolteacher, no doubt! What's that? The Breganze girl? Ah yes . . . . And at this line of questioning, so painful to his tender sensibilities, the *cavaliere* Torchiara scratched his head with one finger and for a third time pushed his spectacles up his nose. Yes, Ms. Breganze, the niece of his friend, Councilman Breganze . . . . No, his influence had nothing to do with it, of course not! It was precedence alone, a question of precedence, you see . . . . Not of ability, no! As far as Ms. Breganze goes, she too is a fantastic teacher, so . . . . But he knew well that the abilities of young Ms. Ajala were incomparably superior . . . . Yes, yes they were!

As Luca Blandino walked the room immersed in thought, his hands joined behind his back, the occasional fragment of a sentence would reach him. What did get through to him at the odd interval only caused him to knit his brow still more vigorously. He understood nothing of the content of this painful dialogue, noting only the expressions of anguished dismay, of profound desperation on the face of Signora Ajala when she eventually rose and bowed her head in salutation.

– Auff! – snorted Torchiara, returning to the study after having graciously accompanied the *signora* to the door. – I can't stand any more of this whole damned business! I feel for her, of course, the poor lady. But what does she expect me to do? If her daughter . . . . You know what I mean! We must bear the curse of living in a small town, where certain things simply cannot be either forgiven or forgotten . . . . I can't take a stand against the whole town, like Horace taking on all of Boeotia alone!

– What's this all about? – asked Blandino.

– Oh, it's nothing, my friend. A trifle. The biggest trifle of all time, unfortunately, that has strolled in wearing a black cloak. What's it about? It's about bread. But what can I do about it, good God in His heaven? I offer my sympathy . . . and that's all I can do!

And he explained to Blandino the reason for Signora Ajala's visit.

– What? And you just sent her away like that? – bellowed Blandino in reply. – You, you, you . . . . I am shocked . . . . How could you . . . ? For God's sake! Action must be taken! We must solve this . . . and quickly!

Torchiara burst into laughter.

– And where do you propose to go now?

The agitated Blandino was now literally running around the room.

– My hat . . . . Where did I leave my hat?

– Your head! Your head! – cried out Torchiara, still laughing. – You should be looking for your head instead!

He seized his friend by the arm.

– Now you see? And you wonder why they call you crazy! First you took the side of the husband, in the duel, and now you defend the wife?

– But I don't judge things the way you do! – Blandino shouted at him. – I judge everything according to its circumstance! I don't draw lines in the sand arbitrarily like you do: up to here is good, but past this point, no, that's bad . . . . Let me act like a crazy person! The first thing I'm going to do is write an insulting letter to Gregorio Alvignani . . . . Oh, that Alvignani, great man that he is, able to escape so easily after having plunged that poor family into poverty and disgrace! Did you know that he used to throw letters down to her from his window, like a smitten schoolboy? Goodbye, Torchiara, goodbye!

And Blandino abruptly left, amidst the forced laughter of *Cavaliere* Claudio Torchiara.

~ Chapter 14 ~

Out of the blue, around three months later, Marta received an appointment from the director of the college.

The old caretaker, Signora Sabetti, who had been so sad to deliver the bad news of the Breganze girl receiving the position that was rightfully Marta's, came in this time shouting joyfully.

– *Signorina! Signorina!* You're coming to our school! To *our* school, my beautiful *signorina*! Here, read this note!

The news was like a sudden ray of sunshine in that time of squalor and misery. Marta's face flamed like burning coal.

– What luck! – old Sabetti went on, gesturing like mad. – One of the teachers, a Ms. Flori, who teaches in the second preparatory, is heading back north . . . somewhere! Her transfer request was granted, God be praised! And the students will be able to breathe again . . . .

– I am to report to the school . . . today! – Marta announced upon having read the note, her voice trembling from the excitement.

– Yes, ma'am! – added the old caretaker. – And you will see that it is just as I've told you! I'm sure of it!

– But how . . . ? – Marta asked. – Was this Ms. Flori really transferred?

– She's been moved, yes ma'am! And it's a good thing, let me tell you, for our girls . . . . What a bore she was! Dull, dull, dull!

– But with the school year already begun? – Marta observed, not knowing what to think.

– Maybe it was Torchiara . . . . – Signora Agata let slip out.

And she relayed the whole story to her daughter of her secret visit to the school inspector.

Not long after, while Marta was dressing to go to the school and the commotion had died down, she asked herself to whom she owed this appointment, late though it was. Could it have come from Rome . . . from him? And she shook at the very thought of it, so badly, in fact, that she suddenly became too weak to fasten her stays.

The battle began again the moment she began teaching.

Already the other teachers at the school, virtuous, plain old maids most of them, quickly came to dislike Marta. The Lord be with you, the Lord be with you; the briefest of greetings in the morning, delivered from tight-lipped mouths, and nothing more. A cold, barely discernible nod of the head, and even that was too much! A disgrace to teachers everywhere! A disgrace to the whole school! The world? Yes, nothing but intrigue, everywhere! People will do anything to get to the top! Yes, but they must do it honestly! Or rather, *honorably* . . . .

And, under their breaths, of course, they commented with biting venom on the way that the director and the other professors of the school had treated this Ajala woman from the very first day! And they lamented the loss of that dear Signorina Flori, whom they would never see again. Poor Signorina Flori, alas!

New and increasingly indignant complaints came from the families of the students, but they were all in vain. And the girls themselves (who had made sure to be absent for a few days after Marta's appointment had been announced by the school) little by little resumed their lessons, but with openly bad manners and wearing their resentment toward their new teacher on their sleeves, behavior all too clearly incited by their parents.

Marta's affability failed to win them over from the very beginning; her care and forbearance counted for nothing. They openly and rudely recoiled at her touch, they were deaf to her kind warnings, they just shrugged their shoulders at the very rare threat. And the worst of them would wait until recess in the yard, when they would speak badly of her just loudly enough for her to hear, or to tease her, they would run to a group of the older teachers and fawn over them, heaping them with praise and attention, leaving her to walk the playground alone.

Returning home after six hours of this punishment, Marta had to make a violent effort to hide her exasperated spirit from her mother and sister.

But one day she returned home early from the school, her eyes ablaze and her face flushed, and trembling with a rage she could barely contain. As soon as her mother and Anna Veronica asked her what had happened, she broke into convulsive sobs, her hat still on her head.

Her patience finally exhausted, and seeing that her kind ways with the students were getting her nowhere, she grudgingly agreed to take the director's advice, and to treat the students a little more severely. For a week now, she had been very careful with one student in particular, who just happened to be the daughter of the same Councilman Breganze, a thin, blonde, irritable girl, who was all nerves. Egged on by her classmates, she had even gone so far as to be directly and loudly impertinent on more than one occasion.

– And I pretended not to hear . . . . But at the end of class today, not long before the lesson ended, I just couldn't tolerate her anymore. I yelled at her. She responded by laughing at me and staring back at me insolently. You should have heard her! "Leave the room, now!" "I don't want to!" "Oh no you don't!" And I came down from the dais to remove her from the classroom myself. But she held onto the bench for dear life and shouted at me, "Don't touch me! *I don't want your filthy hands anywhere near me!*" "Oh, you don't? Out, then, out! Leave the classroom!" and I tried to make her let go of the bench. Then she started screaming in earnest, stomping her feet and twisting her body. All of the other girls got up from their benches and gathered around us. The Breganze girl finally left the room, threatening me all the while, and followed by the rest of the girls. She went straight to the director. He defended me while they were there, but once they had gone he told me that I had crossed the line a little bit, that I must not, he said, raise my hand to any child . . . . Me, harm a child? I never touched her! In the end, he accepted my version of events, but God, God! How can I continue like this? I just can't do it anymore!

The next day, of course, the girl's father, Ippolito Onorio Breganze, senior counselor and *Cavaliere* to the Crown, went in to make a scene in the director's office.

He was furious.

The sheer obesity of his body did not allow him to gesticulate with the vehemence he would have liked. He had short arms and short legs, and he carried with him a rotund globe of a potbelly, which he hauled up and down the length of the office with difficulty, huffing and puffing as his shoes squeaked at every step. What, raise a hand to the face of his child? God Himself, *God Himself* didn't have the right! Even he, who was the child's father, had never dared go so far! Have we perhaps returned to those halcyon days of the Jesuits, when teaching meant little more than striking students across their open palms or backsides with a switch? He wanted swift and ample retribution! Oh yes, in the name of the Lorrrrd! If Ms. Ajala had friends in such high places, then he, *Cavaliere* to the Crrrrown would demand his rrrrightly owed rrrrecompense from an even higher power, *much* higher (and here he attempted to raise his fat little arm, to no avail . . .) – Yes Sir, higher! In the name of wounded Morality, and not only the Morality of the school, but of the whole town!

And *squee, squee, squee*, squeaked his shoes.

The director could not manage to calm him down. It almost made him laugh: in the village, it was widely thought that he was not even the true father of the child. But Ippolito Onorio Breganze, senior counselor and *Cavaliere* to the Crown, now purple in the face, would not be content with a simple reprimand for the teacher, meted out in private. No, he wanted, rather he *demanded* a serious punishment! And not just for the sake of his own dear little innocent girl, but also for the "moral health, *Signor* Director, of the whole of this scandalized town!" Did the director perhaps not fully understand what had occurred? Did he not know the kind of woman to whom he had entrusted those tender minds and delicate souls?

– It is an im-mo-ral-i-ty! – he intoned in the end at full voice, emphasizing each syllable. – If you do not rrrremedy this situation, Sir, I will rrrremedy it myself. I will be making a formal complaint with the school inspector! My rrrregards, Sir!

And clamping his top hat down onto his head, puhm!, he stormed out of the office just as a janitor was entering. They collided with such force that it was only by some miracle that both weren't thrown to the ground.

– Excuse me, Sir.

– Excuse *me*, Sir.

And *squee, squee, squee* . . .

Two days later the director of the school was summoned by the school inspector.

For two months Torchiara had been noting with consternation the serious harm that the appointment of Ms. Ajala was having across the community for Alvignani's political aspirations. "Good Sir," he would remind himself again and again, "the heart has always been the worst enemy of the head!" For *Cavaliere* Torchiara absolutely delighted in formulating aphorisms, and usually inserted the phrase "good Sir" before each, even when he was relating them to a lady, or, as a solitary pastime, to himself.

The visit of a furious Counselor Breganze had thrown him headlong into a sea of turmoil. Would the whole municipality thus be turned against Alvignani? He had naturally promised Breganze reparation and satisfaction and had now sent for the director of the school. Sifting through and evaluating the merits of the contradictory versions of the story, he had written to Alvignani as a precautionary measure and hoping, as the saying goes, to save both the kid and the cabbages. The cabbages, in this case, were the votes with which Gregorio Alvignani had been elected deputy.

The director, although tired at this point of all of the trouble that this teacher, albeit involuntarily, had caused him, as a matter of conscience defended Marta against the allegations set forth by the school inspector.

– I understand, I understand, – responded *Cavaliere* Torchiara. – But sometimes talent, good Sir, and goodwill cannot suffice; sometimes it is necessary to consider . . . to consider a person's private life, which, good Sir, has a definite influence, carries some weight, and a very great weight at that, with regard to the esteem in which the students hold the teacher. Am I making myself clear? . . . which . . . .

But the director had not been a resident of the village for very long, and did not know the teacher's history. Rather, he admired her great ability, and believed that she deserved every consideration!

– And we will of course take that into account! – exclaimed the *cavaliere* Torchiara. – How could we not? We will of course take that into account, and so much the more because I know the sad conditions in which she and her family currently reside, and which . . . . Have no fear; it is nothing that cannot be taken care of with, for example, a transfer that is advantageous to the teacher . . . . In the meantime, good Sir, you need to spend some time in our little community, outside of the school . . . and . . . and pay attention to the claims that the public are making, which . . . . Very well, it seems nevertheless that this teacher, although I certainly do not deny that she was provoked and also that, in a certain sense, her actions might be excusable . . . , it seems that she . . . yes, I mean to say . . . she might have crossed the line just the tiniest little bit . . . . And of course, Counselor Breganze, good Sir, is a person of some importance, eh! . . . and what's more, and I am thinking of what's best for the teacher as well, it would be best to give him some little satisfaction, just to make sure that the matter doesn't escape, shall we say, the confines of the scholastic sphere, if I am making myself clear . . . . Listen, let's go ahead and have you persuade Ms. Ajala to take some time off for illness, shall we say fifteen or so days? And in the meantime, we'll call in a substitute, because of course we don't want the poor students to suffer in terms of their coverage of the curriculum, which . . . . In the meantime, just let me take care of everything. Does that sound alright?

And that very day, he wrote a long, confidential letter to *his dear Gregorio*, imploring him to do everything in his power to obtain a transfer for the "young lady he had recommended"—and who was now poised to do such harm to his political prospects. He, Torchiara, had no illusions as to the difficulties that this request posed. But surely to him, to Alvignani that is, after the splendid speech he had delivered in the Chamber of Deputies in the debate surrounding the budget for public education (a speech with which, in a single blow—and no, he was not saying this to flatter his dear Gregorio!—he had carved out a true place for himself in the Parliament, as all of the newspapers agreed), no difficulty could prove insurmountable. For the rest of that year, at least, Ms. Ajala could serve as substitute in the *Collegio Nuovo* in Palermo (a boarding school where there was a vacancy).

While waiting for this momentous decision to be made, Marta was forced to prolong her "illness" another fifteen days. After around a month, two letters arrived from the honorable Alvignani: one for Marta, and one for School Inspector Torchiara.

Upon receiving that letter, a feeling of acute distress fell upon Marta. Disappointed in her powerlessness in the face of the blatant injustice of everyone around her, revolted by her undeserved punishment, at this point, she felt poisoned with hatred and anger. But that letter also seemed to be a weapon she could use to get her revenge.

It had been composed thoughtfully and carefully; there wasn't a single hint at the past that could have hurt her at that moment. But instead, underneath the bitter reflections on life and on human nature, there was a clear understanding of the state of mind in which she found herself! It was better, much better, to close oneself in an endless dream, high above the vulgarity and the common miseries of everyday life, above the yoke of the law, which pushes everyone under its jurisdiction equally down into the mud, a protective net for dwarves, an obstacle to cut through for anyone who wanted to ascend toward an ideal.

He told her that he knew how much she had been suffering since all of this had started, and he announced news of her new appointment, a transfer orchestrated so as to remove her from the mud in which she found herself mired. He had taken this liberty upon himself, quite of his own accord, certain that he was acting according to her own desires, even if she had never expressed those desires to him directly. And he begged her to leave things as they now stood, to allow him to take watch over her from afar, and to remember her always. Unfortunately, the means he had at hand to show her his high regard were meager and paltry.

And at the top of the page there was his motto, still so clear and easy to read:

NIHIL – MIHI – CONSCIO

Marta, Maria, and their mother had only one regret as they left their hometown: that they had to leave Anna Veronica.

Poor Anna! She was the one always encouraging them to have faith, and not to be afraid, when at the bottom of her heart she was the one who was the most distressed. They would have each other; she would remain alone, alone, alone, abandoned behind enemy lines. She would return to the silence, to the loneliness, to the long, sad, monotonous days . . . .

– But you'll write to me!

And as she continued to say that she wasn't going to cry, she wept and wept. Her lips tightened to try and force a smile, but instead of smiling she unwittingly pushed out her lower lip in a pout and continued to sob.

She insisted on accompanying them to the train station at the foot of the hill on which the village stood. During the cab ride there, no one said a word. It was a humid, gray day, and the old coach bounced over the damp paving stones of the steep, wide road, continuously rattling the poorly hung panes of glass in the carriage windows and causing an unbearable racket.

When the train was finally ready to depart, Anna Veronica and Signora Agata, who had continued clutching desperately to each other, each suffocating her sobs on the other's shoulder, were separated almost violently by the conductor. The steam engine was already whistling, ready to pull away from the platform.

Anna stood there, her face bathed in tears and her extended arms lowering little by little as the black line of train cars receded into the distance. Her eyes focused on the little windows of the car into which her three friends had climbed, and from which they continued to wave their handkerchiefs. One last flicker of white . . . and another . . . .

– *Addio* . . . . *Addio* . . . . – the abandoned woman murmured almost to herself as she waved back . . . .

PART II

~ Chapter 1 ~

A cheerful little house in the Via del Papireto; four rooms on the top floor with plenty of light, floors of Valencian tiles, and wallpaper that, yes, was a little bit faded in places, but wasn't torn, and was of a pleasant enough color. Signora Agata and Maria would share the least narrow of these rooms, and the room adjoining would serve both as Marta's bedroom and study; it suited both purposes beautifully thanks to a balcony that opened onto the Via del Papireto. As for the other two rooms, a dining room and a living room, they would have to be properly furnished as time went on. The most attractive feature of the house was a terrace, complete with pillars and balustrades that looked from the street like a magnificent crown sitting atop the building. Maria could grow such beautiful flowers here!

It was Marta who had found the house, guided by a distant memory. Her father, who had brought her to Palermo on a trip many years previous, had wanted to show her the place where, as a young soldier, he had fought on the very day that General Garibaldi had entered Palermo.

There, at the entrance of that street, he had stood with two other volunteers shooting into a cloud of smoke issuing from the front windows of some far-off houses where the Bourbon soldiers had taken cover. One after the other, his two companions had fallen, while he continued to fire round after round, almost as if waiting for the bullet with his name on it. Suddenly, he felt a light hand on his shoulder, and a voice saying,

– You must move to higher ground, young man; you're too exposed here.

He had turned and had seen *him*. Garibaldi. He was covered in dust, calm, but with furrowed brow, and, as he moved away, was himself exposed without a second thought in the very place that he had judged too dangerous for a mere volunteer.

Marta, in her turn, had wanted to take her mother and sister to that street, to show them that place. By chance, raising her eyes, she saw a sign that read "For Rent" right there, above the door of the house just at the entrance of the street. And so Marta had rented that house in memory of her father, almost as if he had led them to it himself.

Marta felt less alone with that memory to warm her heart, as if someone were watching over her.

Having more or less organized themselves after the inevitable confusion of moving to their new home, all three of them began to stock the house with necessities. The household furnishings that they had managed to salvage from the ruins of their old lives, like poor, sad survivors of a shipwreck to which so many memories still clung, were no longer sufficient for their new home.

The three of them always went out together to buy things, without knowing at first where they were going. They would stop and look in the windows of this or that store, avoiding the temptation to go into the more upscale ones. They would get lost wandering the streets of the city, constantly surrounded by people they did not know and who all seemed to have somewhere to get to, but it was precisely amidst all of that constant motion, all of that constant noise and all of that confusion, that they found a sort of relief. No one here knew them. They could go wherever they pleased and stop to look all around them whenever and for however long they wished, freely and without receiving any hostile glances in return. The fact that her beauty elicited such admiration from the passersby, however, secretly annoyed Marta to no end. Sometimes, in order to be noticed less, she would leave the house without bothering to do her hair.

– That's fine. That will do . . . – Marta would say, quickly putting her hat on and quickly adjusting a few curls on her forehead before going out.

But she noticed, even without wanting it to be so, that this little bit of disorder made her still more beautiful; it enhanced the grace of her appearance—what her fleeting looks in the mirror told her, the looks of the passersby, and her own glances at her reflections in the shop windows, all confirmed.

Meanwhile, at the *Collegio Nuovo*, she had been accepted with kindness by the old director, a true *signora* of manners and cultivation, a woman worthy of presiding over that fine educational institution, where they gathered and cultivated the finest flowers of the aristocracy and of the leading citizens of the area.

Marta's manner and appearance immediately attracted the attention of the old director, who made no attempt to conceal from Signora Agata how pleased she was to have "such a lovely young woman" like Marta as a teacher at her school. The director herself always took great care with her appearance; she was trim, tidy, and tasteful. Furthermore, she firmly believed that everything in this world was made for the enjoyment of young people, and to stir up regret and longing in those poor old people, like herself. She would say this smiling, but who could say from what depths of bitterness that smile arose! As an old woman she was by no means ugly, in part because she was so outwardly kind and affable. But as a young woman, she likely was not particularly beautiful, which made her kindness the more to her credit.

With that simple tenderness that can so often be reassuring, she told Marta about the other teachers at the school, about the three male professors, and about the boarders, painting them all with cheerful language. She spoke about the school schedule, and about a little bit of everything. Finally, she gave Marta four days of vacation, so that she could put her new life in order.

Marta left the school dazzled by this cordial welcome, which she subsequently recounted to Maria, praising everything she had seen: the school building itself, how well appointed the classrooms were, the feeling of order that prevailed there. And after her first day of teaching, she returned home positively beaming at the welcome the students had given her following the flattering introduction of their new teacher by the director.

Echoing Marta's buoyant mood in that happy period, the earth and sky began to give the first hints of renewal: winter was turning to spring. The air was still cold and especially crisp in the morning when she set off to the *Collegio*. But the sky was so clear and cloudless that it was always a pleasure to look upon it, and the air so pure and bracing that it was always a pleasure to fill one's lungs with deep breaths. It seemed that the soul of things, finally made serene by the happy promise of the season, had forgotten the winter, and composed itself into a mysterious, delightful harmony.

And what serenity it was! What freshness of spirit in those days, what inner peace! The clear and happy sense of life that Marta had as a child was now reawakened in her. She was finally getting her due. She had beaten them. She was learning to love life again, and now she wanted only to help others. Oh, the whispered rustling of the new leaves at sunrise, as she passed under the trees of Piazza Vittorio, then in front of the Norman Palace, and finally under those along broad Corso Calatafimi, just beyond Porta Nuova! The cloister of mountains surrounding the city seemed to be breathing up there in the tender blue sky, as if the mountains themselves were not made of stone, but of softer stuff.

And just walking along like that, in no hurry, as Marta thought about the lessons that she would teach, and musing on her newfound sense of well-being, not only did her ideas bubble to the surface unimpeded, but so, too, did her words come rushing to her lips, along with the smiles that accompanied them. She felt a pressing need to be loved by her students, and yet lingering there in the cool air of the street made her enjoy all the more the warmth of their reverent love for her, as it presented itself in the tepid air of the classroom.

The gloomy days had truly, truly passed, and spring had truly returned, for her as well. It was not just the earth that was shrugging off the dark shadows of winter; Marta, too, had found it possible to free herself from the nightmare of those terrible memories.

At home, it seemed to Marta that her mother and Maria were also content, and this pleased her to the very bottom of her heart, in part because she knew that it was she who had made them so. Each of the three of them lived for the other two, avoiding any memory of the past that might have led their thoughts back to the town all three had been born in. One sole image from there remained dear to them: that of Anna Veronica, of whom they spoke often, reading and rereading the long letters she would send. And so Anna continued to remain their only friend, their lone companion even in their almost instinctive separation from the world they knew.

They received only one visit from the other inhabitants of the building, and for a long time afterward, it was the source of much laughter. Marta had only recently realized that she had a talent for discovering and then mimicking the absurdities hidden just below the surface of everything and everyone, and she could reproduce a person's gestures and voice with an extraordinary imitative faculty. The legs of Don Fifo Juè, who lived on the second floor, as well as his wife's manner of sitting, her odd way of speaking, and her extravagant gestures were replicated by Marta with such comic effect that her mother and Maria laughed so much they had to hold their sides.

– Enough, Marta, please!

Don Fifo Juè and his wife, who was called Maria Rosa, arrived at their door dressed in deep mourning, their eyes lowered, contrite expressions on both of their faces, as if they had come back from a funeral at that very moment.

– Courtesy call . . . we are the tenants of the second floor, – they said in faint, mournful voices to Maria, who had opened the door and then stood there perplexed before these two strangers. At which point, both of their throats produced a sort of groan, followed by a brief sigh.

Introduced into what would become the sitting room, Don Fifo, who was tall and thin, sat with his legs pressed tightly together, his feet the same, and just touching the floor with the tips of his shoes. His arms were tightly folded, like those of a boy who had been sent to his room without dinner. His pants were so tight that his legs appeared to have been sewn into them. Donna Maria Rosa, on the other hand, was plump and rosy hued, and had thrown over her shoulder her thick, black veil of crepe fabric that covered her face. As she sat down, she let forth another plaintive sigh.

They had been man and wife for three months. It had been only a year since Donna Maria Rosa's first husband—Don Isidoro Juè, called Don Dorò by all who knew him, the elder brother of Don Fifo—had passed away. And over the course of that long visit Donna Maria Rosa spoke of nothing but her deceased husband and of her first marriage, with tears in her eyes and in her voice, as if Don Dorò had died yesterday. Don Fifo sat motionless and listened with lowered eyes and crossed arms to that interminable eulogy of his brother, as if he himself were the sarcophagus, and his wife the monument.

Oh, but no one, *no one* could list the innumerable virtues of Don Dorò ("VEER-CHOOS," said Maria Rosa in her strong accent, the sound of her dialect creeping in). She and Don Fifo, while Don Dorò lived, had done their best to give Don Dorò the attention and respect that he deserved. He, Don Dorò, had been their guide in life, their teacher. Husband, wife, and brother-in-law had always lived together, one soul in three bodies.

– May he rest in the peace of the angels, *Signora mia*!

And Dorò himself, with his own two lips, bless his soul, as he lay on his deathbed had mumbled to the unhappy pair that was so soon to survive him, – Fifo, – he said, – I leave Maria Rosa to your care! Take care of each other! Take care of each other! From now on, you must live for each other . . . .

– Oh, *Signora mia*! – burst forth Maria Rosa at this point in the story, already full to the brim with emotion, as she remembered those words. She dried her eyes, which were now gushing like two fountains, with a handkerchief stitched with black around the border. – For our part, – she took up again after a few moments, regaining her composure somewhat and loudly blowing her nose, – we, for our part, asked everyone we knew for advice, *Signora mia*. One by one, we asked them to give us the benefit of their experience and tell us what in good conscience we two poor, lonely souls should do, abandoned as we were by that saintly man! And so there we were, related to each other by marriage . . . and we had to live together, under the same roof . . . people would start to talk . . . . And everyone, even the very best people we asked, truth be told, gave us the same advice, to take this next step. All of them! We're both getting on in years, it's true, but you know, *Signora mia*, how people gossip! And if they don't know the truth, they'll just make it up! And in this town especially . . . .

– Oh, it's true everywhere! – sighed Signora Agata.

– Everywhere, everywhere! Well said, *Signora mia* . . . . And so, we were married not long ago . . . . We needed to wait the nine months prescribed by law, although between us, you know, there wasn't any danger, just as I told the gentlemen at City Hall. God did not choose to bless me with children; Dorò was always far too sickly and weak for that, *Signora mia* . . . . In any case, to make a long story short, we got married.

It seemed like all of the parts of Don Fifo's face—his lips, his tongue, his eyelids and nose—were held together with glue, and that if he were to speak, he might just fall to pieces. Only his legs remained firmly glued, each to the other. When all was said and done, of course, he just didn't speak very much. At a certain point, however, he burst out with the exclamation,

– Oh, what sadness, *Signora*, what sadness! Christ only knows!

And it took every ounce of propriety and willpower Marta and Maria had not to burst into laughter, right in the faces of their two guests.

~ Chapter 2 ~

Marta would have liked to have made life as happy and comfortable for her mother and Maria as it had been once upon a time, when her father was alive and the tannery was prospering. And to this end, she spared neither hard work nor sacrifice. She had gotten permission from the director of the college to give private lessons to some of the younger students in the lower grades of the school, and everything she earned from those lessons along with her monthly salary she handed over intact to her mother, whom she prohibited from complaining that Marta was working too hard, as she pointed out daily, without enjoying any of the fruits of her labors. But her mother was deceived. Not enjoying it? Wasn't the renewed faith her mother and sister had found in life, not to mention her own peace of mind, prize enough? Wasn't the sight of the smiles that now would come spontaneously to their lips the "fruits of her labors"? She would have given the very blood from her veins to see them even more content, to see them enjoying those smiles in the presence of other smiles as well. And secretly, she felt intoxicated by her own generosity, all the more because in the depths of her soul she had never gotten over her anger at her father's blind condemnation, at his plunging their family into poverty.

If music was the only thing that Maria truly loved, well then, Maria must have a piano, almost new, that they would pay for in monthly installments. If keeping their little pantry stocked with food and supplies for the month kept her mother calm and content, well then, her mother must be content, and so the little pantry was always well stocked.

Some evenings Don Fifo Juè and his wife would come up to keep the three ladies company, and the deceased Dorò continued to be the main topic of conversation.

It was through them that Marta came to know that Signora Fana, old Pentàgora's wife, was still alive, eking out a meager existence of poverty and squalor.

– We own a house in Via Benfratelli, *Signora mia*, – Donna Maria Rosa mentioned one evening, – and on the top floor, in two rooms, lives a poor old woman who is separated from her husband. He comes from your part of the country . . . perhaps you know him? . . . The name is . . . Fifo, can you remember?

– Fana . . . Stefana, – responded Fifo, seeming to come only slightly unglued as he spoke.

– No, I mean *him*, the husband . . . .

– Ah yes, just a moment . . . Pentàgono!

Maria laughed out loud in spite of herself.

– Pentàgora, – Signora Agata corrected him, to explain and excuse her daughter's laughter.

– Do you know him?

Donna Maria Rosa wanted to know what kind of a man he was and spoke at length about his unfortunate wife . . . .

Neither Marta nor Signora Agata managed to change the topic of discussion for the rest of the evening.

Maria threw herself back into study of the piano again with fervor, and every evening after dinner would play, while her mother sewed and Marta corrected student work in the next room.

Closed off from the others, out of the sight of her mother and sister, Marta would often break from that thankless task and, with her elbows propped up on the little table and her head in her hands, would sit there in a daze, as if she were waiting for something, but she didn't know what. Or sometimes she would be moved to tears by Maria's playing. A deep sadness would overcome her; she could feel it tightening in her throat. She wasn't thinking of anything in particular, and yet she was weeping. Why? A vague, inscrutable sadness, the agony of desires she could not put a name to . . . . She felt a little tired, not in her mind, but in her body: yes, tired . . . . Her mother and sister praised her courage, comparing her to her father for his boundless energy and willpower. On evenings like those, she almost enjoyed her feelings of sadness and disappointment, that indefinable something that softened her and brought her to tears, that heavy languor to which she abandoned herself, feeling her relaxed limbs slip into a sort of voluptuous melancholy. In short, the awareness in that moment of herself as weak, as just a woman . . . . No, no, she was not strong . . . . And really, why was she weeping like this? Come now, come now . . . she was being a baby . . . . And then she would look for a handkerchief, give herself a shake, and get back to work with renewed energy.

Neither her mother nor sister was aware of Marta feeling this way. She was very careful not to give them any indication that there was something wrong, and instead used every trick at her disposal to live up to the conception they had formed of her. This was her task . . . . She had to be this. She even went so far as to hide one of Anna Veronica's letters from her mother, in which the former had spoken at length about Rocco's rage after their departure, his threats of a new scandal, of doing something crazy . . . .

Why inflict that news on her poor mother? And Marta had written back to Anna Veronica, saying that Rocco's actions were no longer her concern, and that she did not wish to hear anything more about him. He had started out a fool, now seemed to be a madman, and had never stopped being pathetic.

Meanwhile, she saw her mother and sister return to their old, comfortable ways, to the calm of once upon a time, to the simple, tranquil life they had led before. And, for the most part, by way of stark contrast, this only brought home to her how very alone, how truly outcast she was. She alone would never regain her place in society, no matter what she did. She alone could never return to the life she had once led. It was another life for her now, another path . . . . Peace, the happiness of the people she loved, her studies, her teaching, the students, this was all that was left for her; this was all that remained on this new path. Nothing else!

Did this make her sad? No, there were only passing moments of sadness. After that gloomy winter, during which the weather had matched her emotional state so well, she was awakening now on this new road in the happy sunshine of springtime. It was just that single ray of sunshine, which had shone through to the many sorrows that lay heaped at the very bottom of her heart and had nudged them awake, had brought them to life; this was why she was sad. Or perhaps it was the effect of Anna Veronica's letter? Or of Maria's music?

– That's enough, Mamma, leave it. It's fine as it is . . . .

And she would push the little swivel mirror on her dressing table away, almost as if she were annoyed by her own image, by the intense radiance of her eyes, by her flaming lips. If her mother then made her sit longer for even a few more strokes of the brush, she would sigh with impatience and become unsettled and anxious, as if she were undergoing torture. Why spend so much time and care on her appearance now? To what end? Didn't her mother understand that now it didn't matter at all to her whether she appeared a little more or a little less beautiful?

And one day when her mother was insistent on trying to make Marta's hair into little ringlets that would fall over her forehead, and this even after she had already done her hair, Marta began to cry.

– What? You're crying? But why? – her surprised mother asked her.

Marta forced a smile and began to dry her eyes.

– Oh, it's nothing . . . . Don't mind me . . . .

– But why, my dear child? You look beautiful with your hair like this . . . .

– No, I don't like the curls . . . . Take them out; take them out . . . . I like it better without.

But any cruelty on her mother's part was unconscious, wasn't it? And anyway, what a baby Marta was being! Crying like that over nothing, and right in front of her mother . . . .

All day long she was even more animated than usual, trying to make up for the impression that those tears must have made on her poor mother's heart.

And now she felt a new sense of discomfort, an incomprehensible fear, a strange anxiety every time she found herself without anyone walking beside her, alone in the open streets, among all of those passersby, staring at her.

No one interfered with her or bothered her, of course, but she felt wounded by their many glances. It seemed to her that everyone purposely looked at her in a way that would make her blush. And she would walk along awkwardly with her chin on her chest, a buzzing in her ears, and her heart pounding out of her chest. But why? And how was it that all of a sudden her presence of mind had locked itself away behind that foolish timidity? Hadn't she laughed so many times at those old maids who refused to go out alone in the city streets, fearing at every step an attempt on their modesty?

But the moment she entered the school, she was back to her old self. She could feel her confidence return as she greeted the three male professors, who could often be found in the teachers' room and with whom she often exchanged a few words before each of them went off to teach their various lessons.

It had become clear to her that two of these professors were, each in his own way, covertly making advances toward her. And rather than be afraid of this, she laughed to herself about it and pretended not to notice anything out of the ordinary. Secretly, in fact, she received great pleasure from the attention, noting the various effects of her actions on the two would-be suitors.

Professor Mormoni, Pompeo Emanuele Mormoni, author of the fourteen-volume (in octavo) *History of Sicily, Including Appendices of Memorable Names and Events, with Dates and Places*, was a tall, heavy, dark man with large black eyes, and a long beard streaked here and there with gray. He was always extremely dignified, and always in his Napoleon coat and top hat. Every chair he sat in seemed to become a pedestal on which he posed, as if to say, "Sculpt me thusly!" Pompeo was spiteful and puffed up with pride like a turkey. Puffed up like this, he always seemed to be saying to Marta,

"You know, my dear, if you don't care anything about me, then I do not care anything about you! Don't delude yourself!" Oh, but he did care. Oh, how he cared! He cared so much! He often felt that he would burst on the spot, and, at such times, he would even lose his monumental posture.

From time to time, Marta would hear the chair in which Mormoni was sitting creak, and she would struggle to stifle a smile. Over the course of a month, all of the chairs in the teachers' room had been damaged in some way: on one, the seat had broken through, another had many of the slats broken.

Attilio Nusco, another teacher vying for Marta's affections, was called by everyone in the college *il professoricchio*, for unlike Mormoni he was extremely small, thin, delicate, always quivering and incredibly awkward. Poor little Nusco, so unsure of finding his place in life! It seemed he was always trying to win the favor of the others with glances, smiles, and the hurried little bows of his wretched little body, so as not to be sent away. And when he sat down, he occupied the least space possible (*Pardon me! So sorry!*). His voice trembled when he spoke, and he never disagreed with or contradicted anything anyone said. It was as if he were continually embarrassed by his own excessive politeness. But in the meantime, his heart . . . . Ah, that Marta! Did she never notice anything?

The poor man would try, little by little, to overcome his timidity, like a threatened lizard crawling out from under its rock; first the tip of his nose, then a tiny bit more, until his eyes were just visible, then the whole of his little head, but always as if he were expecting to be caught in a noose that was waiting for him there.

He had pushed himself to unheard-of boldness, even up to the point of audaciously asking Marta as he sweated, – *Are you cold this morning?* – He would bring to school some early flower of the spring or other, and would twirl its stem between his scrawny, trembling fingers. But he never dared offer it to her.

Marta noticed all of this, and she laughed about it.

One day he had purposely forgotten his flower on a little table in the teachers' room. After an hour, he returned to the room and the flower was no longer there. Ah, finally! Marta had understood and had taken it herself . . . . But when he returned an hour later, he found he had been cruelly deluded: the flower was in the buttonhole of the Napoleon jacket of none other than Pompeo Emanuele Mormoni.

– Farewell, goldfinch! Farewell, violet!

And yet Nusco was no fool. He had a doctorate in literature, was still very young, and among many vying for the position, he had been awarded the post of Professor of Italian at the high school, in addition to his duties at the *Collegio Nuovo.* He also wrote poetry of uncommon taste and elegance.

Marta knew all of this, but what did Nusco want with her? Him *or* this Mormoni, for that matter?

The third professor seemed not yet to have noticed that she existed. His name was Matteo Falcone, and he taught drawing and design. Pompeo Emanuele Mormoni called him "the hedgehog," and, like a Roman emperor, condemned him *ad purgationem cloacarum*—to cleaning the sewers.

Falcone was truly monstrous to look at. What was worse, he was aware of it: a tragic affliction. He was always somber and despondent, detached, and he never looked anyone in the eyes, perhaps so as not to catch sight of the disgust that his figure aroused in others. He most often responded to others in brief grunts, and he kept his head so low it seemed to have sunk between his shoulders. The lines of his face seemed contorted, the result of what appeared to be a furious reaction to his own monstrosity. And to complete the tragic picture, he had two clubfeet, a deformity emphasized by his shoes, which had been specially made to allow him to walk.

Mormoni and Nusco had already grown accustomed to his ways, which were more bearlike than human, and no longer paid him any mind. Despite having been warned by the director, Marta was offended by his rudeness in her first days at the school. And while she paid no attention to the simpering affectations of the other two except to laugh at them, deep down the almost contemptuous disregard of this third man, even if harmless, irritated her to no end.

In the brief time that she spent in the teachers' room before class began, he would immerse himself in the reading of a newspaper, not paying attention to anyone. Marta would often sneak glances at the man's furrowed brow and try to imagine what sort of thoughts must reside in that prickly, obstinate head. Foolish thoughts? No, certainly not. But perhaps brutal.

She heard his voice only once. It was on a morning when Mormoni had gestured with his eyes toward "the hedgehog," who was buried as usual in the reading of his newspaper, and Marta, not wishing to share in the mockery of Mormoni's nodding glance (and indeed wishing to annoy Mormoni, the "great man"), let slip from her tongue, unadvisedly,

– Good morning, Professor Falcone.

– My regards, – he grunted in response, without lifting his eyes from his paper.

Entering the teachers' room another morning, Marta was very surprised to find Falcone and Nusco in the middle of a heated argument. Nusco, his face bright red, a nervous smile on his lips and his hands shaking like mad, was trying to bolster his argument with many a *yes that may be so, but . . .*

which were drowned out by the harsh voice of Falcone. Meanwhile the latter, without paying the slightest attention to his adversary, continued to speak, with his eyes on the newspaper spread out before him. Mormoni listened from the sidelines in one of his monumental poses, not deigning to waste a single word on these "trifles."

Falcone was railing against authors who dress up their verses and their prose with a bitter tinge of irony, while underneath it all they remain entirely obsequious to the prevailing opinions of society.

– You think that these opinions are false? You really think that they are unjust and harmful? Well then, for God's sake, rebel instead of making jokes, tripping all over yourselves and pulling faces, painting over your real feelings with clown makeup! No. On the one hand, you bend your neck to the yoke, and on the other, you deride your own servitude. If this is art, it's the art of sad buffoons!

– That may be so, but . . . . – Nusco repeated. And he desperately wanted to point out that ridicule, too, could be used as a weapon, and that Dickens, Heine . . . . But Falcone would not let him get a word in.

– Sad buffoons! Sad buffoons!

– Let's hear what Signora Ajala has to say, – proposed Mormoni with a gesture consistent with the magnificence of his bearing.

– Women are conservative by nature, – pontificated Falcone, brusquely.

– Conservative? For me, fire and the sword! – exclaimed Marta in a tone of voice that made Falcone raise his eyes and look her in the face for the first time.

Marta remained deeply disturbed by those eyes, which illuminated a face that was absolutely new to her; they were incredibly intelligent eyes, the eyes of an unknown wild animal.

On another morning not long after, Falcone entered the teachers' room with his hat crushed and dirty, its brim broken in the front, his nose scratched, his face white as a sheet, and with a sad smile twisting his lips into a horrible grimace. His jacket was torn down the front, and it too was dirty.

– What's happened to you, Professor? – exclaimed Mormoni, seeing him in that state.

Marta and Nusco turned to look at him in fearful wonder.

– A fight?

– No, nothing . . . – Falcone responded with a trembling voice, but with that sneer of a smile still on his lips. – I found myself passing by the church of Santa Caterina, which was shored up three years ago . . . . This morning, Holy Mother Church was waiting just for me, so that she could throw down a piece of her cornice right on my head.

Marta, Nusco, and Mormoni stood in stunned silence.

– Yes . . . – Falcone continued. – It fell down just like so, grazing my whole body . . . . And so – (here he added a terrible snigger and gestured down toward his deformed clubfeet) – behold and admire the gifts of Mother Nature! If this had happened to you, Nusco, you wouldn't be going out dancing anytime soon! But instead, I . . . I still have these, and I manage!

And with that, he headed off to class.

Did it really seem to Falcone that this was just a terrible response on the part of "Mother Nature" to all of the abuse he had hurled at her because of his own deformity? Did he really feel as if there were a voice that had said to him, "Praise me for the feet that I have given you"?

What was certain was that, from that day forward, little by little, he began to emerge from his usual gloominess. Or was it rather Marta's presence that was the cause of this miracle?

Mormoni suspected that the latter was the case.

– Because, you see, – he said to Nusco, – although it's true that he now greets the two of us, he grunts his greetings, as he did before. He doesn't say "Good morning, Signor Nusco!" with the same, shall we say, Sunday-morning voice he uses to say, "Good morning, Signora Ajala!" A bristly sort of tenderness, I know, but still . . . . And what's more, have you noticed? New shirt collars! And in the latest style! And a new suit, and a new hat! Long live the miraculous cornices of Santa Caterina!

Naturally neither of them could, in all seriousness, be jealous of Falcone, for whom they had nothing but pity, of course! But then again, neither was Mormoni jealous of Nusco, nor Nusco jealous of Mormoni. In Nusco's mind, the great Pompeo Emanuele was too fat and too foolish to be considered a serious rival for Marta's affections, and Nusco had too much respect for her intelligence to fear him. Mormoni, on the other hand, had too much respect for Marta's taste to fear little Attilio, with his poor little poet's soul, always frightened. And so they found common ground in expressing their pity for "the poor Falcone," and in private, they felt pity for each other.

Meanwhile, the discovery of Falcone's new attitude toward her inspired both disgust and fear in Marta. She knew, and she felt, that she could not laugh at him as she laughed at the other two. The repulsiveness of that unhappy and yet bitterly contemptuous man simultaneously aroused both pity and horror in her. He had probably never loved anyone before.

On the one hand, when Marta thought of Falcone being aware, as he was, of his own deformity and yet still insisting on loving her, she felt indignant and offended. On the other hand, she understood how that passion, perhaps the first that had ever begun to flower in that heart, could be strong enough to win over and block out that consciousness itself, as tragically invasive as it was.

Only one thought reassured her, and that was that she had done nothing, nothing at all, to give rise to this monstrous passion.

Now, almost every day at sunset, she saw Falcone pass down Via del Papireto and raise his eyes to the balcony of her room. The first day he had done so, she wished to show him to Maria, but she hadn't expected him to raise his head and stare up at her.

Is he looking up here? But how . . . ?

And that had been the proof of the love he bore her, one of many less clear signs she had not seen, or not wanted to see. From that day on, she made a point of never being seen through the windows, but from some hiding place she could see Falcone walk by every day and look up two, sometimes three times as he passed.

And now, after a night spent tossing and turning, full of terrible nightmares and strange visions, after the harsh shock of opening her tired eyes to naked reality and to the monotony of her existence, even surrounded as she was by the alluring blossoming of the season, every morning her fear of being alone in the city streets grew. Her nerves hummed and jangled as she walked, as if she were hounded by some imminent, unknown danger. And she no longer managed to regain control of herself when she arrived at the school.

How was she to behave in Falcone's presence? She did not want him to know that she had noticed him in her street, but how could she pretend when she was continually full of the horror of her dreams, in which the figure of Falcone appeared almost every night, and at times less monstrous than in reality? If she were to treat him as she had before, she feared that his fascination with her would be bolstered by some innocent compliment, that he would mistake her compassion for passion.

Nor did Mormoni amuse her as he had in those first days. Instead just seeing him now provoked such anger that she might have slapped him. And the painful timidity of Nusco now only irritated and bored her.

"Stop bothering me!" she would have liked to shout in his face, certain that with those three little words he would have slithered back under his rock in shame.

~ Chapter 3 ~

Perhaps even Attilio Nusco himself, in his heart of hearts, felt the deficiency of his own bearing, and how pathetic, even ridiculous his insurmountable shyness must have seemed to all who encountered him. Perhaps he was ashamed of it and was secretly at war with himself, for in his own mind, he surely could not have judged himself an outright fool. But on the other hand, who knows how many people he himself had judged to be fools!

It was in that stretch of days that he had submitted a sonnet for Marta to one of the local literary journals, and they had published it.

Pompeo Emanuele Mormoni had made the discovery. The sonnet bore the mysterious title, "For You."

"'For You'? . . . For whom? . . . There are so many women in the world, more than there are houseflies! I will pretend not to have understood to whom it refers . . . ."

And the next day, taking advantage of Nusco's modesty, he himself gave Marta a copy of the journal, sure that it would irritate her.

– Nusco has published a sonnet: "For You."

– For me? – said Marta, surprised and turning red with embarrassment.

– No, no. "For You" is the title of the poem . . . . But how red you have turned, *Signora*! How such things can give us pleasure, no? Read it; I'll leave it with you . . . . I'll be off now; it looks like rain has stopped for the moment, and I didn't bring an umbrella.

A bow, and off he went, his nose in the air.

Marta's first instinct was to throw the journal away, but she restrained herself, opened it, and read:

FOR YOU

Ere Eros' fervent sighs had scarce begun
To rise up, fluttering in your anxious breast,
Up rose foul Fortune, not to be outdone,
Unleashing her cruel plans with crueler zest.

And those who once lay prostrate at your feet,
Who prayed in vain beneath your distant stare,
They now arise to mock your fallen state,
Your ancient pride too much for them to bear.

But just as you must spurn any less true,
To this one faithful love your heart will cling.
You won't let bitterness embitter you

And yet your radiant smile belies an ache!
It is for this alone my heart must sing:
That you, unfairly tested, do not break.

A furious torrent of rain rattled the windows. Marta raised her eyes from the journal and stared mechanically at the window.

Could these verses be for her? Who had told Nusco all of the details of her life? And what did that line mean: *To this one faithful love your heart will cling?* To which love did he mean? Alvignani jumped to her mind straight away. No, he couldn't be referring to him . . . . *It is for this alone my heart must sing: / That you, unfairly tested, do not break* . . . .

She was so busy reflecting on the sonnet itself that she was no longer thinking about how rude it had been of Mormoni to give it to her to read in the first place.

Then Falcone turned up. Marta shook herself. Her umbrella? Where had she left it? She remembered very clearly having brought it with her when she left the house this morning.

– What are you looking for, *Signora*? – Falcone asked.

– Perhaps I left it upstairs . . . – said Marta, almost to herself. And she called the janitor woman.

– Take mine, – proposed Falcone. – It isn't new, but will do all the same.

He spit out the words as if they were insults. He was more somber and more tense than usual.

Just then the janitor came down. She had checked the classroom and the corridors, but had not found it. Marta became flustered and agitated; Falcone was pushing strongly that she take him up on his offer. It was raining hard, and she couldn't allow Falcone to get soaked on her account.

– Well then, if you'll permit me, I would be happy to accompany you, – said Falcone, his expression suddenly changing. – I live on the same street as you now, just a little bit farther down. – And he added, his chin on his chest as he looked down at his club feet, – If you're not ashamed . . . .

Marta could feel her face flush red. She pretended not to have heard him, and responded,

– I have never much cared what people think. Come, let's go.

– But you've left your journal on the table, – said Falcone, collecting it and passing it to her.

– Oh, thank you . . . There is some of Nusco's poetry in it . . . .

– Idiot! – Matteo Falcone hissed between his teeth.

"How in the world will I manage to walk next to this man?" thought Marta, disheartened.

She could feel both his joy and his embarrassment in that moment, and this troubled her and made her suffer so violently that if he so much as brushed up against her, even unintentionally, she was sure throughout the whole of her trembling body that she would cry out in disgust.

Before exiting onto the street, the janitor brought her a letter.

– For me? – Marta said, pleased that there was something to divert attention from her own embarrassment. – Do you mind? – she added, turning to Falcone, and she tore open the envelope.

The letter was from Anna Veronica. Marta began reading it as she slowly moved toward the door. Falcone gave her a sidelong glance, suspicious. At that moment, he noticed a sudden change come over Marta's face, which grew pale, and her eyebrows furrowed disdainfully. They had reached the main door now. Marta was no longer reading. She was simply watching the heavy drops of rain splash into the mud of the street.

– Shall we go? – he asked somberly, opening his umbrella. Marta shook herself out of her stupor. She refolded the letter and took shelter under the umbrella.

– Ah, yes, of course . . . . I'm ready . . . . I beg your pardon!

She no longer cared that her arm was touching Falcone's, which was inevitable in any case, nor did she notice the painful effort that he was making to keep up with her as they walked. She would have liked to run, not because of him (and Falcone could sense as much) but because of some news delivered in that letter. Consumed with jealousy, he was no longer paying attention to his feet, which, in moving so much more quickly than they were used to, were getting tangled up with each other far more clumsily than usual. He wanted to shout at Marta, ask her who wrote that letter, and what bad news it contained. In the meantime, he let her splash through the puddles and wade in the mud of the street, fearing that any polite request on his part that they slow down would be interpreted by her as a pathetic reference to his obvious inability to keep up with her in that race. His wretched feet were already getting terribly muddy, and he was out of breath, but Marta did not notice either. Why? Why was she running like this?

Suddenly something like a shudder washed over her, and she managed to get ahold of herself. She stopped for a moment, almost as if stifling a scream.

– What's the matter? What is it? – Falcone asked her, stopping.

– Nothing! Come, let's go . . . . – Marta said to him softly, her head bowed, pressing forward.

Falcone turned and looked a little ways ahead of them. On the sidewalk to their right, two men stood under an umbrella staring hard at Marta and him. One was pale, with a gloomy expression on his face, and the other was taller and thinner, and didn't look Italian; an expression of pure derision shot from his light-colored eyes.

It was Rocco Pentàgora and Mr. Madden.

Despite Marta's admonition to the contrary, Falcone shot them a savage look.

– Don't look at them! Don't turn around! – Marta ordered him, choking with rage.

– Tell me who those two men are! – he asked, almost shouting, threatening to stop again.

– Quiet, I said, and keep moving! – snapped Marta in the same tone of voice. – What right have you to ask?

– No right at all, but I . . . . You, you don't know . . . . – Falcone continued in a voice that no longer seemed his own, as if he were weeping, gasping for breath, choking with emotion so violently that he could scarcely get a word out, and then proceeding almost to run after her, painful as it was for him, as the rain began to fall harder. He confessed his love to her and begged for her pity.

Her mind in a tumult that was only made worse by the violence of the rain, Marta could see the half-flooded street whirling round and round as it slipped by below her feet. She ran without listening, hearing only confusedly, and with unbearable anguish, Falcone's breathless words. At last, she reached the door of her house.

There Falcone tried to hold her by one arm, begging her to speak to him.

– Let me go! – Marta shouted at him, tearing away from him and running up the stairs.

It was Maria who opened the door.

– You're all wet?

– Yes, I am going to change right away.

She locked herself in. She threw herself into a chair, pressing, pressing, pressing her temples as hard as she could with both hands, moaning softly, her eyes closed:

– *Oh Dio! Oh Dio!*

She was in the grip of a terrible dizziness, but it wasn't just the room that seemed to be spinning around her now; it was her whole life, whirling and whirling before her eyes. Her ears rang with the pounding of the rain, but also with the words of that gasping monster, weeping as he shuffled along behind her.

And those two who had taken their posts on the sidewalk, keeping tabs on her! But what could they possibly want of her? What did they take her for? And those other two, those other two as well, that big imbecile and that little one who publicly addressed those lines of poetry to her . . . .

Ah, and Anna's letter? She looked for it and read it again, skipping the parts that didn't seem important at the moment.

> You know, my dear Marta, as I wrote . . . . But I have not seen him again, not since that *furious* visit, about which I . . . . I have heard from the Miracoli family, though (Niccolino calls on them often, and people in town are saying that he will marry Tina Miracoli . . .), that *he* left this morning to find you. He wants to know (or so Niccolino said to his fiancée) what you're doing in Palermo and is convinced that there must be *a very good reason* for you to stay, *a serious impediment* to your returning here to the countryside. Tina, although like any other well-bred, God-fearing young woman she must pretend she doesn't understand, made it very clear through her mysterious tone of voice what I was to understand by *very good reason* and *serious impediment*. Well, you can imagine how I received the news, and how I responded to her! But she says that she doesn't know anything, that she doesn't believe these things herself, and that she's only repeating what she heard the Pentàgoras themselves say. As you

> know, when your father—may he rest in peace—was still with us and you were rich, Signora Miracoli was your mother's closest friend. Now, with this proposed marriage between Tina and Niccolino, she has cozied up to Antonio Pentàgora, who, by the way, doesn't seem to want anything to do with this marriage. But anyway, back to your husband . . . . If he (Nicola keeps saying) discovers anything, he'll run to the nearest court of law and ask for a legal separation. Remember, of course, that these are perhaps just arrogant words spoken by a boy for effect, in the presence of his bride-to-be . . . .

So, another fistful of mud. Still attacked, even from far away. More slander, more malice.

Marta rose from her seat, quivering with rage and contempt, her eyes flashing with hatred.

In spite of her innocence, here she was, judged guilty again. And for what? For naïvely defending herself from temptation in the first place! Guilty despite the proof of her fidelity! The result? Infamy. The result? The blind condemnation of her father! And then all of the consequences that followed that had also been deemed her fault: the collapse of her family, their ruin, the fall into poverty, her sister's shattered future . . . and more! A whole crowd's pitiless public insulting of an innocent old woman, a sick woman dressed in widow's black. She had wanted to vindicate herself in noble fashion, to pull herself up from this undeserved disgrace by dint of her own intelligence, with hard work and study. But no! Her humility was met only with more insults. Her pride was met only with the public stoning of slander. This was her reward, the prize for her hard-won victory! Bitterness, injustice, and that meaningless existence of hers. Exposed to the horrifying desires of a monster, exposed to the pathetic, timid longings of a weakling, exposed to the pompous cowardice of the other. Oh, stones and thorns everywhere on that long road leading away from life . . . .

She was startled by a knock at the door. And then the voice of Maria . . . ,

– Dinner, Marta.

Dinner, already? She hadn't even changed her clothes. How could she eat now, how could she hide all of this from her mother and sister? She tore off her wet things in a fury. She hadn't even taken off her hat when she came in. She bathed her burning eyes and face in the basin.

– It smells wonderful! – said Maria, who was already at the table as the steam rose from the bowl.

And her mother proceeded to tell her about the extreme measures that she and Maria had had to take up on the terrace to save the plants during that sudden deluge.

~ Chapter 4 ~

"Now he'll think that that monster is my lover! That's just like him . . . ." thought Marta after dinner, when she had once again locked herself in her room.

And she said it to herself in just that way: *my lover*, since that was the way her husband had thrust her into the arms of another man, that man! But how much more ghastly now these words seemed to her when they referred to Falcone!

Was Rocco so embittered with contempt for her, then, that he wanted to take a new vengeance on her now? The threat had been made explicit in Anna Veronica's letter.

A new scandal . . . but where was the proof? Oh God, that monster . . . . Yes, it was likely that that monster Falcone would offer him all of the "proof" that he needed if they met again in the street . . . . He would make some scene and as quick as that her name would be in the paper alongside Falcone's.

Marta was wringing her hands with fear and disgust; she couldn't stay still. And she would have loved to shout at

Maria to stop as she continually played some old, simple passage on the piano in the next room, much to the delight of her mother.

Ah, the tranquility of her mother and sister, the calm of their new home, the music, the muffled conversations of others: how they made her suffer in that moment!

Yes, there was her work, of course. But could no one understand at what cost came that martyrdom? Now that the past was dead and buried, were they never to speak of it again? Her mother and sister had made it through, and now a new life had begun for them, one that was calm and modest. But for her? Was her life, her youth to remain buried there, in the past? Was her life not to be spoken of ever again? What was done, was done—was that it? Was she dead? Was everything finished now for her? Was she only living now so that she could keep other people alive? Yes, yes, she could have been content, she hoped, even cast out as she was from life. But only if she had been able to enjoy in peace the sweet, quiet spectacle of that little house, the house that had been built atop her grave . . . . At least let them speak about it a little bit; let them feel at least a little sorry for the fact that her youth was dead, that her life was shattered! Especially given that it was so unjust that her life had been shattered like this, without any reason, her youth cut off so soon! And no one would even talk about it?

A shadow had fallen, and here she was, being attacked again! Persecuted still! The next day, she was sure she would see her husband again at his post, just as she would see Falcone again at school.

"If he continues to harass me, I will speak about it to the Director," Marta suddenly thought to herself with an impetuous surge of energy, and she began to undress for bed with trembling fingers. – And as for those other two, if they don't cut it out, I'll put them in their place myself! And as for you, oh you just wait, – she was more breathing the words than speaking them as she thought of her husband. She turned down the covers and put out the light.

In the dark, curled up into the fetal position under the blankets, Marta tried to collect her thoughts, but she couldn't manage to come up with a precise course of action against her husband. She said to herself, "Yes, I know how to handle Falcone if he persists . . . . The director can't stand him and is looking for an excuse to get rid of him anyway. I'll give her one . . . ." And as she mechanically repeated these sentences, she continued to try to determine what she could do to her husband. Nothing? Really? She couldn't come up with a single means of getting back at him? And, in her impotence, she felt her hatred begin to boil and foment into a growing rage. Although she perceived no physical pain as a result all of that useless tension, her brain finally gave in as if it were in some torture chamber; unable to find the thought she was seeking, it began to offer her other, unrelated thoughts instead, confusing and distracting her. Marta, however, was determined to find what she was looking for, and as soon as one of these extraneous thoughts would appear, she would shoo it away. One thought finally succeeded in capturing her attention: the thought of her umbrella . . . . Yes, . . . now she remembered exactly what had happened . . . . She had leaned it against the frame of her classroom door while she adjusted her hat. Yes, and then she had forgotten it up there . . . . Falcone must have recognized it and hidden it as he passed through the corridor. Oh, there was no doubt about it! Yes, of course, he did that so he would be able to offer her his, to have an excuse to accompany her . . . . It was him, yes, there was no doubt! And that was the reason he was so anxious when they had run into each other downstairs in the teachers' room. Where could he have hidden it?

Not long after, Marta fell asleep.

She woke up early with a terrible headache, but with a mind sustained by a nervous energy that was unlike the energy she had gained before from her self-assurance. She could not see where her road would lead, but she would follow it to the end, whatever the cost; she was waiting, ready to pounce upon any new obstacle that wished to overtake her.

That morning, she had no apprehension about walking the streets on her own. After the rain of the day before, the green of the trees had come to life, and they looked almost festive. Even the houses and the streets themselves seemed to have a festive aspect in the clear cool of the morning air.

Meanwhile she made sure to look ahead to see if her husband was there at his post, and she felt certain that if he were, she would have had the courage to pass by him with her head held high.

"But of course, he'll be sleeping at this hour," she thought suddenly, and a derisive smile came to her lips as she walked along. "He's never in his whole life seen the sun come up . . . ."

In her mind's eye, she saw him lying next to her again in their bed, his thin, blond mustache uncombed above his dry, pale lips.

She quickly abandoned such thoughts, however, and as she was on her way to school, the more immediate object of her spite became Falcone. She no longer thought about or took an interest in her own suffering.

What would she do, what would she say if he dared make even the slightest reference to what had happened the day before?

She did not yet know. But she could see with extraordinary clarity the teachers' room of the school, into which she would be entering momentarily; in her mind, she was already entering . . . . She could see Nusco and Mormoni, spectators of the scene that she was going to act out there inside . . . . She could see Falcone waiting for her there, more sullen than usual.

She stood before the door of the school, went down the few little steps, and she entered.

The teachers' room was empty.

~ Chapter 5 ~

Matteo Falcone had not gone into school that morning.

If Marta had turned around as she ran up the stairs the day before, she would perhaps have felt a little bit of pity for him standing there at the door as if he had turned to stone. He had hoped that as she hurried away, she would at least turn and glance back at him one time. And then he moved on in the rain, almost staggering, attracting stares from the people he passed.

He had never felt such ferocious hatred of himself. Sneering derisively and shaking his umbrella violently enough to break the frame in two, he kept muttering to himself, – I, love! *I*, love! – among other, less intelligible words. And then at the top of his voice, there in the middle of the street, with his face contorted and his eyes locked on the face of some passerby in a sinister stare,

– You're lucky you didn't laugh at me!

But then he laughed instead. It was a terrible laugh, and people turned and looked, as shocked as if they were looking at a madman.

In the end, soaked through with rain, he had nowhere to go but home.

Falcone lived with his mother and an aunt, who were both decrepit and senile. The three of them shared an enormous old house cluttered with piece upon piece of cheap furniture that was lined up along the walls and, in some cases, stacked one on top of the other, giving the house the feeling of a furniture store: enormous armoires of painted wood, tables of every shape and size, huge boxes, chests, lockers, shelves, coatracks, cane chairs, chairs upholstered in faded fabric, and several canapés in the old style with ornamental rolls of wood at either end.

The two sisters, his mother and his aunt, had opted to live together after the deaths of their respective husbands, but neither was willing to give up a single stick of furniture from her original home, hence this useless abundance, more an encumbrance than a treasure.

In their senility, the two old women no longer remembered having ever had husbands, and each firmly believed she was waiting for the death of the other, at which time she could finally marry some imaginary suitor.

– Why won't you die? – they would ask each other simultaneously, right to each other's faces, every time they met each other, as each clung to the back of one of the house's numerous chairs for support. And so, chair to chair, they made their way around the house.

They lived their lives completely separate from each other, at opposite ends of the house. And every so often, over the course of the day, but also often at night, one would ask the other in a long mournful wail,

– What time is it?

And the other invariably answered in a drawn-out, somber voice,

– *Seven o'cloooooooooooock!*

It was always seven o'clock!

And whenever some neighbor woman would climb out onto her terrace to laugh at them behind their backs, the two old women would raise their arms in the air and shake their wrinkled hands at her, admonishing,

– Why aren't you married! You need to get married!

It seemed to them that there was no other refuge in life, no other salvation. And each of them had known for a thousand years that her much-awaited wedding day would arrive eventually. But alas, the other one refused to die! In the meantime, they would have their neighbors dress them up and adorn them with dresses in the old style, from their heyday. And the neighbors naturally chose fabrics that were the most garish, most laughable, the oldest and most out of tune with the old age of the two senseless old birds. Because the gowns were far too large now for their shriveled bodies, they would tie a mangy boa around the waist of one, or a wide ribbon around the waist of the other. And the poor, foolish old things would put paper flowers in their hair, along with cabbage leaves and lettuce leaves and false curls, and cake their faces in powder, or redden their sunken, ruined old cheeks with blush.

– Just look at you! You look like a fourteen-year-old girl!

– Yes, yes . . . – the old woman would respond, delighted, laughing with her toothless mouth in front of the mirror and trying hard to keep her head still so as to avoid letting the fine edifice balanced on her head collapse. – Yes, yes, but close the door quickly! Because *he* is coming, and I don't want her to see him come in . . . . Close it! Close it quickly!

When Matteo Falcone came home from work, he often found them awkwardly and garishly costumed in this way, neither of them able to move under the weight of hair and trimmings.

– Oh, Mother!

– Go over there! Go over there! That's your mother over there! – his irritated mother would respond from underneath her costume. – I don't have any children! I'm just twenty-eight . . . . I'm not married . . . .

And his aunt, for whom he also had filial respect and compassion, would respond in exactly the same way.

– Only twenty-eight . . . . I'm not married!

In his aunt, however, there arose and often weighed on her the dark suspicion that Matteo really *was* her son, for from time to time in her benighted memory, there stirred a vague sense of loss. This was caused, in fact, by the loss of her only son, many, many years previous.

– But how can that be! – the neighbors asked her. – If you have never had a husband?

– Yes . . . . And yet . . . . And yet *perhaps* Matteo is my child, – the old woman would respond, smiling maliciously, and with an air of mystery. – *Perhaps!*

– But how?

The old woman would take the neighbor by the arm, draw her in close, and whisper in her ear,

– By the blessing of the Holy Spirit!

And she would burst into peals of laughter.

Who is to say how much that continuous spectacle in Falcone's home contributed not only to his awareness of his own ugliness, but also to the formation of his horrendous conception of life and of human nature?

He had not come to understand unhappiness as something that the mind creates for itself, whether as a result of doubting or of the fever of wanting to know everything; for him, poverty was a bearable and surmountable ill. No, for Falcone only two things could truly ever constitute unhappiness, and they were reserved for those on whom Mother

Nature exercised her merciless injustice: ugliness and old age. And these were forever destined to be mocked and disdained by youth and beauty.

Wasn't it possible that the only reason his mother and aunt kept on living was to serve as a source of amusement for their neighbors? And he, why had he even been born? Why take away people's ability to reason and leave them alive, when there is nothing left for them but to die?

He was so profoundly obsessed with and upset by this idea that he often felt his whole being urged to vindicate the victims of such injustice: to slash the faces of the beautiful, to release the old from the agony of life. And at times, he must have had to do real violence to himself in order to resist the impulse to commit such crimes, while his very clear mind would represent these acts to him visibly, already committed. A crime? No. It was reparation!

And how many times, tearing himself away from these criminal urges with sudden force and going to his mother, as if to compensate for the cruel plan he harbored for an instant against her by treating her with exaggerated care, did she not see the danger, and, greeting him with an unknowing laugh, say to him,

– Put your feet on straight!

The old woman believed that he wore them that way on a whim, or to make her laugh. And she would insist, laughing,

– Put your feet on straight!

And then he would laugh too. Oh, to go mad staring in the face of his mother's senility!

– Yes, of course, Mother! I'll fix them now!

And the old woman would watch him, laughing and laughing at him as he leaned against the wall, trying to straighten his feet.

That day of his disdainful rejection by Marta he didn't even stop by the room of his aunt and mother, as he usually did when he got home. He did not have dinner, he did not go to bed that night, he didn't even take off his suit, which had gotten drenched in the rain. As soon as dawn broke, he went out for one of his long walks, which he habitually took after one of his violent attacks (much to the torture of his feet and body). Monte Cuccio, the highest mountain of the Conca d'oro, was his goal. Having reached the summit, he turned to look out over the city and spat out with all the force his soul could muster,

– I am a rat, and you are a rat's nest!

He came back down later that day exhausted, worn out, almost calm. It was late. At that hour, classes at the school would already have ended for the day. He deemed it prudent to go there, to explain his absence. In reality, he was going there in hopes of meeting Marta on her way home.

And in fact, he did meet her a few steps from the gate of the school. She was walking slowly, reading a letter. Another letter . . . . Who was writing her every day? And how flushed her cheeks were! It was a love letter; there could be no doubt!

Falcone could not have been more certain if he had torn it from her hands and read it himself.

And in fact, it had been his instinct to do just this when he had first caught sight of her. But he had held himself back. He let her pass before him slowly and turn into her street, happily absorbed by what she was reading.

"She didn't see me . . . ," he said to himself. And he turned down a side street, no longer thinking about going to the school to excuse his absence.

~ Chapter 6 ~

As soon as Marta stepped through the little door of her house, she tore the letter that Falcone had seen into tiny pieces, and threw them away before going up the stairs. Together with the letter, she tore up a printed ticket of admission; then she passed her hand over her eyes and over her burning cheeks, and stood there a little perplexed, as if she were trying hard to remember something.

She felt every vein in her body pulsing and, in that moment of indecision, her inner turmoil grew until it clouded her mind, almost making her feel inebriated. And in fact, as she stood there at the foot of the stairs smiling with her face lit up and her eyes sparkling, she could have easily passed for drunk.

What was keeping her from going up the stairs? What was she waiting for?

To regain her outward calm, at least, for her mother and sister must not notice a thing!

She eventually ran up the steps, as if by hurrying, she hoped to escape the thoughts that plagued her troubled mind. She was prepared to improvise some lie to her mother and sister, to tell them anything but the truth. Wasn't she already lying to them every day by concealing her own bitterness?

She had destroyed the letter. But the words that it contained followed her as she climbed the stairs, just as if those little pieces of paper had somehow rematerialized and were now whirling around inside her head and echoing in her ears. She heard those words bouncing around inside of her confusedly, not in the voice of the man who had written them, but in a voice she herself had given them at that moment. There were no sweet, caressing tones here; there was only anger, revolt against anything and everything that she had suffered up to that point.

As soon as she was alone in her room, the pain she felt at the lies she was forced to tell in her own home became even more pronounced. And she felt more deeply how detached she had become from her mother and sister. Hadn't they, with their restrained, dignified humility, with their timorous regard and constant concern for what other people thought of them, hadn't they both already been readmitted to that world that had so savagely cast her out, so remorselessly condemned her?

A new wrinkle had appeared on her forehead as this new and pronounced revolt against her family arose within her. She tried to nip it in the bud, tried to suppress the fact that her confusion was joining forces with the feelings of anger and hatred that instinctively surged inside her, and powerfully enough to take over everything, to suffocate the apprehension that had plagued her before.

But why did she have to be a victim? She, who had won, who had beaten them? Was she dead, she who made others live? And what had she done to lose the right to live? Nothing . . . , nothing . . . . Why suffer, therefore, the flagrant injustice of everyone? And not only their injustice, but their insults and slander as well. That unjust condemnation could never be repaired now. Who now could believe her to be innocent after the way her husband and father had behaved? There would be no recompense, then, for the war that they had waged against her, no reparation. She was lost forever. But innocence, *her* innocence, shook her, crying out for vengeance. And her avenger had arrived.

Gregorio Alvignani had come. He was in Palermo. He had written and included with his letter a card inviting her to the lecture he was giving at the university the next morning. "Come, Marta!" he wrote in that letter, which Marta remembered almost word for word. "Come, and bring the director of your school. Come, and with you there to hear them, my words will catch fire!"

No. No. How could she go? She had already torn the invitation to pieces. But then again . . . .

But she would see him again the next day in any case. He wrote her that he would visit her school himself in order to hear from her own lips whether she was happy with his lecture. He knew that she would never have written to him, would never manifest any desire to see or hear from him . . . . At this point in the letter, he seemed especially troubled . . . and it was precisely for this reason that he had come to her.

Why was she trembling so? Why now? She stood up, raised her hand to her forehead, and haughtily pushed her curls to the side. Her face was burning, and she was restless, as if a surge of new blood were careening through her veins. She opened the balcony door and gazed out at the sky, illuminated so brilliantly by the sunset.

Was she to remain outside of life forever? To bring nothing to that brilliance but shadows and fog? To smother the feelings that recently had begun to well up inside her again so confusedly, feverishly, like anxious aspirations to those blue skies, to that springtime sunlight, to the joy of swallows and flowers, the swallows that had built their nests above the balcony, and the flowers that her mother had scattered here and there throughout the house? Was it not time for her too to come back to life?

"To live! Live!" said Alvignani's letter. "That is the cry that burst from my heart, even among all of the empty, meaningless anxieties and the silly intrigues and the problems and annoyances; the sad art form that they have made of fiction and falsehood in the pandemonium of our nation's capital. To live! To live! And so, I fled . . . ."

Marta was bowled over by that unexpected letter, which read almost like a hymn to life. She was suddenly overcome with a painful desire to weep. With her eyes full of tears, she quickly drew back from the balcony and sat, hiding her face in her hands.

~ Chapter 7 ~

Gregorio Alvignani's letter was, like every other manifestation of his sentiments, sincere, at least in part.

It was true that, while in Rome, he had heard what he referred to in the letter as "the sincerest voice of our nature—yours and mine . . ." speaking to him.

He was exhausted. The combination of too much sedentary work, endless mental activity, the enormous and unflagging effort required not only to sustain the gentleman's lifestyle to which he had grown accustomed, but also to develop and put into action his own ambitions to political power, not to mention justifying them to other people, had worn him into the ground. All of this, compounded by his not getting sufficient sleep and taking only the occasional holiday, had resulted in a serious strain on his nerves.

And one morning, as he stood in front of his mirror, he suddenly took note of the pallor of his tired face, the wrinkles at the corners of his eyes, the sad lines running down from his mouth, his thinning hair; he was profoundly troubled by all of this. He then entered his study and sat at his desk, which was covered with thick dossiers, all neatly stacked. But he could not find it in him to lift a finger; he had lost even the slightest motivation to continue with the work he had begun. And so it was in this manner that the awareness of his inability to go on had been imposed upon him, quite without warning, and he had come to the conclusion that a long rest was unquestionably in order.

It did not help matters that he was disgusted at the underhanded and treacherous war against the prime minister that some of his colleagues were mounting for trivial reasons at that time in the houses of Parliament and in the newspapers. He, too, was in the opposition, but the bad-faith attacks of these few threatened to drag the entire opposition down and draw the disgust of the general public. He foresaw that, as a result, the House would soon close for the purpose of a brief suspension of parliamentary session, which, in fact, is precisely what came to pass only a few days later.

He therefore devised to leave Rome, the better to reinvigorate himself with a good, long rest, and to prepare himself in this manner for the approaching political struggle. The mirror, too, had something to say about distressing feelings that were agitating him. He was already on the downhill slope of life's mountain and had even started his descent. He was afraid of going too fast, of falling. He felt that he needed something to hold onto.

In his brief parliamentary career, he had been very fortunate. He had managed to make it into the public eye almost from the start, and had elicited both envy and sympathy, earning precious friendships and arousing serious hope in people. Having too easily won victory after victory in this way, he was beset by the unavoidable disappointments and discouragements of political life, which were all the more troubling because he had no one around him in any intimate sense with whom to celebrate his triumphs, just as he had no one to comfort him in his defeats. He was alone.

He hurried to make his preparations to leave Rome, and as soon as he had departed, he felt a sudden calm, almost greater than he had hoped for, as if the fog that enveloped him had all at once lifted. Behold the sun! Behold the new green of the fields! And the train chugged along. He drank in the rushing air in large gulps as it poured into the little window of his train car and shouted to himself even before he shared his thoughts with Marta, "To live! Live!" And this feeling of triumphant exultation had only grown as his voyage went on. He had seemed to see the world, and life itself, in a new light: in the broad sunlight, without complications, full of immense happiness. The blues and greens of the sky! Of the sea! Of the countryside!

Only a few days after his arrival in Palermo, he managed to find a house that suited his disposition perfectly. It was down a deserted street, just outside the Porta Nuova on Via Cuba, far from the city center, almost in the country.

The small villa was only one story high but of quite a stately appearance, with a central balcony flanked by two windows on each side.

– A paradise! No one could die here . . . – said the caretaker as he opened the little door below the balcony. As soon as he had crossed through the foyer and set foot on the first of three small steps that led into a wide courtyard paved with bricks that was walled in but open to the sky, Gregorio Alvignani was suddenly startled by a loud flapping of wings and looked up to see doves lining the tops of the two surrounding walls, cooing softly.

– So many doves!

– Yes, *Signore*. They belong to the owner of the house. I am only taking care of it for him . . . . If the *signore* does not want them here, I can take them away.

– No, that will be fine; leave them. They don't bother me.

– As the *signore* wishes. I come to feed them twice a day and clean up after them.

And the old caretaker whistled to them with a call all his own and with a snap of his fingers. Upon hearing this call, first one, then two together, then three, and then all of the birds descended upon the courtyard, cooing and extending their necks, bowing their little heads so that they could look sideways.

On the left, along the outer side of the wall, there rose a staircase in two short, easy flights. The double staircase, in that courtyard, with those doves gave the house a rustic air that was at once modest and cheerful.

– No surprises here . . . . The *signore* is free to have a nice long look around. No eye can see here inside these walls: only God and the creatures of the air, – the old caretaker explained.

He climbed the stairs in order to view the inside of the house. There were eight rooms, each furnished with at least an attempt at style. Alvignani was pleased.

– Does the young *signore* have family?

– No, I am alone.

– Ah, very well. And so, if you wish to have this double bed exchanged for a smaller one . . . . The owners live just around the corner, on the Corso Calatafimi. If the *signore* would like to take his meals at home, they can also provide board. The *signore* can, in short, have anything he likes.

– Yes, yes, we understand each other perfectly . . . . – said Alvignani.

– But wait . . . ! the terrace! The *signore* must see it! It's a real treat. The mountains, my young *signore*, it's as if you could touch them with your hands, they're so close.

Ah, yes, yes. This was just the refuge he needed: there, in the shadow of the mountains, and in view of the countryside.

He moved in two days later.

– Here I will finally be able to rest.

As he went into the city each morning down Corso Calatafimi, he passed the *Collegio Nuovo*. He looked at the large outer doors, at the windows of the huge building, and thought to himself that Marta was in there, somewhere. And he promised himself that he would see her again, if for no other reason than curiosity. But he had to find an opportunity. He thought, "I could just walk right in, even now. I could simply have myself announced, and then see her and speak to her. No. Suddenly like that, no. Better to give her some warning. She doesn't even know that I am in town and living so close to her. And who knows how I shall find her? Perhaps she has changed . . . ."

And so he would pass by, happy to have a nice bit of deserted road before him before he entered the city proper, where he would undoubtedly meet a lot of bores.

He was deeply convinced of his own worth, of his importance. But for now anyway, the air of slightly petulant self-confidence to which he so often abandoned himself when he was far from work and far from Rome pleasantly mitigated the absoluteness of this conviction in the eyes of others.

He had not yet decided entirely how he was going to occupy his time during his stay in Palermo. Could he remain idle? No, no. For him, idleness and boredom went hand in hand. Besides, having nothing to do could prove extremely dangerous. Yes, from the moment he had arrived he had thought of one thing, and one thing only: seeing Marta again.

"I will buy some new books to read, and I'll read them. And then if the mood strikes me, I'll prepare a few more notes for my lecture on *Relative Ethics*. That should do it. We'll see . . . ."

He tried not to think about any one thing for too long; his soul was bathing itself in this new sense of well-being, renewing itself.

"Come now, no one wants to die! Even when the mind is clouded with thoughts, the body finds plenty to enjoy in the sweetness of each season: a cool swim in the summertime, a roaring fire in the winter; sleeping, eating, going for walks. They enjoy these things, our bodies, and nary a word to us. And when do we speak? When do we reflect? Only when we are forced to by adverse circumstances. Meanwhile, when the world is most pleasant, our spirits rest and are silent. And so it seems that the world is only ever full of pain and malice. A brief hour of pain leaves a long impression; a whole day of serenity passes and doesn't leave a trace."

This reflection struck him as being both extremely true and original, and he smiled to himself with satisfaction. But how could he find the opportunity and the means of seeing Marta again? However much he tried to distract himself, the thought was never far from his mind, and he continually tried to devise a way to facilitate that encounter without compromising either himself or Marta.

He left the house. And as he walked, he thought, "If only I could at least catch a glimpse of her in the street first, without her seeing me! But what if she noticed me? Everything will depend on that first encounter . . . ."

Everything—what did that mean? Gregorio Alvignani avoided that thought.

"Everything will depend upon that first encounter . . . ."

The occasion did present itself, eventually, and it seemed to him a propitious one. He was invited to give a lecture on the subject of his choice in the great hall of the university. Although he had only brought a few books with him and indeed had found himself entirely unprepared, he accepted the invitation anyway after being practically begged to do so. He had always been tempted to undertake a thorough, eloquent examination of the modern conscience, and he had brought with him his notes for a study that he had begun but which had then been interrupted entitled "Future Transformations of the Moral Idea"—that would do nicely. From the examination of the moral conscience, he intended to pass to the examination of the various manifestations of life, principally of the artistic life. "Art and the Conscience of Today"—there was his title.[1]

"I will write to her. I will invite her to come to the lecture. That's how I'll see her; she'll be sitting right in front of me as I speak."

He was absolutely certain this plan would be a success. For when had he not succeeded? And it tickled him to think that that was where Marta would see him again for the first time, graciously receiving the applause of what he was sure would be a large and receptive audience.

He drew up an outline of his lecture and pored over it point by point since he intended to speak it, not read it. And when the concept was fully fleshed out and his line of argument clear, then, he wrote the letter of invitation to Marta, very pleased with himself.

The triumph his oratory met with the day of the lecture was even greater than Alvignani himself could have expected.

But one thing his triumph did not meet with was Marta. He scanned the expansive hall, packed with people. He caught sight of the director of Marta's school. She was alone. Marta had not come. And he didn't even think to acknowledge the applause with which the whole of that vast audience greeted him as he entered.

~ Chapter 8 ~

– Come, just a little walk . . . . Your headache will go away. Can't you see what a beautiful day it is? Just two steps . . . .

– I shouldn't have come . . . .

– Why do you say that?

– I should have sent word . . . . But to where?

– Why? – Alvignani insisted.

He too was flustered. He had not expected to find Marta so extraordinarily beautiful, nor so embarrassed and tremulous in his presence. He could not explain the ease with which she seemed to want to allow herself to be led. And he was almost disappointed at this. He feared he might be deceiving himself; he forced himself to doubt and was afraid to believe. He was afraid that an imprudent word, or gesture, or even smile might, in a single moment, break the spell.

Marta was walking beside him with her chin on her chest, blushing deeply. She had not managed to take her leave of him at the gate of the school, and having acquiesced to his suggestion that they take a short walk together, she had made sure to turn up a street upon which it would become less and less likely that they would meet anyone. She would certainly never have gone with him if they had been walking toward the city, and toward people who might know them.

She left the school two hours earlier than usual; at that time of day, her husband wouldn't yet be at his post, nor was it likely that Matteo Falcone should see her. She was trembling all the same. It seemed to her that everyone must be aware of his indiscretion, indeed, of his temerity. And how could anyone fail to notice the extreme agitation with which she followed him? She looked as if she were under some spell or being led as a blind person is led.

And she was not able to grasp the meanings of the words he was saying to her, in that trembling voice, but she heard them. His ardent, impassioned words elicited feelings of shame and confusion in her, but along with a sort of indefinable pleasure. He told her that he had never stopped thinking about her, no matter how far away . . . .

And she repeated his words involuntarily, with an incredulous air,

– Never . . . .

– No, never!

What was he saying now? That she had not responded? When? What letter? She began to raise her eyes to look him in the face, but quickly lowered her head again. Yes, it was true: she had not responded. But how could she have responded at that time?

Disjointed thoughts raced through her mind; the two little children she usually tutored on that day, the latest threat of her husband recounted in Anna Veronica's most recent letter, the monstrous love and tremendous jealousy of Matteo

Falcone . . . . But none of these thoughts managed to penetrate her troubled consciousness, or the anguish she felt pressing inside her chest with every heartbeat.

She felt that she belonged to this elegant, daring man who was walking beside her, who had suddenly come to take her. And she walked beside him as if he really did have some sort of natural right over her, as if it were her duty to follow him.

Great rushes of blood pounded in her brain, and then, all at once, she felt as if her limbs were drained of all energy. She had, in a very deep sense, lost all consciousness of herself, of everything. And so she walked beside him without a will of her own, and without any hope of releasing herself from him, as he drew her in with his web of impassioned words.

He, too, was caught, entirely at her mercy, as if under the sway of some hypnotic charm or love potion, and he spoke without quite knowing what he was saying, but with the feeling that every word she uttered, its sound, its inflection, was in perfect harmony, and so rang with a sort of immediate and infallible persuasion. He, too, had stopped thinking. He was aware of one thing and one thing only: that he was close to her, and that he would never leave her.

It was as if the air surrounding their bodies had become inflamed, and it enveloped them entirely, blocking out every perception they might have had of life continuing to go on around them. Their eyes were unable to see any object, their ears no longer able to discern any sound.

He had begun addressing her with the familiar "*tu*," just as he had in his last letter, the one that had been discovered by her husband. And this time she accepted it almost without noticing.

The road had been deserted for some time. The yellow dust shimmered in the afternoon sunlight—a cascade of innumerable blinding sparkles that made it seem that the very ground beneath their feet was shimmering. The sky was an intense, immaculate blue.

Then suddenly they came to a halt. He stopped first. Marta looked around her, confused. Where were they? How long had they been walking?

– Have you ever walked this far up the road?

– No . . . never . . . – she responded timidly, continuing to look around her as if she had just awakened from a dream.

– Over there . . . – Alvignani said to her as he took her lightly by the wrist and motioned toward a cross street to his left.

– Where? – she asked, forcing herself to look at him and drawing her arm, which he would not release, back a little bit.

– Over here, come . . . – he insisted, gently guiding her with a slight, tremulous smile on his dry lips, his face very pale.

– But no . . . now I must . . . . – she tried to keep her defenses up but was more awkward and agitated than ever as she noticed his trembling hands, his nervous smile, his colorless face, and the impetuous look in his eyes, the pupils of which had now darkened and dilated.

– Only for a moment . . . this way . . . . As you can see, there's no one . . . .

– But where? No . . . .

– Why not? You'll be able to see the magnificent enclosure of mountains, and Monreale high up above us . . . , and below us, the countryside with everything in bloom . . . in one direction you have the sea, and Monte Pellegrino . . . and in the other, the whole of the city stretched out before your eyes. Here, we're at the door. Come!

– No, no! – Marta refused more emphatically, eyeing the door, almost as if she did not yet understand that he lived here, and certainly not finding the strength to free her wrist from his hand.

But he kept drawing her forward. Once she had crossed over the threshold, she heaved a deep sigh; within the walls of that short, narrow foyer she felt a moment of peace, as if washed over with cool air on a hot day.

– Look, look . . . – Gregorio said to her, pointing out the doves that were all cooing in unison, now strutting forward with their chests puffed out as if to defend their territory, and now backing away, fearing Marta's voice as she bent down, calling to them.

– Oh, how beautiful they are . . . . And so many . . . .

As Gregorio watched her bent over like this, he was overcome by an uncontrollable desire to embrace her, to pull her close to him and not let her go, not ever let her go again. It seemed to him that he had always, always desired her, from the first day he had seen her.

– And look over here, two little steps . . . . Let's go up onto the terrace . . . .

– No, no, I really must be going now . . . – Marta responded immediately, straightening up.

What? But you've only just got here! Just two little steps . . . . You really must see the terrace . . . . You're already here . . . .

Marta once again allowed herself to be led. But as soon as she had set foot inside the house, the spell that had held her transfixed up to that point was suddenly broken. Her vision clouded over and a dizzying confusion took hold of her. She was lost! And as if in a nightmare, she felt powerless to save herself from this imminent danger.

– The terrace? Where is the terrace?

– Here we are . . . . We will go there now . . . . – Gregorio responded, taking her hand and pressing it to his chest. – But first . . . .

She raised her anxious, pleading eyes to his.

– Where is it? – she repeated, drawing back her hand.

She could not see any way out now.

Gregorio led her through a series of rooms, and then they climbed a narrow flight of wooden stairs.

The view was truly spectacular. The great wall of mountains loomed before them, dark and majestic under the brilliant sky. The outlines of their formidable backs were put into sharp relief by the well-defined shadows. Monreale seemed to be a snow-white herd pastured halfway up the slope. And down below stretched the countryside, dotted with little white houses, dark now in the shadow of the mountains.

– And now this side! – he said.

And just as dark and as imposing as the view of the mountains had been on the other side of the terrace, so did the view from the opposite side spread out before her, as vast and bright as any she had ever seen. She could see the whole of the city; the wide expanse of rooftops, cupolas, and bell towers, among which the bulk of the *Teatro Massimo* stood out, gigantic, offering themselves up to her eyes. And then there was the sea, pushed into the background, sparkling in the same sunshine as Monte Pellegrino, all rosy now as it seemed to lie down blissfully, ready for sleep.

For a moment, Marta was lost in contemplation of this vast spectacle. Then her eyes searched out the campanile of the Duomo, behind which sat her house. And suddenly at the thought of her mother and sister waiting for her there, her distress grew sharper, her remorse grew more acute, and she felt a deep and desperate distrust of herself. She drew up her handkerchief and hid her face.

– You're crying? But why, Marta? Why? – he asked her with affectionate concern, pulling the two of them together. – Come, let's get down from here . . . . You can go now . . . .

– Yes, yes, . . . right away . . . . – she said, controlling herself only with great difficulty. – I should not . . . I should not have come.

– But why do you say that? – said Gregorio again, clearly suffering, wounded by her words, as he helped her down the stairs. – Why do you say that, Marta? My Marta, *Marta mia* . . . . Wait, wait . . . . Here we are! Please don't cry . . . . Sit here a moment and get ahold of yourself.

And as he dried her eyes, he embraced her trembling body.

– No . . . no . . . . – Marta tried to defend herself, but her strength was gone.

When he embraced her, all of her limbs shook violently, and a sob broke from deep inside her, like the wailing of one who concedes without conceding.

~ Chapter 9 ~

– When, when will you come back? – Alvignani asked her passionately as he held her tightly in his arms on the staircase.

She let him hold her and did not respond. She was strangely inert, almost comatose. Had she tried to speak, she would not have found her voice. Come back? But now she no longer would have wished to go away; not only so as not to break his embrace, but because by then, she felt that she had reached her inevitable destination. She had finally sunk as low as she could, straight to the bottom where everyone, everyone had pushed her, or rather in a fury of blows had beaten her down, struck her from behind, tripped her until she had fallen. How could she ever raise herself up again? How could she ever recover from this? How could she even take up the fight again? It was over! She had finally arrived at the place everyone wanted her to end up. And the one who had been waiting there all along, he had taken her; he had come to get her, just so, quite simply, as if all of the injustices she had endured somehow granted him this right over her. That was why, right away, from the moment she had seen him again, she was unable to resist him, why she had found herself suddenly without a will of her own, and in front of him, who was all confidence. Without will! This was her overwhelming impression of herself.

– Mine . . . mine . . . mine . . . – Alvignani insisted, pulling her in more and more tightly.

Yes. His! His like a thing. Like a thing she had given to him.

Not understanding her abandon, or rather, interpreting it otherwise, he bent down as if he were drunk and whispered into her ear, entreating her to stay, to please stay just a little while longer . . . .

– No, I must go, – she said, suddenly rousing herself and almost wriggling out of his arms.

He took her hand.

– When will you come back?

– I will write to you . . . .

And she left. But as soon as she was alone on that same street she had walked not an hour before, next to him, she was beset again by those same feelings that she had left by the roadside on her way there. It was as if they had remained there in hiding, ready in ambush, waiting for her to come back and retrace her steps.

Almost in shock, she turned back to look at the street she had just left, and then she took up again, moving forward hurriedly, her mind a jumble. And as she walked, she reflected on her own honesty, trying to defend her actions by calling forth all of the reasons, the excuses, and arguments that she could muster. It was almost as if she were trying to mount an attack against this man who had suddenly robbed her of that honesty, while at the same time freeing herself from the idea that most dismayed and humiliated her: the idea that she had almost without any resistance allowed herself to become guilty of the very crime that she had so unjustly been accused of committing in the first place. She forced herself to see, to feel, to sense in that sudden and unexpected fall of hers, which so shocked her, an act of vengeance that she had committed on purpose, her revenge against everyone for having been wrongly accused before.

At the sight of the school on her right, she managed with some effort to raise her spirits a little bit. She was now back on that stretch of the *Corso* that she was used to passing through every day. She slowed her pace, and pressed on more calmly, more sure of herself, as if she had literally left her guilt behind her by virtue of the fact that anyone who saw her now would simply think, "She is just going home from school." All the same, she still felt weighed down by some indefinable something, a fear that if anyone so much as breathed close to her, or looked at her, or spoke to her, she might betray herself. She tried to rid herself of this aggravating sensation by reading the familiar signs of the shops as she passed them, just as she did every day, and with that, she finally felt reassured. She was suddenly struck with terror that if she were to speak to anyone her voice would tremble. And then a sigh came quickly to her lips. – Oh, so tired! – As she spoke these words, she listened carefully to how they sounded, pretending that they really did express what she was feeling, and weren't just an experiment she was carrying out, brought about by the sudden onset of fear. It was her usual voice, yes. But the words did not seem to be coming from her own mouth; rather, they sounded like an imitation, as if she were doing an imitation of her own voice.

She noted with relief that nothing on the street had changed at all, that everything, in sum, was just as before, and she made a conscious effort to bring herself into line with the workaday rhythms of the shops and newspaper stands she walked past every day. And here she was, finally passing beneath the Porta Nuova, just as she had yesterday, just as she had the day before that. And as she approached her house, little by little she felt her sense of calm returning by sheer force of will and concentration.

Maria was on the terrace and, looking down between the urns of flowers that lined the balustrade, she caught sight of her sister in the street. Marta waved to her, and Maria smiled. Nothing new at home either.

– How . . . but why are you so early today? – her mother asked.

– Early? Yes . . . I canceled one of my tutoring sessions . . . I had a little bit of a headache.

What she was saying was true. Her voice was steady. She had fittingly remembered the headache. She smiled at her mother and added,

– I'll go and change. Maria is on the terrace . . . . I saw her from the street.

Alone in her room, she was amazed at how calm she had seemed, as if she had been in complete control of herself all along. She was amazed at how well she had managed to deceive her mother. And with that amazement there came a kind of satisfaction. For the rest of the day, she seemed more cheerful to her mother and sister than they could remember having seen her in a long time.

As evening fell, however, it became clear to her that she did not need to pretend for the others so much as she needed to pretend for herself. In order to avoid her own feeling of uneasiness and not to be left alone with herself, she quickly took out from one of the drawers a stack of schoolwork to correct, and pencil in hand, she set herself to reading the papers and marking the errors, just as she did every night, focusing all of her attention on the task at hand. Her effort was in vain, however; there were too many thoughts bouncing around inside her head. She couldn't even manage to stay seated and went to press her burning forehead against the cool glass of the balcony window.

There, with her eyes closed, she tried to recreate clearly in her mind every last detail of that afternoon. But the lucidity of her soul was clouded even now, as she recalled the walk to Alvignani's house. He lived way up the mountain, and he had led her, ignorant of his intentions though she was, all the way there, all the way to his house! She should have taken her leave of him when they had reached the corner of the street. But how could she have? She hadn't even been able to say a word! In her mind's eye, she revisited the courtyard full of doves, the open staircase. There . . . if only the stairs had not been out in the open like that . . . perhaps she would never have gone up them in the first place . . . . Ah, yes, of course! And again she saw the magnificent spectacle of that expansive cluster of mountains. And then as she lingered on the memory of having searched from Alvignani's terrace for her own little rooftop in the shadow of the Duomo, she had a strange sensation: she seemed to find herself looking down from that terrace once again, and seeing herself as she was right now, there, in her room, with her forehead pressed against the glass of the balcony window.

– It's what they all wanted . . . – she murmured to herself sharply, trying hard to keep the emotions that she could feel tightening in her throat in check. – I will write to him, – she added, furrowing her brow. Then with a sudden change of heart, she shrugged, and ended her thought, – Well, it was bound to end this way, whatever happened.

And she wrote a long, desperate letter that revolved almost entirely around the two phrases, "What have I done?"

and "What will I do now?" She expressed her remorse at her sudden fall with an aggressive pouring forth of passion in the phrase especially repeated and underlined: "*Now I am yours!*" almost as if she were trying to frighten him.

"As I walked up that hill next to you, I had no idea . . . . You should have told me; I would not have come. It would have been better, so much better, for me . . . and for you too! If only you could imagine how much I suffered when I had to return here alone, how much I am suffering at this very moment, here with my mother and sister! And tomorrow? I feel like I have been thrown physically out of anything that resembles life, and I don't know what I will do, or what will become of me. I am the sole provider for two poor women. And I myself am lost, without a guide . . . . Can you not taste how bitter it is, the fruit of our love? Merely to think at all poisons it. But how can I *not* think, in my condition? You are free; I am not! The freedom of spirit that you speak about is nothing but torture for a body in chains . . . ."

The letter terminated abruptly, almost as if it had been choked off at the foot of the page by the lack of space. "We must see each other again. I will let you know when . . . . Farewell."

~ Chapter 10 ~

– Oh, *mia cara*, when I say, "My conscience will not permit me," I am really saying, "People will not permit me, the world will not permit me." My conscience! What do I suppose it really is, this conscience of mine? My conscience is just other people talking, *mia cara*! My conscience simply repeats to me what the others say, what society says. So then, hear me out! My conscience absolutely gives me permission to love you. And you, you examine your conscience, and you will see that the others have given you permission to love me as well. Yes, just as you yourself said, precisely because of all of those things that they have made you suffer unjustly.

In this way, Alvignani would twist his words in order to quiet his doubts, as well as Marta's guilt and fear. Indeed, he often repeated this argument in various formulations because it made it seem clearer and more convincing, especially to himself. And the rising passion of his words sometimes managed to silence even his own doubts, his own guilt, and the fear that he had not yet openly—or secretly, for that matter—admitted to himself.

Marta would listen in silence, hanging on his every word, letting herself be wrapped up in his warm, colorful language. She wanted to believe, but she was not convinced. She knew all too well what those secret visits to his house were costing her, what torment she felt at school, and what anxiety and anguish it caused her at night! She knew that her confused, agitated state, with her thoughts and feelings turning over and over in her mind, each dissociated from the next, would eventually betray her, one day or another. She desperately wished she could have some hope for the future. But what was left to hope for? She could not have said, even to herself. But she knew that she could not last much longer in that state, living that kind of life. She no longer had any place where she could find even a moment of peace: in her own home, it was all lies; at school, it was torture; at his house, guilt and fear. Where could she flee to? What was she to do?

She went to Alvignani's for only one reason: to hear him speak, to hear him say the things that in her heart of hearts she truly wanted to believe were true—that she had not given in, had not been beaten. That this man had not taken possession of her by means of the violence others had visited upon her, but that she herself had willed it, and, at this point, she had to stand by the situation she had created since it was she who had given herself to him. Her soul was suffering, her mind was reeling, and it was only in his words that she could find some slight relief.

– If you loved me more, you would think about all of this less, – he would say to her. – Love means forgetting everything else.

– You make it sound as if I want to think about all of this! – responded Marta, irritated.

– Look, I only think one thing—that you are mine, and that we mustn't let anything get in the way of our loving each other. Look me in the eyes. Do you love me?

Marta looked at him for a moment, and then lowered her eyes, her cheeks turning a bright crimson as she responded,

– I wouldn't be here . . . .

– And so? – he asked as he took her hand and pulled her closer to him.

She did not try to pull away, but rather abandoned herself, shamefaced and trembling, to that embrace. And then she hurried away, believing, once she had awakened from her momentary loss of memory, that she had stayed too long with him.

In the meantime, as he saw her off, he no longer lingered unsatisfied and fascinated on the last step of that staircase, as he had on her first visit. Now, just as soon as she had turned to go out through the little foyer, waving a sad, small goodbye, he quickly drew a deep breath, almost as if of relief, or perhaps of pity for her, and slowly made his way back up the stairs, deep in thought.

Thus did that first almost dreamlike stupor vanish, little by little, as did the first happy upheaval he had initially felt upon seeing Marta and at the unhoped-for ease with which his sudden, blazing hot desires had been fulfilled. He now realized how and why he had managed to take possession of her so quickly, and he also realized the extent of Marta's feelings for him. No, she did not love him, and she had not given herself over to him for love. Perhaps under different circumstances, yes, she might have fallen in love with him. But not now. In the chaos of her sudden fall, she had clutched for him as one clutches for someone else in a shipwreck: desperately, and without hope of being saved.

How would it end?

"Will she want to come with me to Rome?" Alvignani thought.

This would certainly have made him happy. But what about her mother? And her sister? Would they come with her? He would have no objection to that. But how would he propose it to her? She was so proud . . . , and under no circumstances would she bend to the conditions that he was able to offer her. And this proposal was the only one he had to offer. What, indeed, could he do for her? He was ready to do anything, but she had to give him a sign.

In the end, Alvignani deemed it better to put subtlety aside, and take a more direct approach, so as not to have anything to reproach himself with later.

– I bore you, don't I? – she would ask him bitterly. – You're thinking of leaving . . . .

– But no, Marta! Why on earth would you say that? You've misjudged me . . . . As long as you don't want to go with me . . . .

– Go with you? If it were just me, perhaps! But don't you see? This means that you *are* thinking of going away!

Gregorio shrugged his shoulders and sighed.

– But if you refuse to understand what I say to you . . . ! I am here, and I will stay here, with you, until we have come to some decision about our future. I only want you to be happy. I am not thinking of anything else . . . .

– But how? How? If only I knew!

– I know; I understand what you mean. But can you also see that as long as I am with you . . . .

– Yes.

And Marta had to agree. But what should she decide? Everyone had a road stretching before them, whether a sad or happy one. She alone had no road at all. She alone did not know what remained for her to do.

For nearly two months, their relationship dragged on in this way, darkened and saddened by the shadow of the guilt that her conscience continually cast over them. He had tried in vain to remove it, to shake off this shadow with his impassioned words. Now he suffered its oppressive force in silence, as it added its weight to their shared sadness with its own heavy inertia, and they awaited the day that neither of them would be able to bear it any longer.

– It is your decision. As I have told you, I am ready for anything.

Going away, returning to Rome, coming up with a letter that put forward some excuse—the sudden call of some urgent professional matter? If he had taken any of these options, perhaps she would have found a little bit of calm. And perhaps in that calm she could come to a decision. No. After much reflection, he rejected this plan as too violent. Maybe it would have been better simply to propose to her directly that they end things; not so much for his sake as for hers, as she was already suffering so much. But this plan too was rejected by Gregorio Alvignani, as he wished to avoid the distasteful scene that would almost certainly follow. No, better to wait until some step was taken by her, of her own accord.

Then there arrived a piece of unexpected news that upset both Alvignani and Marta, albeit in very different ways. Anna Veronica announced in a long letter that Rocco Pentàgora was gravely ill with typhus, and his case was so severe that by doctor's orders he had been placed in hospice care.

Marta went white as she read the letter, which seemed to her like a direct, odious response to the desperate wishes she had made on those long, sleepless nights, wishes that, in the depths of her conscience, she knew to be wrong, since, because of her more recent actions, she no longer had any right to wish for her husband's death. And yet how many times as she tossed and turned in her bed had she prayed,

– Please God, if only he would die!

And now he was dying. He was really dying.

In a state of terrible agitation, she went to communicate the news to Alvignani.

He stood there perplexed, watching Marta as she eyed him piercingly. They stared at each other for a little while, and he almost got the impression that the silence of the room was waiting for him to say something, as though death itself had entered and dared their love to speak.

~ Chapter 11 ~

– You, in Palermo? But how?

And Gregorio Alvignani found himself standing before Professor Luca Blandino, who was walking, as usual, with his eyes half-closed, lost in thought, with his stick under his arm, his hands behind his back and a long cigar lying lazily on his beard.

– Oh, my dear man! – said Blandino, looking up at Alvignani without the least bit of surprise, as if he were simply continuing a conversation they had been having for the past hour. – Up, up! Raise your chin a little . . . . Yes! How much are they?

– How much are what? – Gregorio asked, laughing.

– Those collars . . . how much a piece? They're a little too high for me . . . . What are you laughing at, you scoundrel? Are you making fun of me? I want to buy three of them. Come now, you must help me. I have a call to make, and in my present state I am not at all presentable. I've only just arrived . . . .

And with that he took the arm of Alvignani, who was still laughing, and set off with him.

– Oh, speaking of which, what are you doing here?

– Speaking of what? – Gregorio Alvignani asked him, and began to laugh again.

– Oh nothing, nothing . . . I just wanted to know, – Blandino responded, suddenly becoming serious and furrowing his brow ominously.

– The Camera is closed . . . . – said Alvignani.

– I know it is . . . . And you, why are you here? I don't want to make another mess of things . . . . Tell me the truth.

– What mess of things? – asked Gregorio, becoming serious himself and struggling to understand.

– I'll tell you all about it . . . . Let's go in here, – Blandino responded, directing them into one of the many shops that lined the street. – I can buy those collars.

– I gave a lecture at the university . . . . I'll be heading back in a few days . . . .

– To Rome?

– To Rome.

– Collars! – Blandino demanded of the young man behind the counter. – Look here . . . like the ones my friend here wears, but a little lower.

The purchases made, Gregorio Alvignani suggested that he and Blandino go to his house (Marta would not be coming by that day), and so they climbed into a carriage.

– Now would you please explain to me this "mess"?

– Ah, of course! So, a lecture? And then you'll be leaving soon?

– I hope to . . . .

– I would have preferred not to find you here.

– And why is that?

Alvignani believed he understood, but he assumed an expression somewhere in between pained and surprised. There was a faint smile playing on his lips.

From this smile, Blandino, who was a singularly acute reader of people, could tell immediately that Alvignani was already on his guard.

– Why? Because your presence here arouses my suspicions.

– Oh, of course it stands to reason that I should never visit Palermo again! But you, why have you come here? And for goodness' sake, what suspicion?

– Haven't you understood me? – Blandino asked, holding his gaze.

– No, I suppose I haven't . . . . That is, I can't imagine that you would even think of suggesting . . . . Yes? Really? Still? My dear man, water under the bridge . . . .

– Word of honor?

Gregorio Alvignani burst once again into a peal of laughter, and said,

– Do you know something? You become more foolish every time I see you.

– You're right! – confirmed Luca Blandino with the utmost sincerity, shaking his head and closing his eyes. – Every day I am more forgetful and stupid than the day before. I can't even teach anymore; I no longer remember anything . . . . Eighty, eighty, and eighty—that's two lire forty, correct? Wait, no, I think I've made an error . . . . I bought three collars, correct? Two lire forty . . . the thieves! How much change did they give me back? No, no—this is right: forty and sixty make one hundred—three lire, that's right. Very good. Anyway, what were we talking about?

– How many more years do you have to work before you can retire on your pension? – Gregorio Alvignani asked him.

– Oh, too many. Let's not talk about it, I beg you, – Blandino responded. – We must focus now on reconciling Rocco Pentàgora and his wife.

At first, Gregorio Alvignani didn't think that he had heard correctly. Then he turned pale. That jesting little smile never left his lips, however.

– Oh yes? But why on earth, after . . . ?

He broke off, feeling that perhaps his voice was not entirely steady.

– This is why I have come, – added Blandino, studying him closely. – That's the reason I told you that I would have preferred not to find you here.

– But what does it have to do with me? – cried Alvignani with an astonished air.

– Oh, be quiet and you'll see; this has to do with you, – exclaimed Blandino with a sigh. – But please, let's not talk about it any longer . . . now we need to think about this reconciliation.

– Are you sure it's even possible? – Alvignani asked, feigning naïveté to perfection.

– Let's hope so . . . . Why not? Her husband wants her back.

– Oh, so he was finally persuaded, eh? – added Gregorio Alvignani with an air of indifference.

The two men continued their journey in silence.

– This way, driver. It's Via Cuba, the first house . . . . – Alvignani finally broke the silence to direct the driver.

Not long after, once they were standing in the large room that opened out onto the balcony with its balustrade and pillars, they resumed their conversation.

– You really are incorrigible! – Gregorio exclaimed, laughing. – You really don't know how *not* to ask for trouble, do you?

– Eh, I know, I know. But what can I do? It's my fate . . . . Everyone comes to me for help. I don't know how to say no, and . . . . This time, however . . . . Did you know that poor boy has been sick? He almost died.

– Pentàgora? Really?

– Rocco, yes. Typhus . . . I live, I don't know if you knew, in the Pentàgora house, as a tenant. He sent for me . . . . Poor boy, he's unrecognizable, just skin and bones. "Professor," he says, "you must help me . . . . The letters are no good . . . . You must go to Marta's mother and tell her my condition. I want Marta back! I want her back!" And so, here we are my dear Gregorio! Let's hope we can bring this tragic story to an end.

– Yes, of course . . . . – affirmed Alvignani as he paced up and down the room. – That would be the best thing, without a doubt.

– Wouldn't it?

– Yes. It would have been better if nothing unfortunate had happened in the first place, as indeed nothing should have happened. I told you this at the time, do you remember? When you found the courage to present yourself to me as Pentàgora's second. He acted like a child, trying to provoke me like that. I did not need a second scandal, and so could not avoid the duel. From then on, I knew that this would be the solution. Perhaps it's taken him a little long . . . . But enough; in any case, he is trying to remedy the situation now. And he does well.

– Did you know that since the death of Francesco Ajala, *he*, her husband I mean, has tried many times to reconcile the two of them? She would hear nothing of it . . . .

– Too late, or too soon perhaps, – Alvignani observed. – Because you really ought to have some sympathy for the wife, it seems to me! I know it's not my place to say so, but just between us . . . . In any case, now everything is over and done with, or will be shortly. And disgrace her they have! If some blame . . . that is, blame . . . let's not say blame! If there has been some . . . mistake, some, shall we say, tiny mistake on anyone's part, it was mine. And I have regretted my part in this matter most bitterly. I still do. It was a momentary lapse on my part, I confess. Her convenient proximity, my sudden and intense feelings for her . . . the closed nature of my life, always buried in my work . . . it was a moment, in sum, of uncontrollable, if cordial . . . excitement, and nothing more. By the grace of her own virtue and honesty, I would have soon returned to my life of books and work, if as a result of the husband's incredible lack of judgment, things had not suddenly turned out . . . well, as they turned out. Ah, we must never linger so long in dreams, my dear friend, that we are overcome by the shock of reality! I have told myself that time and time again . . . . But I bring this up only to point out that if he, this husband of hers, God save him, had died, I myself would have quickly repaired the evils that, from every side, brought the poor woman so low. You know me, and you know that I am not the kind of man who runs around having affairs! You yourself once wrote me a rather brash letter on her behalf, do you remember? But I did not hold it against you. Rather, I immediately did everything in my power to help her . . . which was too little, unfortunately, given the circumstances, but still, I did everything I could. And now you bring me this encouraging news. She will be granted justice in the eyes of society; it is this that you must make her understand . . . . Yes, because she . . . well, I imagine . . . will not be disposed to respond well to the husband's change of heart, not right now. And rightly so; she has suffered so much, the poor thing. But if you want it to succeed, you must make her the proposal, it seems to me, from this angle. And this will take a great deal of tact, passion . . . . I am sure you can manage that! This truly is the way out of this mess, the only real recompense for her, the proof, the recognition of her innocence on the part of all of those who accused her and condemned her with their eyes stubbornly closed! Don't you think so? This, *this* is what you will have to argue when you see her!

– Yes, yes, of course . . . – Blandino agreed, distracted. – Just leave it to me . . . .

– Don't you think so? – Alvignani repeated, still lost in his reasoning, as if he were trying to persuade himself in particular. – It's precisely the ending one would want to this terrible, tragic story—the just ending, the natural one. You cannot imagine, my dear friend, how happy this makes me . . . . You must understand how I feel: this whole situation was initiated by me, and brought to bear on an innocent woman, without rhyme or reason, and it has been weighing on me terribly. Just knowing that this poor lady, thrown out of her home, still so young and beautiful, exposed as she has been to the evils of society . . . it has been, believe me, a source of continual regret for me . . . . Are you going?

– Yes, I'll be leaving now, – responded Blandino, who had already stood up.

Let's see each other this evening . . . . I would like to know . . . . Shall we have dinner together?

They made arrangements to meet, and Luca Blandino left. Not long after, as Gregorio Alvignani opened his bedroom door in the near darkness, he felt these two words strike him in the face, like blows.

– Coward! Coward!

He took a step backward.

– You? Here? Marta!

He entered and quickly closed the door behind him.

~ Chapter 12 ~

– Yes, here. I heard everything, – Marta shot back, quivering with disdain.

– And just what was it that I said . . . ? – Gregorio Alvignani stammered, almost to himself.

– It was all I could do not to open that door, not to rush in and unmask you in front of that imbecile! Even from here I wanted to shout out to him, "Don't believe him! I am here, in his house!"

– Marta! Are you crazy? – shouted Gregorio. – What do you want me to say? Is it my fault that he brought up your husband?

– And did he maybe also ask you to teach him the best way to get me to fall into his trap? Or how to present this proposal to me? Oh, you are really pleased with yourself, aren't you?

– Me? Well . . . yes! I did what I did for you!

– For me? And what other cowardly acts would you like to commit for me now? For me, you say? And what have

I become to you? Now that you have grown tired of me you want to push me back into the arms of my husband? Is that it?

– No, no! Not if that isn't what you want! – Gregorio protested.

– Whether I want it or not. And do you really think that it's possible now, after what has happened between you and me? And to discover that you have been hoping for it? That you're happy about it? God! Is this what they have turned me into? What have I become? You waited for me . . . . I came, here, to your house, of my own free will, and now that you have had me, you think you can just pass me back to this other man?

– How can you think such terrible things of me? – Alvignani exclaimed, crestfallen.

– Oh, how can I? How can you think that of me? The fact you would hope that . . . . But you don't even know the worst yet! Oh, my head . . . my poor, aching head . . . .

And Marta pressed her trembling hands hard against her temples.

– The worst? – asked Gregorio Alvignani.

– Yes, yes. There's no way out of this for me, not now. You might as well know. Death alone.

– What are you saying?

– I am lost! You've destroyed me . . . . I came with the purpose of telling you that.

– Destroyed? What are you saying? Explain it to me!

– Lost. Don't you understand? – shouted Marta. – Lost . . . lost . . . .

Gregorio Alvignani stood still as if perplexed, staring Marta in the face with terrified eyes, and stammered,

– Are you sure?

– Sure, absolutely sure . . . . How could I make a mistake like this? How could I have deceived myself like this?

– Marta responded, collapsing in a chair. – This is what I came to tell you. How can I hide my condition from my mother? My sister? They'll see right away . . . . No, no, I'd rather die! It's all over. Death is all that's left for me now.

– God, what a blow this is, – murmured a crushed Alvignani, covering his face with his hands.

– How can we fix this? What remedy is there? – said Marta desperately through her tears.

– Please don't cry like that! We'll look for a solution together . . . .

– Oh, for you! For yourself! I see how it is . . . . You've already found a way out for yourself!

– For me? What? No . . . no . . . . Stop blaming me . . . . How was I to know? Forgive me! Listen, I'll run and catch up with Blandino. I'll tell him that . . . I'll tell him the truth! . . . And that he no longer needs to worry about . . . .

– What! And then what's your plan?

– Then you will come with me . . . .

– That again? Why must you torture me? It's useless, and my heart can't take it! Or are you saying this on purpose because you know that it can't possibly be what I want?

– And again with your suspicions! Marta, for God's sake, can't you see that my pain is sincere? I know you don't want it, but what other option do you have? What do you propose to do?

– I don't know . . . . I don't know . . . . Go with you, yes. Yes, at this point I might as well, now that all is lost . . . . But my mother? My sister? You know that I provide for them. After everything they've been through, do you really expect me to add this new shame? Can't you understand? You know how proud my mother is.

– And so? – asked Gregorio, irritated, trying to rise above his discouragement by sheer force of reason. – Can't you see that there's no way out? Either you go with me, or with him, your husband!

Marta rose to her feet, contemptuously.

– No! – she said. – This last act of cowardice, no! I would never stoop so low!

– And so? – Gregorio repeated.

After a moment of silence, he continued.

– Not with me, and not with him either. But while by some act of providence he is giving you the chance . . . . Just hear me out! Think about it. You don't have the courage to come with me . . . because of your mother and sister, correct? That's fine. So what will you do? Either you sacrifice yourself for them by reuniting with your husband, or they are the ones sacrificed, and you come with me. But tell me this . . . . Did you somehow seek out the olive branch that he is offering you now? No, he, your husband, is offering it to you himself, of his own accord.

– That's true, – returned Marta. – But why? It's because he knows that I am innocent, just as I was before, and because he is sorry for having punished me unjustly.

– And didn't he truly punish you unjustly?

– Yes.

– Well then? Why does it suddenly seem like you are defending him now?

– Me? Who is defending him? – shouted Marta. – But I can no longer accuse him now, don't you see?

– Now you're accusing me instead.

– Yes, you. And myself, and everyone, and my unhappy fate.

Gregorio Alvignani shrugged his shoulders.

– I offer you my hand, and you push it away . . . . You also heard what I said to Blandino in there. If your husband had died, I would have married you . . . . What other proof could I give you of the honesty of my intentions? But instead you insist on seeing me as someone . . . someone out to profit from your misfortune. It's not true! I am not what you insist on thinking that I am. I am ready, now as I always have been, to do anything you wish . . . . What else can I say to you? Why insist on blaming me?

– I blame myself and myself alone, – said Marta somberly. – It was I alone who became your lover . . . .

The moment he heard this word Alvignani suddenly started. Pulling Marta close, he took her forcibly by the arm.

– My lover? No, my dear! Oh, if only I had ever seen in you, in your eyes, the least bit of love! I would go to your husband, and I would say to him, "You kicked her out although she was innocent, you defamed her without any cause, you ruined her because I loved her? And now that she loves me, you want her back? No! Now she is mine, mine forever, all mine. One man in her life is enough!" But you, love me? No . . . . You, my lover . . . no! And yet this is why I embraced this proposal that you and your husband reconcile. Because I thought that you wouldn't be able to last much longer in that situation—a situation of my making. Understand, it's not unbearable for me, who loves you, but for you, because you don't love me! You have never loved me. You have never loved anyone, ever! Whether this is through some defect on your part or is the fault of others, I don't know. You admitted as much yourself when you said that you felt that everyone had pushed you into my arms . . . . And now, look what we have here; this is your real revenge. And if I were in your shoes I wouldn't hesitate a minute! Think about it! Even though you were innocent, they punished you, defamed you, drove you out. And only now that you have been pushed and persecuted by everyone, now that you have committed this terrible sin—don't look at me like that, I know that's what it is to you!—the sin they accused you of when you were innocent, and not because of any passion on your part, or even because you particularly wanted to! Now they want you back! Well, go then! Go back! You will be punishing them all, just as they deserve!

The eloquent, impetuous resentment of his speech struck Marta dumb. She stood for a moment staring at him, and then her eyes made their way to the window and she suddenly realized that darkness had fallen. She jumped to her feet.

– Evening already? What will I do? It's dark out now . . . . Oh God, what will I tell them at home? What excuse can I find . . . ?

– What you need to find is a solution to this problem, – said Alvignani sullenly, not paying attention to Marta's distress at the lateness of the hour. – Think, think about what I have said!

– You can argue all you want, – sighed Marta. – But I . . . . Let me go, let me go now . . . . I must go . . . . It's already evening . . . .

– I will be waiting for you here tomorrow, – Alvignani told her. – Whatever you decide, know that I will be ready for anything. *Addio!* Wait . . . your hair . . . at least fix your hair a little . . . .

– No, no . . . there, like that . . . . *Addio!*

Marta hurried down the street, rubbing her eyes, straightening her hair, and thinking of excuses she could put forward for the great lateness with which she was returning home.

As she rounded the corner in the semidarkness, she suddenly found herself face to face with Matteo Falcone.

– Where are you coming from?

– You! What do you want with me?

– Where are you coming from? – Falcone repeated, so close to her that their faces were almost touching.

– Let me pass! What do you think you're doing, accosting people in the street like this? Are you spying on me?

– I'll show the world what you really are! – Falcone roared between clenched teeth.

– Brute! Taking advantage of a woman out on her own in the dark?

– Where are you coming from? – said Falcone again, out of his mind with jealousy, clutching at Marta's arm.

– Leave me alone, *villano*! I'll scream!

– Scream then, and make him come down! Even the way I am, I have an iron grip, by God, the better to wring his neck like a chicken's! Is it that skinny blond fellow from before?

– Yes, my husband! – said Marta. – Why don't you go and find him?

– Your husband? What? That man is your husband? – exclaimed Falcone, taken aback.

– Get out of my way . . . . I do not have to answer to you . . . .

Marta rushed down the street, followed by Falcone.

– He's your husband? Listen . . . , listen, please . . . . You must forgive me . . . .

– You're driving me mad! – Marta shouted at him, turning and stopping for a moment.

– You, mad? No, I am the mad one! You must forgive me, have pity on me . . . . I deserve compassion, not contempt . . . . I am not the monster; the world is the monster, a crazy monster that has made you so very beautiful and made me . . . like this. Let me shout for my vengeance! Can't you see? I need you in order to pay back this hateful world in kind, with hate! You were to be my revenge! It is revenge . . . revenge . . . .

Marta was trembling all over with both fear and disdain as she ran. She had left Falcone behind, still shouting and gesticulating wildly in the middle of the deserted street.

– Revenge! Revenge!

Windows were thrown open, people appeared in their doorways. It was not long before Falcone was surrounded.

– He's crazy! – someone yelled from a window.

Marta turned around for a moment and saw in the dim evening what looked like a scuffle. Falcone was screaming, inveighing against the people who were trying to grab hold of him; he shouted and shouted as he tried to wriggle free. The street had come to life and was full of people running in every direction. And Marta, too, began to run, down, down, toward her house, while in that supreme agitation one foolish, petty idea continued to pop up in her mind: "I'll say that I wasn't feeling well at school, and so I stayed . . . ."

When she had run far away, and was already close to Porta Nuova, she suddenly froze, as if fear had stopped her dead in her tracks. Surely Falcone would not, in the madness that had overtaken him, mention her name?

Marta felt what seemed like a deep abyss open up inside her chest, and, in that whirling dissociation of ideas and feelings, she stood there perplexed for a moment, unsure whether to turn back or to press on toward home. An energy she was not conscious of coursed through her. She was not thinking. She no longer felt anything. She turned and continued on her way home, as though she were following the voice in her head that kept repeating, "I'll say that I wasn't feeling well at school, and so I stayed . . . ."

~ Chapter 13 ~

The next day, Marta entered the teachers' room of the school nervously to find the immaculately dressed old director in conversation with Mormoni and Nusco.

– Have you heard, *Signora*?

– What? – stammered Marta.

– About poor Professor Falcone!

– Falcone . . . the *signora* knows. It was to be expected! – exclaimed Pompeo Mormoni, slicing through the air with one of his usual gestures.

– He's gone mad! – The director continued. – Or at least he gave signs of a serious mental imbalance last night, right out on a public street.

Marta stared into the director's eyes, then into the eyes of Mormoni, then into the eyes of Nusco.

– He started shouting, – she added, smiling nervously. – Then he started attacking the people around him . . . .

– Where is he now? – Mormoni asked the director.

– Perhaps at the asylum, or at least . . . . Last night, they took him to the police station first. He wasn't drunk; he never drinks wine . . . . Maybe he was coming back from Monte Cuccio? Because he was in the habit of making pleasant little climbs up the mountain in the evening . . . . And with those feet of his, just think! The sun would have been beating down on his head, and who knows what sort of crazy idea finally snapped in his brain. Apparently he was shouting for revenge.

– Let's just hope that by now, – little Nusco hoped out loud, – he's come back to himself, poor fellow!

– Yes, – said the director. – And in the meantime? To be honest, I must confess that at this point, I would be afraid to have him back here among our girls. I can't help but hope that they send him somewhere else, when and if he does come back to his senses, which I certainly hope he does!

"He'll lose his position!" thought Marta as she listened. "And I will lose mine as well . . . ."

And she delivered her lessons that day almost automatically, with a mind every so often attacked, beaten, dragged away from her work by the violent thoughts about which she had tossed and turned in her bed all night long.

Marta was trapped, caught between those two vile options Alvignani had given her. The only way out, it seemed, was death, which had dominated her thoughts all night long, and continued to do so. But the image of her actually taking her own life filled her with such horror that it almost made her dizzy. Against the invading darkness of this thought, however, there trembled inside her a glimmer of hope—the hope that she was not, in fact, in such a desperate position as so many fearful signs seemed to indicate that she was. This faint glimmer of hope illuminated in that horrendous darkness a single way out. The only way. Oh, how she wished she could throw herself down that path! But something held her back, as if she were under some spell. She forced her eyes to scrutinize that solitary road from which there is no return, far from Alvignani, far from her husband. She yearned, and, at the same time, she looked deep within herself, inside her own body, for some sign that could give her reason to continue to hope.

When she returned home after her lessons, she found that they had guests: the Juès, their neighbors from the second floor.

She could tell immediately from the eyes of her mother and her sister that Blandino had already been there. Her mother's eyes were shining, and her cheeks were bright red. As soon as she saw Marta, she suddenly grew very cheerful, struggling to contain her joy in front of their two inopportune guests.

Marta having said to the Juès that that she had been ill and that she continued to feel under the weather, Signora Juè turned to Signora Agata and expounded,

– Ah, it comes with the season, it comes with the season, *Signora mia*; it's nothing out of the ordinary . . . . Half the city is ill this time of year . . . . Do you remember that tenant of ours I was telling you about who rents the house in Via Benfratelli? The poor lady separated from her husband? Well, she can't so much as get out of bed! The other day, Fifo went to collect that little bit of rent we charge her (a pittance, really), and, wouldn't you know, he had to return empty-handed . . . . Ah, if you only knew, *Signora mia*, how much that blessed little house has made us suffer! Of course, it's because we're too bighearted . . . . You tell her, Fifo . . . .

And Signor Juè, seated as usual with his legs pressed tightly together, his arms folded across his chest, unstuck himself just enough to repeat his favorite phrase.

– Christ only knows!

A little while later, the husband and wife opted to "eliminate the inconvenience" of their presence. As soon as they had left, Signora Agata threw her arms around Marta's neck and held her in a tight embrace, pressing her close to her breast, kissing her again and again on the forehead.

My dear daughter, my dear daughter! Here! Here it is! You've finally gotten your reward! Justice has finally been served!

Her eyes filled with tears as she continued.

– Didn't I tell your father (bless his soul) that evening that it would happen? Light will win out over darkness, I told him, and your daughter's innocence will be recognized! Wait, wait . . . . Oh, if only he were alive to see it! Don't cry, don't cry my dear . . . . What's wrong? Oh my goodness, Marta, what's the matter?

Marta had collapsed into a chair, pale, sullen, and trembling.

– You know, I don't feel at all well . . . , – she murmured.

– Yes, but now you don't need to cry anymore! – her mother replied. – Do you know who paid us a visit this morning? Perhaps you don't know him. Blandino . . . Professor Blandino. And do you know why he came? Do you know who sent him? Your husband! Did you know that he was at death's door?

– I know, – said Marta, her eyebrows furrowed.

– You know? But how could you know?

– Anna Veronica wrote to me about it.

– Ah, in secret?

– Yes, I asked her never to mention him in the letters she sent to you.

– Yes, yes, but now . . . . Tell me, did you also know that . . . .

Marta pulled herself to her feet with difficulty, exhausted.

– He wants a reconciliation, doesn't he? – she said.

– Yes, yes! – confirmed her mother with joy. But that joy fell away immediately, when she saw Marta's somber expression.

– Do you think that's possible now? – she asked, spitting out every syllable deliberately and looking her mother straight in the eye.

– What? Why do you say that? – her mother exclaimed, astonished.

– Why? He wants me back. But I no longer want him.

– But how can you . . . . And don't you think . . . . But how? – stammered her mother. – If this means reparation for you! Don't you see, this means justice in the eyes of the world! And you want to refuse? How?

– Justice . . . . Reparation . . . . – Marta interrupted her. – Do you really believe that, Mamma?

– And why not? If Blandino came here . . . .

– Oh, I know that Blandino came here . . . . Mamma, it's no use! I ask you again: do you really believe that what they've done to me, first him, Rocco, and then Papà, do you really think that can just be undone? No, Mamma, no. It can't be repaired . . . . And you can be sure that in the eyes of the people, I will remain exactly what I am, no more and no less . . . . Do you know what they'll say? They'll say that he has forgiven me and leave it at that! And they will laugh at him, as they would at an imbecile . . . . I will always be the guilty one . . . . And why not? "If she were really innocent," they'll say, "then why did her father lock himself away out of shame for months and months in the dark, in his room, until it finally killed him? And why did her husband throw her out?" Oh, go on! Reparations, yes . . . . And your father, Maria? Who's going to give him back to you? And everything we've suffered through? Who will lift that heavy burden from our hearts? You can't be serious! Are these wounds that can just be patched up? No, Mamma. I cannot, I must not accept his penitence.

– But even if now he publicly acknowledges that he was wrong?

– No one will believe him.

– No one? Why, everyone will believe him, my dear! Who would have any right to speak if he does right by you?

Marta could feel herself withering under the gaze of her mother and sister and remained silent, listening.

– Yes . . . yes . . . , – she said. – I'll think about it. Let me think. I can't say anything more about it now.

– Think it over, Marta, think it over, for pity's sake! You will see that it is the right thing, and you'll agree. I'm sure of it! In the meantime, tell me, what response shall I give to Blandino?

– For now, none. Tell him . . . tell him that I need time to reflect on all of this . . . yes . . . . Give me time, and I will think about it.

But what was there to think about? Was she to wait until that flicker of hope, which grew dimmer day by day, finally disappeared, and the darkness and the void extended more and more, both within her and all around her?

She soon recognized that she could no longer deceive herself. And so, confronted with the horror that the idea of death aroused in her, she was forced to make a decision.

There was no distraction from this question, not even for a moment. She was penned in, pressured from all sides. She decided that her existence could not and should not last more than a few more days: one, two, three days to go . . . and then? Her blood felt frozen in her veins. She pulled herself back from the balcony railing for fear of giving in to a sudden impulse to cut short that agony. Oh no, no, that was not the death for her, no! But there were no firearms in the house. Poison! It would be better to die of poisoning. But how could she get her hands on some?

She was losing her mind, and with the last of her vital energies she grappled with these material difficulties, making them loom larger and larger. She could hear her mother talking in the other room, and would ask herself, "What will she do? Will they take pity on her and Maria when I am gone?" But how was it possible that her mother considered this proposed reconciliation and her husband's sudden remorse to be such a prize, recompense for all that they had suffered? She wanted to scream at her, "Is this what you call justice? You believe that I am innocent, and then call it justice when the person who wrongly accused me has a change of heart? And if I really were as you believe me to be, how could his repentance make up for what I have gone through? Does it seem to you that I could ever just smile at the idea of returning to live under the same roof as a man who has treated me so unjustly, and who doesn't understand me? A man I don't respect and don't love? Is this the reward for my innocence?"

She wanted to see Alvignani one last time. She had no illusions as to whether he could help her, but . . . who knows! Perhaps in speaking with Blandino or by reflecting on the problem himself, he had been able to come up with some solution, some other way out.

– I was just writing you! – said Gregorio, seeing her come in. – See, the letter is right here!

Marta reached out her hand to take it from him.

– No, it's useless now . . . . I'll tear it up. It's full of nonsense anyway. You never came back . . . .

He took a long look at her and, reading the desperation on her face, added,

– Poor Marta!

And then he asked, but almost without much hope of a response,

– Have you made a decision?

Marta sighed, opening her hand with a small gesture of despair, and she sat down.

He went back to looking at her, and he felt all of the enormous, unbearable weight of their situation. He was struck by that silence, that oppressive, inert irrationality, as if by a blow. In order to shake her out of it, he said,

– Will you come with me?

But she only turned and looked at him. Then she closed her eyes and tilted her head back, desperately weary.

– Nothing, then, nothing, – she said. – You haven't found anything.

– But what is there to find? – he responded quickly, passionately. – Day and night I have thought only of you. I have waited and waited for you to come . . . . It's useless to look anymore, Marta! Look here, I had just written to you, "Decide, and decide soon: there is no time to lose. You have already waited too long . . . . Give Blandino your response. Tell him right away, yes or no, and if the answer is no . . . ." And look, here I propose to you that . . . . Do you want to read it yourself? . . . Read it; read it . . . .

– Alvignani held the letter out to her, indicating the point at which she was to begin reading, and Marta took it. But after only a few lines she dropped her hands to her lap.

– Read it to the bottom of the page! – he exhorted her.

Marta raised the letter to her eyes once more. For all of the bad she had expected to find there, as she read, her face betrayed how desperate she was to find on that page even a single word that would give rise to a new hope in her; the desperation of a weary traveler, dying of thirst, searching a dry bed of stones for a trickle, even a drop of water. And in those words of Alvignani's she found nothing more than dry, heavy stones, which she sifted through without finding anything at all beneath them. She shook her head no, no, no disconsolately.

Having finished reading the letter, she stood up with a sigh and said nothing.

– Well, what do you think? – he asked her.

Marta shrugged her shoulders and handed him back the letter, exclaiming,

– Let's not rehash the same useless argument from last time . . . please, or my brain will just . . . .

– But what do you want to do?

– Don't you see? What else can I do?

– You're crazy!

– Crazy? I should have done it a long time ago, while my father was still alive . . . . And then . . . then it wouldn't have been as . . . as *ugly* as now! Now I've got my back against the wall.

– But you're the one who keeps yourself there! – shot back Alvignani, harshly.

He took both of her hands in his, and continued,

– But think this through with me. Who is the one who should be punished? Should *you* perhaps be punished? No, it's him, him, him!

– And how do I do that? – said Marta. – By betraying him? That would no longer be a punishment for him, but it would be for me! Aren't you listening? Can't you see how much this horrifies me? For me, for me it's horrifying! Don't you understand? If I were some sort of unthinking, unfeeling object . . . . But I am a human, and I think and feel! *I* know that I have been with you, *I* know what I have done . . . and I can't, I just can't! It horrifies me!

– Listen, there is no way, – said Alvignani resolutely, rising to his feet, – no way at all that knowing what I know I can allow you to commit this double crime. So you are no longer figuring your mother and sister into the equation? I will write to him!

– To whom? – asked Marta, suddenly coming around.

– To him, to your husband, – Alvignani responded. – I can't leave you alone in your current state, abandon you to your own devices, to your own despair . . . .

– Are you mad? – Marta interrupted him. – What on earth would you write to him?

– I don't know. I'll speak my mind, my conscience. I know only one thing: that you are not the guilty one. Either he or I must be punished, whichever one of us is left standing, it will fall to him to amend things.

– What idiocy! – Marta exclaimed. – No . . . listen . . . listen to me . . . .

She broke off. An idea suddenly struck her, and her face immediately lit up. She almost smiled.

– Don't write him. – She took up again. – I will write him . . . . Leave the writing to me . . . . I've got it! I've got it!

– What are you saying? – Gregorio asked anxiously. – What will you write him?

– I've got it! – repeated Marta joyfully. – Yes, that will solve everything . . . . You'll see! I'll explain everything to you after . . . . For now, let me go . . . .

– No, tell me first . . . .

– After, after . . . . – said Marta. – I am telling you, everything will work out fine . . . . Let me go . . . . I'll explain everything afterward . . . . Promise me you won't write him!

– But I want to know . . . – Alvignani objected, perplexed.

– There's nothing to know. Just leave me to do it . . . . Promise me.

– Well alright, I promise . . . . When are you coming back?

– Soon. And don't worry, I'll be back. For now, *addio*!

– *Addio!* See you soon!

Marta went away. And as she made her way home, the idea that had flashed in her mind slowly began to take on a more concrete, precise shape. In the excited, almost delirious state in which she found herself, she could not see the absurdity of the solution that had come to her so suddenly. And she said to herself, as she walked along, "I do not accept his forgiveness, the forgiveness of someone who should be asking for forgiveness himself . . . . I do not accept it . . . . I deserve to be punished? Fine! I'll make sure that I am punished. But first he must pay for all the terrible things he did to me, unjustly . . . . That he owes me . . . . Alright, so I will just remove myself from the situation. And with me out of the picture, why can't he marry my sister? Maria is wise . . . . Maria is good . . . . She'll do it for her mother's sake . . . . They'll make a nice little family, along with Mother . . . . And so everything will be alright . . . ."

She was hurrying now, talking to herself. She felt that an enormous weight had been lifted from her. She looked around her with bright, cheerful eyes, and really almost laughed at everything her gaze chanced upon. She felt that a perfect calm had descended upon her spirit.

And that was her state of mind when she reached home.

– Have you made a decision, Marta? – her mother risked asking.

– Just now, Mamma, – she responded. – I thought about it for a long time. I must write to him. Don't worry, I'll write tonight or tomorrow morning. I am thinking of the two of you!

– Of us? But you must think about yourself, my child . . . . Do you see what you have been reduced to?

– I am thinking of myself and of you . . . . – said Marta. – Don't worry.

~ Chapter 14 ~

Around daybreak, Marta finally managed to get some sleep. She had spent the night formulating the letter to her husband, weighing every word, excluding from it every phrase tinged with self-pity, or that recriminated him. She had then tried to imagine in great detail what life would be like for the others without her there: the tears and the despair of her mother and sister; the comfort that he, her husband, would rush to bring them; the remorse and surprise of those who knew her; the mourning . . . . Then, as time goes on, the desolate calm in which that grief finally slips away unnoticed, as if it were falling asleep. And little by little, the strange surprises of seeing and of feeling that life has indeed gone on, that it has simply followed its natural course, and that we who remain . . . we have done so too. The dead? The dead are far away . . . .

After just two hours of sleep, Marta awoke very calm, as if, during that short rest, her spirit had been purged of her violent intentions. Nor did this calm come as a surprise to her; she had thought about this for a long time, weighed and mulled it over for a long time, and always with her mother and sister in mind. She felt, therefore, no remorse. She was prepared. She was ready. Yes, after breakfast, she would write the letter. And then, as evening approached, she would go out and post the letter with her own hands. And then . . . then she would never return to that house. At this point, all of the difficulty she had felt regarding the way in which she would take her own life seemed silly; she would go to the nearby train station and throw herself down onto the tracks, her head between the wheels of a train. Or perhaps she would go to the beach and drown herself in some lonely spot.

– What a gorgeous day! – said Maria as she came out of her room. – I left the blinds open so that I would wake up as soon as it was light out . . . , but wait, wait . . . the sun never rose . . . .

In fact, the sky was cloudy and threatening for the first time after a long season of beautiful weather.

Marta was incredibly sweet with her mother and sister that day, in every word and in every glance she gave them. She was almost cheerful at the table. After breakfast was over, she announced to her mother that she would be writing to her husband.

– Yes, my dear . . . and may God be your guide!

Her mother was sure that Marta had acquiesced to her husband's proposed reconciliation, and with Maria's help, attended calmly to the usual household chores.

By afternoon, the sky had darkened ominously. Heavy storm clouds gathered over the city, and a strong wind began to blow. At every gust, the panes of the windows rattled violently, until it seemed that they must give in to the fury raging outside with a deafening crash. Upstairs the terrace door would slam every now and again without warning. Suddenly there flashed in the darkness a blinding light, and almost simultaneously the thunder exploded, rending the air with a formidable roar. Marta ran from her room with a scream and threw her arms around her mother, pale and shaking like a leaf.

– Were you afraid? – her mother said to her, stroking her hair. – Look how nervous you are! What a baby!

– Yes, yes, I know . . . , – said Marta, wracked with shivers that soon turned into sobs. – I can't write today . . . . I'll write tomorrow . . . . I'm shaking all over . . . .

– You just stay here with us, – her mother advised.

Stay there with them? There, in that sheltered little kitchen, getting a taste once again of that safe, narrow, blessed life of the family, of home? It was no longer for her.

She had torn up sheet after sheet of paper. That letter, so easily formulated in the delirious excitement of the night before, seemed weak and disjointed to her now that she had sat down to write it. She tried to think of how she could reformulate it, but it was all in vain! It felt as if her soul itself were struck dumb, her brain all dried up, and her body was restless, rebelling against the task imposed on it by her will. Her body felt the imminent threat of the weather: the electricity crackling in the air, the violence of the wind. Her eyes turned, almost against her will, to look out the window. She saw herself at the mercy of that wind, blown along a deserted stretch of shoreline, and the angry heaving of the ocean, howling at her as she looked on. She saw herself searching for a suitable place to throw herself down into those hideous, crashing waves. And with her soul thus suspended, as she was following every step until that last one, until the moment of taking that plunge, there was suddenly a blinding flash of lightning and an explosion of thunder.

A moment later, she was laughing instinctively at what her mother and Maria were saying as they tried to calm her down, making light of her fear of the storm.

Night fell like a pall over the city. Marta, her mother, and Maria had gathered for dinner when they heard a frantic ringing at the door, prompting all three to exclaim at once,

– Who can it be at this hour?

It was Donna Maria Rosa Juè, who entered with her hands raised in the air, shaking her head and shouting,

– *Signora mia! Signora mia!* I have so much to tell you! Why must everything happen to me? And what have I done, dear God, to offend You? What have I done? That poor old woman, my tenant down on Benfratelli street . . . *Signora mia*, she is dying . . . *Gesù! Gesù! Gesù!* Dying there just like a dog, but for the fact that she is baptized, of course . . . . I sent the doctor at my own expense, and I bought her medicine, although surely these are fakes, *Signora mia*, which won't do anything at all, but I did it anyway, so no one could say that I hadn't done everything I could . . . . She hasn't paid her rent . . . . But enough of that . . . . As I was saying, surely this poor old woman has some family down south, in your part of the country . . . . I don't mean for the rent, which is nothing, or the doctor or the medicine . . . but for the funeral, *Signora mia*! Who will pay for the burial? Fifo and I have already done more than we should have, out of the goodness of our hearts, and for charity's sake, "love thy neighbor" and the rest of it . . . . And in this terrible weather, too! Oh, *Signora mia*, wind that could blow away a house . . . . We came back just for a moment to grab a quick bite to eat . . . . We're heading back there now to keep vigil, probably all night long . . . . Why are we doing it? We are Christians! Ah, husbands, husbands! I'm not speaking of mine, of course; I, by the grace of God, have had two, unworthy as I am, and each one better than the other: that saintly soul who was my first, and this one, who is the spitting image of his brother, identical, with the same good heart. That will be our downfall, *Signora mia*, that good heart . . . . But could you write to someone, if you know of any family she might have down south?

– Yes, we'll write to her son . . . . – responded Signora Agata, dazed by the flurry of words with which Juè had imparted the news as much as by the news itself.

– What! – exclaimed Donna Maria Rosa. – That poor lady has a son? And her son is just letting her die like this, like a dog? Oh children, children! They're worse than husbands! Write to him, for goodness' sake . . . . tell him that she really is not long for this world! I'll see to it that the priest gives her the Last Rites tonight . . . . Are we Christians or not? We are not heathens!

– I'll go with you, – said Marta, getting up from her seat.

Her mother and Maria turned to look at her.

– Do you really think you should? – her mother asked. – You have been feeling so poorly, Marta, and with this weather . . . .

– Let me go . . . . – Marta insisted, heading toward her room.

Signora Agata said nothing more. She admired her daughter for responding in that way, with an act of generosity toward the husband who had treated her so badly. It also seemed to her that with this visit to her dying mother-in-law, Marta could respond to her husband's proposed reconciliation, and set a seal on the peace his offer promised.

Marta, on the other hand, was searching for her hat and shawl in the darkened room, and thinking to herself, "She must be a victim too. I want to see her, to get to know her . . . ."

– I'm ready.

– You must pin your hat on well, or better still, leave it here, mark my words, – Donna Maria Rosa advised. – Wrap a scarf around your head, as I have done . . . .

Don Fifo was waiting on the second-floor landing, half-dead, shivering with cold, his hands in his pockets and his collar up for warmth.

As soon as they were out on the street, Marta heard the extraordinary fury of the wind, which roared through the street, as if it were trying to blow all of the houses away. She looked up at the raucous sky, overrun by enormous storm clouds that looked as if they had themselves been torn to shreds. Through these gashes, the moon would appear every now and again, looking as if it were fleeing the scene, rushing away in fear for its very life. The street was almost completely dark as the wind had blown out several of the streetlamps. At the knoll, farther down Via del Papireto, a tree had been split in two, and the others were twisting and bending in the wind. The two women leaned into that furious wind as they made their way slowly up the street, their dresses impeding their progress at every step. Don Fifo was holding his hat onto his head with both hands so tightly that he was pulling it down almost to his shoulders.

Where the Corso turned toward the Duomo, they saw something none of them had ever seen before: a deafening torrent of dry leaves that seemed to be growing every second as it whirled around and around. It was as if the wind had stripped every last leaf in the countryside and now in a forceful rage, in a vehement excess of destructive force, was dragging them from Porta Nuova to the very bottom of the street, and then all the way down to the sea.

The two women and Don Fifo got caught up in the whirlwind as they turned their backs to it, and they, too, were pushed down, and then almost lifted up with the leaves themselves. Suddenly, Don Fifo let loose a scream, and Marta saw him leap like a grasshopper, throwing himself after his hat, which had just disappeared in the churning eddy of leaves.

– Leave it, Fifo! – shouted his wife from somewhere over his shoulder.

But now Don Fifo, too, had disappeared into the whirlwind of leaves, in the dark.

– This way, over here! – shouted Signora Juè to Marta, rounding the corner of Via Protonotaro, which was out of the path of the wind, and in which huge piles of leaves had taken refuge. – He'll catch up to his hat back at Porta Felice, if he makes it that far! Of course that would happen! Just what we needed! All this, and now a new hat!

They crossed the little Piazza Origlione, and soon found themselves in Via Benfratelli.

– Here it is, the entrance is here, – exclaimed Donna Maria Rosa, ducking into an entryway.

They climbed the steep, narrow staircase in the dark, all the way up to the top floor. Signora Juè drew an enormous key from her pocket, blew into the keyhole, guided the key to the lock with her fingers in the darkness, and opened the door. As soon as she opened the door she shouted,

– *Gesù-Maria!* The windows!

The three rooms that comprised the squalid abode of the dying woman had been invaded by the wind, which had forced the window frames and broken all of the glass out of the windows. The little lamp in the bedroom had blown out, and in the darkness Fana Pentàgora was wheezing, terrified.

– The window panes! Every single one of them is broken! I offer them up to you, oh Lord, in penitence for my sins! – exclaimed Signora Juè, putting all of her strength into closing the shutters against the wind.

Marta had remained at the threshold, terrified, with her ears intent on the old woman's dying wheeze.

With the shutters now closed and the room silent, that wheezing became unbearable.

– And the matches? – exclaimed Donna Maria Rosa. – Of course, Fifo has them . . . running after his hat and leaving us here in the dark with nothing to do. Ah, what a man! Just the opposite, sometimes, of his brother, may he rest in peace. I'll go and look for some in the kitchen.

Marta groped her way to the bed, as if she were drawn by the old woman's wheezing. She moved to lean her hand on the bed, but then quickly drew back in disgust, for in doing so she had inadvertently touched the woman as she lay on the bed. She bent over her and called to her in a whisper,

– Mamma . . . Mamma . . . .

The only response was that labored wheezing.

– I am Rocco's wife . . . . – Marta continued.

– Rocco . . . . – Marta seemed to hear the dying woman mumble with rasping breath.

– Rocco's wife . . . . – she repeated. – Don't be afraid. I'm here now . . . .

– Rocco, – said the dying woman. There was no mistaking it this time, and the wheezing stopped for a moment.

The silence became terrifying.

– You stay quiet now . . . . – Marta responded, gently admonishing her, as one would a sick child. – Your landlady is here . . . .

Holding a lit match in one hand and shielding it with the other, Donna Maria Rosa was moving about the dark room like a will-o'-the-wisp.

– Where is that lamp? Ah, here it is!

Having lit the lamp, Donna Maria Rosa stood with all ten fingers splayed, examining them.

– Lord, what filth! I got it all over me in the kitchen . . . . Just look at what a sty this place is!

The shards of glass from the window had been blown as far as the center of the room.

At the same time, Marta looked on, trembling with horror as the dying woman slowly raised her head from where it lay buried deep in the pillows, scanning the room with dull, lifeless eyes. It was as if she were amazed by the light, and by the sudden silence after the darkness and the terrible howling of the wind. There was a milky film covering the pupil of her right eye, and the skin of her face, but especially of her nose, was dotted with small, black pockmarks that stood out against the extreme pallor of her sweat-drenched skin. Her coarse gray hair lay in a curly, thick mass across the pillows, which had begun to yellow with age. Marta's eyes paused on the woman's enormous hands, the hands of a man, really, as they lay there motionless at her sides. The thin sheet beneath her was even dirtier than her shirt, which lay open, exposing her dry, bony chest. It was horrible to see.

– Rocco . . . . – the dying woman murmured once again, her eyes fixed on Marta's face, thirsty for information.

– What's she saying? – asked Signora Juè, who was bent over, her skirts raised up above her knee as she yanked her stocking from where it had fallen down around her ankle up over her thick calf.

– She's calling her son's name . . . . – Marta responded, drawing close to the old woman once again as she said under her breath, – He will come, don't you worry . . . . I will write him right now to come quickly . . . .

But the dying woman did not understand, and kept repeating in a weak voice, her eyes searching all around the room,

– Rocco . . . .

– A telegram, yes? – said Signora Juè. – Fifo will go to the telegraph office . . . . There's no time to lose. Ah, here in this drawer there should be paper and everything you need to write with . . . . *Mio Dio*, how it smells in here! Do you smell that? What smells so bad in this room?

On the little table closest to the window, there was a glass half-full of a greenish mixture, which was giving off a noxious odor.

– Ah, here you are! – said Signora Juè, pointing out the glass with her stubby index finger. – And now let's throw you away!

Marta ran over to her.

– No, don't! What is it?

– It must be poison, – said Donna Maria Rosa, taking note of Marta's nervous expression.

– It might prove useful . . . .

– Just what purpose do you want it to serve, my dear? It will just sit there smelling terrible all night, uselessly . . . .

And she went to the kitchen to pour it out.

Marta pulled herself up to the little table and began writing the telegram. Almost without thinking, she wrote simply, "Your mother is ill. Come quickly. MARTA."

– Ah, you two must be close, – observed Signora Juè, reading the telegram. – Are you perhaps related?

Marta blushed red, not sure how to answer, and tenuously nodded her head several times in assent. Donna Maria Rosa noted that sudden confusion and embarrassment and suspected that there must be a story lurking behind it . . . .

– Or, of course . . . from the same part of the world . . . , – she said. And, in an awkward attempt to mitigate the indiscreet question, added, – At any rate, I hope he comes soon . . . .

They heard a knock at the door.

– That will be Fifo!

Don Fifo entered bareheaded, his hair a mess, shouting and gesturing broadly,

– That was no hat; it was a devil!

– Yes, alright . . . , – said his wife. – And right now, we need you to run off to the telegraph office! Look, even the window panes are all shattered!

Don Fifo leapt back in surprise.

– Me? To the telegraph office? Now? Not even if they made me pope!

– Idiot! I told you, all of the window panes are shattered! – shot back Donna Maria Rosa, really getting angry now. – Now get yourself to the telegraph office!

– Oh *Cristo mio*! – exclaimed Don Fifo. – Outside all of the devils of hell are roaming around free . . . . Where do you want me to go? And must I go without my hat?

– You can wrap my shawl around your head . . .

Don Fifo looked at Marta and his mouth curled into the smile of someone used to being fooled.

– Yes, sure, your shawl . . . . You just want everyone to laugh at me . . . .

– Who do you think is going to see you at this time of night, in this weather? Come on, out you go! Out!

And she threw her shawl over his head, adding,

– Then you can go home and go to bed.

– By myself? – asked Don Fifo, adjusting the shawl on his head.

– What, are you afraid?

– Afraid? Me? I don't know the meaning of the word . . . . But you here, and me there . . . oh, nothing. Look, I'd rather just stay there in that corner over there . . . . I wouldn't get in your way . . . . Alright, be patient. I'm going, and I'll be right back.

And off he went. He returned around a half an hour later. Marta had continued keeping a close eye on the dying woman, who had, in turn, continued to sink further and further into her lethargy. Signora Juè, on the other side of the bed, had already dozed off, her chin resting on the steep slope of her ample bosom. Don Fifo looked at her for a little while, and then turned to Marta and said softly,

– Oh God help us all, she's beginning to snore . . . .

He shook his clenched fists violently, and added,

– She'll bring the whole house down!

He hadn't even finished his sentence, however, when Donna Maria Rosa gave her first proper snort, her mouth falling open wide. Don Fifo ran over to her and called to her, shaking her gently,

– Mararrò . . . Mararrò . . . .

– Ah . . . what is it? . . . What do you want? . . . Did you send the . . . . Alright . . . .

– No . . . I was trying to tell you . . . – Don Fifo went on timidly. – We must be quiet . . . . You see, the sick woman . . . .

– Stop bothering me, Fifo! – Donna Maria Rosa interrupted him and began to drift off again.

Don Fifo shrugged his shoulders and raised his eyes to the ceiling with a sigh.

Not long after, he, too, was asleep next to his wife, who was once again snoring formidably. And after a little while he began to snore himself, but in weak, timid little snorts, accompanied by a soft whistling that came from his nose. In this way, husband and wife seemed to be playing in a sort of harmony: one a bass tuba, the other a muted violin.

Marta, in the meantime, was completely absorbed by her contemplation of the dying woman, a horrible image of her own imminent demise.

"Tomorrow he will come," she thought. "He will see me here, and he will believe that I want . . . that I am able to accept his proposal. But I was not thinking of him when I came here. Perhaps he, when he knows everything, will even suspect that I came here just to endear myself to him. No. No, tomorrow morning, before he arrives, I will go away . . . so that he doesn't see me . . . . I will go away . . . ."

She stood up from her chair and tiptoed close to the figure lying in the bed, who seemed already to be dead. She leaned in close, trying to hear if she was still breathing, and then returned to her seat, thinking,

"How peaceful she is! And she is dying . . . . Death is already inside of her, inside that sleeping body . . . . Go away? No, I can't go away . . . . I must speak to him first . . . whatever the cost . . . . It is a sacrifice I must make in order to ensure that he faces up to his duty: he must help my mother. And so he will find me here, next to his! I will tell him everything . . . everything . . . ."

The little light was dying on the table next to them. The shadows of the two sleeping figures grew larger and larger on the wall and leapt grotesquely at every flicker of the flame. Marta was afraid that at any moment they would be plunged into complete darkness, and she got up to wake Signora Juè.

– The lamp is going out . . . .

– What's it doing? Ah, it's going out? . . . OK then, let's just . . . .

She pushed herself up from the chair, stumbled over to the little table, and blew the lamp out, remarking,

– It smells bad . . . . There's no oil left . . . . Now where's my chair?

– Ah! – shrieked Don Fifo in the darkness. – You've massacred one of my feet!

– My chair . . . . Here it is! Patience, my dear Fifo. Tomorrow night with any luck we'll be able to sleep in our own bed . . . . In any case, it will be daylight soon enough . . . .

And indeed, not long after a cock's crowing broke the silence. Marta, wrapped in that darkness, listened intently. Another rooster, this one farther off, responded to the call of the first. And then a third sounded, farther off still. But not so much as a ray of light shone through the slats of the shutters.

Dawn finally broke. Signora Juè woke up, stretching and almost whinnying as she asked Marta for an update on the dying woman. Only Don Fifo, sitting there in his corner with his head sunk onto his chest, his arms crossed, his legs pressed tightly together, and looking very miserable indeed, continued to snore his timid little snores with the whistle at the end, now unaccompanied.

– She's cold! She's cold! – said Signora Juè, still half-asleep, as she placed her hand on the forehead of the dying woman. – We must send for the priest right away . . . . Fifo! Fifo, wake up!

Don Fifo woke up.

– Run over to Santa Chiara right away . . . or this unhappy woman will die without the Last Rites . . . . Are you listening to me Fifo?

Don Fifo had scrambled to his feet and was wandering around the room, his eyes glazed over with sleep.

– What are you looking for?

– I'm looking for . . . . Ah yes! No hat, *santo Dio*! Even if I had a little cap . . . anything! Do I have to go like this?

– Go! Go! Run . . . . There's no time to lose, – Donna Maria Rosa shouted at him, and turning to Marta, added, – Meanwhile you and I will tidy up the room a little bit. The Lord is coming!

Marta looked at Signora Juè completely stunned. The Lord? Suddenly an image of Anna Veronica came to mind, and she almost looked around the room for her. And she even saw a little bit of Anna Veronica in herself in that moment. Should she bow down and beg God to pardon her sin and her shame, just as Anna had done? Ah, no! No! Never! Since the Lord would be there soon, she would kneel, but only to pray for the health of her spirit.

While Signora Juè tried to arrange the blankets, the dying woman opened her cloudy, sightless eyes. Marta watched those eyes and that face and saw that they were suffused now with a serenity that seemed somehow more than human. It seemed that only her broken-down body lay in that bed, and that she no longer perceived the squalor and misery that surrounded her. She was without sadness, without memory.

The Viaticum finally arrived but went unnoticed by the dying woman. Fana Pentàgora stared at the priest in precisely the same way she had been staring at the ceiling of that room. She did not respond to his questions. The onlookers were on their knees around the bed, murmuring prayers. Marta wept, her face hidden.

Not long after, the Rites were over. Marta raised her tearstained face, and she looked around herself, disillusioned, almost nauseated, as if she had just taken part in some meaningless, incredibly vulgar scene. That? That was the coming of the Lord? A blond, cold, insipid priest, hastily put together for the occasion? And to think that for a moment she had actually considered throwing herself to her knees and praying for guidance . . . .

– I'm afraid that he won't arrive in time . . . . – sighed Signora Juè, referring to the dying woman's son.

Don Fifo, after the Viaticum, had left the room and was pacing the adjoining room in consternation, his arms folded tightly across his chest. He grumbled to himself every so often as he waited for his wife to come out and announce the death of their tenant. From the threshold, he impatiently craned his gaunt face toward the bed, and gesturing toward the woman with a nod, asked, – Is she still alive?

Donna Maria Rosa explained to Marta,

– After the death of Dorò, God rest his soul, that man just can't bear to see anyone die . . . .

~ Chapter 15 ~

As the hours dragged slowly on, Marta became more and more anxious. The waiting grew a little more painful with each passing moment.

Early that afternoon, Rocco Pentàgora finally arrived at the door of the apartment. He was out of breath, and almost seemed lost.

It appeared to Marta that he had grown taller, most likely a result of the weight he had lost during his illness. His fever had also made much of his hair fall out, and now soft, extremely fine little curls had started to grow in again. His forehead too seemed to have broadened, and his skin had brightened, although he was still as pale as ever. And in his eyes, he carried a new expression, a sort of cheerful glimmer, almost childlike.

– Marta! – he shouted as soon as he saw her, and he ran to her.

Shaken by the sight of her husband thus transfigured and indeed almost refined by his convalescence, not to mention by his spirited bounding toward her, without thinking, Marta stopped him dead in his tracks with a subtle gesture that he keep quiet, and pointed him to the bed where his mother lay in agony.

The son immediately turned to the bed and bent over his mother, calling out to her,

– Mamma! Mamma! Can't you hear me, Mamma? Look at me . . . . I've come!

The dying woman opened her eyes and looked up at him bewildered, as if she did not recognize him. He went on,

– Can't you see me? It's me . . . . I've come . . . . Now you'll get well again . . . .

He kissed her softly on the forehead and wiped the tears from his eyes with a quick movement of his hand.

His dying mother continued to stare at him intently, every now and then closing her eyelids arduously, as if her body no longer had the strength to give any other sign of life. Or was that slow movement of her eyelids the final, faraway gesture of a spirit already well on its journey to death?

With difficulty, Marta held back her tears, but only because of the shame of breaking down in front of Signora Juè, who was making a proud, simpering display of her own tears.

Little by little, however, the eyes of the dying woman grew more animated, or animated enough, as if from those depths of death some far-off residual of life were surfacing again. She opened her mouth, and her lips moved.

– What is it? – asked her son with palpable apprehension, leaning down even closer to her.

– I am dying . . . . – breathed his mother, almost imperceptibly.

– No, no . . . . – he comforted her. – You're getting better, now . . . . I'm here now . . . . And Marta is here too . . . . Didn't you see her? Marta, come here . . . come over here . . . .

Marta went to the other side of the bed, and the dying woman turned her head to stare at her just as she had first stared at her son.

– Here she is . . . . Do you see her? – he added. – Marta is right here . . . . It's her . . . . Do you remember how much I talked with you about her last time?

The dying woman drew a breath with difficulty. She seemed not to understand and stared up at Marta with confused eyes. Then her pale, waxen cheeks slowly began to show the slightest hint of their former pink, and she moved her hand under the covers. Marta quickly lifted the blankets out of the way and placed her own hand in the hand of the dying woman, who now gestured with her other hand as best she could, staring at her son. Rocco then followed Marta's example, and with effort, his mother then succeeded in joining their two hands together and heaved another deep sigh.

– Yes, yes . . . . – Rocco said to his mother, deeply moved. He squeezed Marta's hand, and she could no longer manage to hold back her tears.

Astonished, the two Juès looked on slack-jawed from their post at the edge of the bed, their gaze shifting from Marta to Rocco and back again.

Not long after, the dying woman closed her eyes again, slipping back into those mysterious depths, where death was waiting for her.

Marta timidly withdrew her hand from the hand of her husband.

– She's resting again, – said Signora Juè, under her breath. – Let's let her rest . . . . Listen, Signora Marta, Fifo and I will take advantage of this moment of calm to run back home. There is so much to be taken care of . . . . I'm not one to boast, but I know how to manage these things . . . . Fifo, you tell them . . . . Of course, this is a time of grieving and loss, but, how to say it? An empty sack cannot stand on its own, and after so many hours on the train, poor Signor Rocco must be desperate for some refreshment . . . .

– No . . . no . . . . Nothing for me . . . .

– Just leave it to me . . . . – Signora Juè interrupted him.

– Rather Marta, perhaps, – said Rocco.

– Just leave it to me! – Repeated Donna Maria Rosa. – I'll take care of everything . . . . And I'll also take a little care of myself and this soul in Purgatory over here . . . . We haven't had so much as a sip of water since yesterday. How does one do it, I ask you? Best be patient . . . . Goodbye now, goodbye . . . . And try to keep your spirits high, eh?

The two Juès went away.

On the one hand, Marta would have liked for them to stay, by force if necessary, so as not to be left alone with her husband. On the other hand, however anxious the looming thought of that dreadful confession made her, she now considered it inevitable, and she longed to get it over with as soon as possible.

– Oh Marta! Marta *mia*! – Rocco exclaimed, opening his arms and calling her to him.

Shaking terribly, Marta rose from her seat and said to him,

– In there . . . in the other room . . . . No . . . wait . . . . I want you to hear everything I have to say right now . . . . Come . . . .

– What? You mean you don't forgive me? – he asked her, following her into the next room, which was almost completely dark.

– Wait . . . . – repeated Marta without looking at him. – I . . . I have nothing to forgive you for, if you . . . .

She trailed off. Her face contracted and her eyes closed, as if just below the surface she were in the throes of some unbearable convulsion. Then she turned to her husband with a look of pity and continued, resolutely.

– Listen to me, Rocco. You knew . . . .

She suddenly stopped short again, noticing the long scar on Rocco's cheek, all that remained of the injury he had sustained in his duel with Alvignani. She felt her courage falter, and she pressed both of her hands hard to her face.

– Forgive me! Forgive me! – he begged her insistently, laying his hands lovingly on her arms.

– No, Rocco! Listen to me. I won't ask anything of you for myself . . . . – Marta began again, uncovering her face. – I want to say just one thing to you. Remember that father left us in poverty. Mamma and Maria . . . they hadn't done anything wrong . . . and this was your fault. All alone . . . three poor women, left to fend for themselves out on the street and attacked on all sides by the whole town . . . .

– So you don't forgive me? You don't want to? You'll see, Marta, you'll see how I'll make it up to you . . . . Your mother, Maria, they will come with us . . . live in our house . . . that goes without saying, doesn't it? Isn't that obvious? With us, always! Is that all you wanted to say to me? Come, Marta, let's not dwell on the past . . . . Are you crying? Why?

Marta, her face once again hidden in her hands, was shaking her head no, sobbing. And in vain Rocco pressed her to tell him the reason for her tears, and for that mute denial.

– Oh, for Mamma . . . for Maria . . . – she finally said, uncovering once again her flushed face, now streaked with tears. – Listen to me, Rocco . . . .

– Again? – he asked, perplexed, bewildered, hurt.

– Yes. I am leaving you free, free to do what you will, from this very night forward . . . . You can't ask anything more of me . . . .

– What!

– Yes, I am leaving you . . . . I leave an open road before you so that you can do your duty for my mother, for my sister, like a good, honest man . . . . I ask nothing for myself! Listen to me . . . . Try to understand what I am saying . . . .

– I don't understand you! What do you want from me? You're leaving me free? What does that mean? . . . But just ask me, and I will do anything you want . . . . Stop crying! I should be the one crying . . . . I'll agree to anything, but forgive me . . . . I'll accept any terms, as long as you forgive me . . . .

– Oh *Dio*! Not now, Rocco! Not now . . . . Before . . . you should have asked me to forgive you before, with this same voice. I wouldn't have turned you down . . . . But now, no. There's nothing I can do for you now!

– Why?

– I must die. Yes . . . . And I will die. But . . . *Dio* . . . *Dio*! If I weren't able to take care of myself . . . if that anger had stayed in my heart . . . . What am I now? Look at me! What am I . . . ? I have become what people, thanks to you, believed I was, and what they still believe I am, and what they will always believe I am, even if I were to accept your repentance. It's too late now, you understand? I am lost! You see what you have done to me? I was alone . . . you all persecuted me . . . . I was alone with no one to help me . . . . And now I am lost!

He stood and stared at her, speechless, afraid of understanding, afraid of having understood.

– Marta! But how . . . you . . . . Oh, *Dio*! . . . You . . . .

Marta fell forward into her hands, and nodded her head several times in between sobs.

Rocco then grasped her arm, trying to pull her hands from her face, and still shocked, still almost unable to believe it, he shook her.

– So then, you . . . so after we . . . with him? Speak! Explain yourself! Ah, so it's true after all? Is it true? Speak! Look me in the face! That miserable . . . . Don't you have anything to say? Oh that dirty . . . . – he exploded then. – It *is* true! And I made myself believe . . . and I came here to ask for forgiveness . . . . And now . . . tell the truth, an affair before too? Huh? Tell the truth . . . with him?

– No! – screamed Marta, burning with disdain. – Don't you understand? It was you, you yourself with your own two hands, and all, all of the rest of them with you, who finally reduced me to the point that I had no other choice but to accept help from him! Among all the bitterness and scorn that you and everyone else heaped upon me, all the injustice with which you treated me, you made it so that in the end, he and he alone was the only person who offered me a single word of comfort, an act of honesty and fairness. Oh you . . . no, you of all people have no right to reproach me for anything! I know well what I must do now . . . . Just remember that I have fallen in a war that you started . . . . But I don't care about that because this is not about me! You . . . you also must do your duty and make things right! Do you know what my mother and my sister have been reduced to because of you? They've become entirely dependent on me alone. What will become of them? How will they live? Before I do anything, I have to know . . . . This is the reason that I have confessed everything to you . . . . I could not have said anything, or I could have lied to you . . . . Be grateful to me at least for that . . . and in return, help them . . . help my family, because it wasn't me, but you! You're the one who reduced them to this sorry state!

Rocco had sat down with his elbows on his knees and his face in his hands; he was repeating to himself softly and without expression, as if his brain could no longer handle the strain of it all,

– That bastard . . . . That bastard . . . .

In the silence that had suddenly overtaken the room, Marta heard a deep, labored wheezing coming from the adjoining room, and she hurried to the bed of the dying woman.

He followed her, and there, ignoring his dying mother entirely, he demanded wildly, his eyes fixed on Marta,

—Tell me . . . tell me everything! I have to know it . . . . I have to know everything! Tell me!

– No! – Marta responded with a bold firmness. – If I am to die by my own hand, I won't give you the pleasure.

And with that she bent over the bed to adjust the pillows under the head of the dying woman, who, from the depth of the coma into which she had fallen, continued to emit the dull death rattle.

– Die? – he asked with scorn. – And why? Why not go to him? He's helped you before, hasn't he? He'll continue to help you . . . .

Marta did not respond to this bitter attack. She only closed her eyes slowly, and then wiped away the icy sweat from his mother's forehead with her handkerchief.

Rocco went on,

– There's a way out for you! Go to Rome! Why die?

– Oh Rocco! – said Marta. – Your mother is still here . . . . Please stop this, for her sake . . . .

He was quiet, and he turned pale, contemplating his mother. The idea of death, made all the more manifest by Marta, suddenly came roaring to life, as terrible images filled his head. Pressing his hands against his temples, he left the room without a word.

It was already almost evening. In the encroaching darkness, Marta stared mechanically at the empty lamp on the little table. Who would have thought that this poor woman's agony would be drawn out so long? She sat close to the bedside, her eyes fixed in that darkness on the face of the dying woman, almost as if waiting for the plan itself, that terrible plan that she had so long been turning over in her mind, allowing it to ripen, to give her the push she needed to get up and put it into motion. The regular footsteps of her husband pacing in the next room rang louder in her ears now than the labored breathing of the dying woman, and she waited, as if the sound of those footsteps might reveal what he was thinking. She intuited, she could sense that in that moment he was going over thoughts from the past, experiencing their pain anew, assailed in that darkness by memories and by regrets . . . . Ah, regrets . . . everyone had earned them. Everyone, that is, except two people: Maria and her mother. And Marta expected her husband to do right by them, to act justly. She expected nothing less as she sat, listening to his footsteps.

Then suddenly there was silence from the next room. Had he made his decision? Marta rose to her feet and felt about her for her shawl. She found it, and just as she began to move to the doorway to call to him, she heard a knock at the door. It was the two Juès returning, followed by a servant boy carrying a box of provisions.

– Oh, in the dark? – exclaimed Donna Maria Rosa as she came in. – I brought you a candle . . . . Oh, I'm sorry . . . but where is Signor Rocco? Fifo, light the candle!

Don Fifo lit the candle, and he suddenly appeared in the room looking completely lost, carrying a long bundle of four funeral tapers in his arms.

Marta leaned over the bed and examined the face of the dying woman.

– How is she? How is she? – Signora Juè barked insistently.

Marta, frightened by a long, harsh gurgling noise coming from the throat of the dying woman, raised her frightened face and stared at Signora Juè, perplexed. Then she resolutely went to the doorway of the other room and called into the darkness,

– Come . . . . Come . . . . She's dying . . . .

Rocco came running and both of them bent over the bed. Don Fifo left the room on tiptoe with his bundle of tapers, signaling to the boy with a wave of his hand to follow him.

Rocco raised his eyes from his mother's face to Marta's and stared fixedly at her, at first with his eyebrows furrowed, then with surprise, almost amazed. Marta held one of his mother's hands in her own, and was bent over her, holding herself close to her, as if she were trying to infuse the dying woman with her own living breath.

Then all at once a very pale Signora Juè said softly,

– Come, Signor Pentàgora . . . .

– Is she dead? – asked Rocco, watching as Marta released his mother's hand and straightened up. And he cried out loud, his voice convulsive, – Mamma! Oh Mamma! My mother! – He was shouting then and breaking into sobs as he pressed his face into the pillows next to his mother's.

– Fifo, Fifo, – called Signora Juè. – Come in here, Fifo, and take him with you . . . . Take him with you into the other room, in there. Courage, courage my boy . . . . That's right . . . . It's alright . . . . Come now . . . . Go with Fifo . . . .

And with her husband's help she managed to tear Rocco away from the lifeless body of his mother.

– I've taken care of everything . . . . – said Signora Juè quietly as soon as they were alone. – It couldn't last . . . . I expected it . . . . I've brought four fine funeral tapers . . . . But first let's tidy her up a little bit, then we'll dress her . . . .

Marta couldn't take her wide eyes off of the dead woman's face and hadn't understood any of the many, many words that Signora Juè had said to her, the same words that perhaps Don Fifo was saying right now to Rocco.

– If you could just move a little bit . . . . And now we can dress her.

Marta moved away from the bed, mechanically. And as she dressed the dead woman under Marta's horrified gaze, Signora Juè never once stopped talking in veiled terms about the expenses that she had incurred, without forgetting a single one—not the medicine, nor the doctor, nor the broken glass of the window, nor the dinner, nor the tapers, nor the rent that the deceased had not paid—and all so that Marta could then deliver an itemized list to Rocco. Having dressed the body, she covered it with a sheet and placed the tapers at the four corners of the bed.

– There we are, all done, – she said then. – All clean! I don't mean to brag, but . . . .

And she sat next to Marta, admiring her work.

They passed many hours that way. In that room, it seemed that the only living things were the four tapers, which slowly burned down. Every so often Donna Maria Rosa would get up, remove a drop of wax from the shaft of one of the tapers and feed it back into the flame.

Finally, Don Fifo appeared in the doorway and gave his wife a signal that Marta did not see. Signora Juè responded with a signal of her own, and shortly thereafter said softly to Marta,

– We'll be going now. I'll leave this pair of shears here so that you can trim the candles every so often . . . . If you don't trim them, you see, they'll sputter and the sheet might catch fire, so pay attention . . . . Goodbye for now. We'll be back tomorrow morning . . . .

– Please, *Signora*, will you tell my mother not to come . . . . – Marta said to her, as if in a dream. – Tell her we will stay here with this woman . . . her son and I . . . . tell her . . . to keep the vigil of the dead . . . and that she and Maria must stay calm, and . . . and give her my love . . . .

– I'll take care of everything, never fear. Oh, listen . . . if by chance, later, Signor Rocco . . . and you too, of course . . . the basket we brought is there in the other room . . . I mean, if by chance . . . I don't have any appetite at all. Believe me, *Signora mia*, it's like I have a stone right here in the pit of my stomach. I am very sensitive, you know . . . . Anyway, goodbye for now. I'll just call Fifo ever so softly and we'll be on our way. Courage, my dear, and goodbye!

Now that she had been left alone, Marta strained her ears to listen to what her husband was saying in the next room. Was he crying in silence? Was he thinking?

"I don't mean anything to him anymore . . . ," Marta said to herself. "He doesn't even care enough to see whether I am still here, or whether I have gone away . . . . And yet he knows where I must go . . . . I'll go now . . . . I've told him everything . . . well, not everything about the child . . . . But the child is mine . . . mine alone . . . just like the other one that died because of him was mine and mine alone . . . . Oh, if only he had lived . . . ."

She turned her eyes to the bed, over which the four tapers cast a warm, yellow light. A few stiff folds in the sheet showed that a body lay below it in the heavy immobility of death.

With one hand, Marta fearfully drew back the sheet and uncovered the face of the dead woman, already transfigured. She fell to her knees next to the bed and let loose an enormous torrent of grief in an unending flood of tears, covering her own mouth with her hand so as not to scream, not to cry out.

And she wept there, until Rocco came in from the next room. Then she got to her feet, with her shawl under her arm, her face in her hands, and moved toward the door.

Rocco held her by one of her arms, and asked her in a somber voice,

– Where are you going?

Marta did not respond.

– Tell me where you're going, – he repeated, and unsure what to do, he extended his other hand and held her by both of her arms.

Marta partially uncovered her face.

– I'm going . . . . I don't know . . . . Let me go, I beg you . . . .

He did not let her go on. In a rush of passion, almost as if in fear, he pulled his face up to her face and burst into tears, embracing her.

– No, Marta! No! No! Don't leave me alone! Marta! Marta! Marta *mia*!

She tried to push him away and drew her head back, but she could not manage to free herself from that embrace. Pressed so close to him, she trembled.

– Rocco, no . . . it's impossible . . . . Let me go . . . it's impossible . . . .

– But why? Why? – he asked, still holding her close, more tightly still, and kissing her with abandon. – Why, Marta? Is it because you told me?

– Let me go . . . . No . . . . Let me go . . . . You didn't want me . . . . – Marta went on, choking with emotion, suffocated by that passionate embrace. – You didn't want me anymore.

– I do want you! I want you! – he shouted desperately, blinded by his passion.

– No . . . let me go . . . . – Marta implored, still trying to shield herself from his embrace, but already almost overwhelmed by his strength. – Let me go, I must go away . . . . I beg you!

– Marta, I forget everything! And you should too! Forget it! Leave it in the past! You're mine, Marta! Mine! Don't you love me anymore?

– It's not that, no! – Marta moaned, overcome with grief. – But it's too late! Believe me, it's not possible any longer!

– But why? Do you still love him? – Rocco cried out angrily, pushing her away.

– No, Rocco, no! I never loved him, I swear it! Never! Never!

And she erupted into sobs she could no longer control. She felt her strength fail her, and she collapsed into his arms, which he instinctively stretched out to support her once again. Exhausted with grief, he almost toppled over under her weight. But exhausted as he was, he held her up with an almost furious effort, clenching his teeth, contracting his facial features, and shaking his head desperately. And as he did so his eyes moved to the uncovered face of his mother on her funeral bed, between the four candles. It was as if the dead woman had turned to look him in the face.

Managing to overcome the shudder that his wife's body, as much as he desired it, instilled in him, he held her close to his chest once again, and with his eyes fixed on the body of his mother he stammered, suddenly taken with fear,

– Look at her, Marta . . . . Look at my mother . . . . I forgive you . . . . I forgive you . . . . Stay here. Let's keep the vigil together . . . .

Monte Cavo, 1893
Trans. Saint Paul, Minnesota, July 2022

Letter from the Author to Luigi Capuana

The following letter from Pirandello to the Italian novelist Luigi Capuana served as the dedication page for the 1908 Fratelli Treves edition of *L'esclusa* and is included in the appendices of most subsequent editions. The author referenced in the second paragraph of the letter, Francesco Berni, was a prominent poet in the early sixteenth century.

My illustrious friend,

You know the story of this novel and know that it represents my first attempt at the art of narrative (now some fourteen years ago). And that it was—in its earliest form—dedicated to you.

But "one who strives to publish great works," as Berni would say, often claims that the chicken is born before the egg, that is, that a writer can gain fame before publishing the book that would give it to him. And for a long time, my little Outcast seemed destined to remain ignored by both the publishing houses and by the public. Until, that is, it appeared in *La Tribuna* of Rome, the first Italian novel to appear in the pages of that journal.

I don't know how to gauge the effect it has been able to have on the patient, pampered readers of that journal—dramatic scenes are certainly not lacking in this novel, even if the drama itself takes place more in the souls of the characters—but I have strong doubts that in a reading so forcedly sporadic one is able to realize the most original part of the work; the part that is scrupulously hidden under the completely objective representations of persons and events; in sum, at the essentially humoristic core of the novel.

Here, every will is excluded, although characters are left with the complete illusion that they are acting voluntarily; while an odious law guides them, or rather draws them along—always hidden, but inexorable—and makes it so that an innocent woman (driven out of society, later to be readmitted) must first pass under the forks of infamy, truly committing, that is, that sin of which she had been unjustly accused.

There was nothing to devise, however, or to put together beforehand or to modify for this final secret. And here there are in fact many unforeseen obstacles, both serious and less serious, that oppose and limit and deform the characters and the lives of individuals. Nature, without—or at least apparently without—order and full of contradictions, is often very far from works of art in which all of the elements visibly cohere and cooperate with each other. Thus they show a life too concentrated on the one hand, and too simplified on the other. In real life, aren't the actions that make a character stand out portrayed against a background of ordinary events and common details? And these ordinary events, these common details—the materiality, in sum, of life in all its variation and complexity—do they not severely contradict all of those ideal and artificial simplifications? Do they not force people to act? Do they not inspire thoughts and feelings that contradict all of that harmonious logic of the facts and of the characters conceived by authors? How many unforeseen and unforeseeable events occur in life, sudden hooks that tear at our souls for a fleeting moment, of meanness or generosity, in a noble or shameful moment, and then hold them suspended, whether on the altar or in the stocks, for their entire existence, as if their lives could be summed up by that moment only, of passing drunkenness, say, or of reckless abandon?

And this by way of explaining (and excusing) the humble and minute representations, which occur frequently in my novel.

I have, my illustrious friend, lovingly revised it from top to bottom, and in large part have reforged it. And in presenting it to the public for the first time in a single volume, I dedicate it to you once again.

Yours,
L. Pirandello
Rome, December 1907

Notes

Part I, Chapter 2

1. The common misconception that a broad forehead indicates intelligence is one of the hallmarks of phrenology, a pseudoscience developed by the German physician Franz Joseph Gall at the turn of the nineteenth century. The idea was very popular and finds its way into several nineteenth-century novels.
2. Roughly, "I am not aware of being guilty of any crime."

Part I, Chapter 6

1. . . . *percotendosi le anche* (archaic). Although the expression is no longer in use, slapping or hitting one's hips or thighs indicated grief or profound sadness.

Part II, Chapter 7

1. Pirandello's essay "Arte e coscienza d'oggi" was published in September 1893 in *La nazione letteraria* of Florence.